Indecent Exposure

Tom Sharpe was born in 1928 and educated at Lancing College and at Pembroke College, Cambridge. He did his National Service in the Marines before going to South Africa in 1951, where he did social work for the Non-European Affairs Department before teaching in Natal. He had a photographic studio in Pietermaritzburg from 1957 until 1961, when he was deported. From 1963 to 1972 he was a lecturer in History at the Cambridge College of Arts and Technology. He is married and lives in Dorset.

Tom Sharpe's novels *Riotous Assembly*, *Porterhouse Blue*, *Blott on the Landscape*, *Wilt*, *The Great Pursuit* and *The Throwback* are also published in Pan.

Also by Tom Sharpe
in Pan Books

Tom Sharpe
Indecent Exposure

Pan Books
in association with
Secker & Warburg

First published 1973 by Martin Secker & Warburg Ltd
This edition published 1974 by Pan Books Ltd,
Cavaye Place, London SW10 9PG
in association with Martin Secker & Warburg Ltd
12th printing 1981
© Tom Sharpe 1973
ISBN 0 330 23922 8
Set, printed and bound in Great Britain by
Cox & Wyman Ltd, Reading

CHAPTER ONE

It was Heroes Day in Piemburg and as usual the little capital of Zululand was quite unwarrantably gay. Along the streets the jacarandas bloomed unconscionably beside gardens flamboyant with azaleas while from a hundred flagpoles Britons and Boers proclaimed their mutual enmity by flying the Union Jack or the Vierkleur, those emblems of the Boer War which neither side could ever forget. In separate ceremonies across the city the two white communities commemorated ancient victories. At the Anglican Cathedral the Bishop of Piemburg reminded his unusually large congregation that their ancestors had preserved freedom from such assorted enemies as Napoleon, President Kruger, the Kaiser and Adolf Hitler. At the Verwoerd Street Dutch Reformed Church the Reverend Schlachbals urged his flock never to forget that the British had invented concentration camps and that twenty-five thousand Boer women and children had been murdered in them. In short Heroes Day provided everyone with an opportunity to forget the present and revive old hatreds. Only the Zulus were forbidden to commemorate the occasion, partly on the grounds that they had no reputable heroes to honour but for the most part because it was felt that their participation would only lead to an increase in racial tension.

To Kommandant van Heerden, Piemburg's chief of police, the whole affair was most regrettable. As one of the few Afrikaners in Piemburg to be even slightly related to a hero (his grandfather had been shot by the British after the Battle of Paardeberg for ignoring the order to cease fire) he was expected to speak on the subject of heroism at the Nationalist rally at the Voortrekker Stadium and, besides, as one of the town's leading officials, he was obliged to attend the ceremony at Settlers Park where the Sons of England were inaugurating yet another wooden bench in honour of those who had fallen in the Zulu wars some hundred years before.

In the past the Kommandant had been able to avoid all these engagements by pleading the impossibility of being in two places at the same time but since the police had recently been allocated a helicopter, this year he was denied that excuse. At intervals throughout the day the helicopter could be seen chattering across the city while the Kommandant, who disliked heights almost as much as he did public speaking, sorted through his notes in an effort to find something to say whenever he landed. Since his notes were ones he had used annually since the Congo Crisis years before, their illegibility and general lack of relevance caused some confusion. At the Voortrekker Stadium Kommandant van Heerden's speech on heroism included the assurance that the citizens of Piemburg need have no doubt that the South African Police would leave no stone unturned to see that nothing disturbed the even tenor of their lives, while at Settlers Park his eloquence on behalf of the nuns who had been raped in the Congo, coming as it did after a passionate plea for racial harmony by a Methodist missionary, was considered not to be in the best of taste.

Finally, to round the day's business off, there was a parade of his men at the Mounted Police Barracks at which the Mayor had agreed to award a trophy for conspicuous bravery and devotion to duty.

'Interesting what you had to say about those nuns,' said the Mayor as the helicopter lifted off the ground at Settlers Park, 'I'd almost forgotten about them. Must be twelve years ago that happened.'

'I think it's just as well to remind ourselves that it could happen here,' said the Kommandant.

'I suppose so. Funny thing the way kaffirs always seem to go for nuns. You'd think they'd like something a bit more jolly.'

'It's probably because they're virgins,' said the Kommandant.

'How very clever of you to think of that,' said the Mayor, 'my wife will be relieved to hear it.'

Below them the roofs glowed in the afternoon sun. Built in the heyday of the British Empire, the tiny metropolis still possessed an air of seedy grandeur. The City Hall, redbrick Gothic, loomed above the market square while, opposite, the Supreme

Court maintained a classic formal air. Behind the railway station, Fort Rapier, once the headquarters of the British Army and now a mental hospital, stood outwardly unaltered. Patients shuffled across the great parade ground where once ten thousand men had marched and wheeled before departing for the front. The Governor's Palace had been turned into a teacher training college and students sunbathed on lawns which had once been the scene of garden parties and receptions. To Kommandant van Heerden it was all very puzzling and sad and he was just wondering why the British had abandoned their Empire so easily when the helicopter steadied itself over the Police Barracks and began to descend.

'A very fine turn-out,' said the Mayor indicating the ranks of police konstabels on the parade ground below.

'I suppose so,' said the Kommandant, recalled from past splendours to the drab present. He looked down at the five hundred men drawn up in front of a saluting base. There was certainly nothing splendid about them, nor about the six Saracen armoured cars parked in a line behind them. As the helicopter bumped to the ground and its blades finally stopped turning, he helped the Mayor down and escorted him to the platform. The police band broke into a rousing march while sixty-nine guard dogs snarled and slobbered in several iron cages vacated for the occasion by the black prisoners who were normally confined in them while awaiting trial.

'After you,' said the Kommandant at the foot of the steps that led to the platform. At the top a tall thin luitenant was standing, holding the leash of a particularly large Dobermann Pinscher, whose teeth, the Mayor noted with alarm, were bared in what appeared to be an immutable snarl.

'No, after you,' said the Mayor.

'I insist. After you,' said the Kommandant.

'Listen,' said the Mayor, 'if you think I'm going to dispute these steps with that Dobermann . . .'

Kommandant van Heerden smiled.

'Nothing to worry about,' he said. 'It's stuffed. That's the trophy.' He lurched on to the platform and pushed the Dobermann aside with his knee. The Mayor followed him up and was introduced to the thin luitenant.

'Luitenant Verkramp, head of the Security Branch,' said the Kommandant.

Luitenant Verkramp smiled bleakly and the Mayor sat down in the knowledge that he had just met a representative of BOSS, the Bureau of State Security whose reputation for torturing suspects was second to none.

'I'll just make a short speech,' said the Kommandant, 'and then you can award the trophy.' The Mayor nodded and the Kommandant went to the microphone.

'Mr Mayor, ladies and gentlemen, officers of the South African Police,' he shouted, 'we are gathered here today to pay tribute to the heroes of South African history and in particular to honour the memory of the late Konstabel Els whose recent tragic death has deprived Piemburg of one of its most outstanding policemen.'

The Kommandant's voice amplified by the loudspeaker system boomed across the parade ground and lost in the process all trace of the hesitancy he felt in mentioning the name Els. It had been Luitenant Verkramp's idea to award the stuffed Dobermann as a trophy and, glad to see the thing moved from his office, the Kommandant had agreed. Now faced with the prospect of eulogizing the dead Els, he wasn't so sure it had been a wise decision. In life Els had shot more blacks dead in the course of duty than any other policeman in South Africa and had been a constant offender against the Immorality Laws. The Kommandant looked down at his notes and ploughed on.

'A loyal comrade, a fine citizen, a devout Christian . . .' To the Mayor, looking down at the faces of the konstabels before him, it was clear that Konstabel Els' death had indeed been a great loss to the Piemburg constabulary. Certainly none of the faces he could see suggested those admirable characteristics which had evidently been so manifest in Konstabel Els. He was just coming to the conclusion that the average IQ must be in the region of 65 when the Kommandant finished his speech and announced that the Els Memorial Trophy had been won by Konstabel van Rooyen. The Mayor stood up and took the leash of the stuffed Dobermann from Luitenant Verkramp.

'Congratulations on winning this award,' he said when the

prizewinner presented himself. 'And what did you do to be so highly honoured?'

Konstabel van Rooyen blushed and mumbled something about shooting a kaffir.

'He prevented a prisoner from escaping,' the Kommandant explained hurriedly.

'Very commendable, I'm sure,' said the Mayor and handed the leash to the konstabel. To the cheers of his fellow police-men and the applause of the public the winner of the Els Memorial Trophy staggered down the steps carrying the stuffed Dobermann as the band struck up.

'Splendid idea giving a trophy like that,' the Mayor said as they sipped tea in the refreshment tent afterwards, 'though I must say I would never have thought of a stuffed dog. Highly original.'

'It was killed by the late Konstabel Els himself,' the Kommandant said.

'He must have been a remarkable man.'

'With his bare hands,' said the Kommandant.

'Dear God,' said the Mayor.

Presently, leaving the Mayor discussing the advisability of allowing visiting Japanese businessmen to use Whites Only swimming pools with the Rev Schlachbals, the Kommandant moved away. At the entrance of the tent Luitenant Verkramp was deep in conversation with a large blonde whose turquoise dress fitted her astonishingly well. Under the pink picture hat the Kommandant recognized the features of Dr von Blimen-stein, the eminent psychiatrist at Fort Rapier Mental Hos-pital.

'Getting free treatment?' the Kommandant asked jocularly as he edged past.

'Dr von Blimenstein has been telling me how she deals with cases of manic-depression,' said the Luitenant.

Dr von Blimenstein smiled. 'Luitenant Verkramp seems most interested in the use of electro-convulsive therapy.'

'I know,' said the Kommandant and wandered out into the open air, idly speculating on the possibility that Verkramp was attracted to the blonde psychiatrist. It seemed unlikely somehow but with Luitenant Verkramp one never knew.

Kommandant van Heerden had long ago ceased trying to understand his second-in-command.

He found a seat in the shade and looked out over the city. It was there that his heart belonged, he thought, idly scratching the long scar on his chest. Since the day of his transplant operation Kommandant van Heerden had felt himself in more ways than one a new man. His appetite had improved, he was seldom tired and above all the erroneous belief that at least a portion of his anatomy could trace its ancestry back to the Norman Conquest did much to alleviate the lack of esteem he felt for the rest of himself. Having acquired the heart of an English gentleman, all that remained for him to do was acquire those outward characteristics of Englishness he found so admirable. To this end he had bought a Harris Tweed suit, a Norfolk jacket and a pair of brown brogues. At weekends he could be seen in his Norfolk jacket and brogues walking in the woods outside Piemburg, a solitary figure deep in thought or at least in those perambulations of the mind that the Kommandant imagined to be thought and which in his case revolved around ways and means of becoming an accepted member of Piemburg's English community.

He had made a start in this direction by applying for membership of the Alexandria Club, Zululand's most exclusive club, but without success. It had taken the combined efforts of the President, the Treasurer and the Secretary to convince him that being blackballed had nothing to do with the colour of his reproductive organs or the racial origins of his grandmother. In the end he had joined the Golf Club where conditions of membership were less rigorous and where he could sit in the clubhouse and listen with awe to accents whose arrogance was, he felt, authentically English. After such visits he would return home and spend the evening practising 'Jolly good show' and 'Chin up.' Now as he sat dozing in his chair he was well content with the progress he was making.

To Luitenant Verkramp the change that had come over the Kommandant since his operation suggested some sinister and secret knowledge. The advantage Verkramp had previously enjoyed by virtue of a better education and a quicker wit had quite disappeared. The Kommandant treated him with a lordly tolerance that infuriated the Luitenant, and greeted his sarcastic remarks with a benign smile. Worse still, Verkramp found the Kommandant continually interfering with his attempts to stamp out Communism, liberalism and humanism, not to mention Anglicanism and Roman Catholicism and other enemies of the South African way of life in Piemburg. When Verkramp's men raided the Masonic Hall Kommandant van Heerden raised the strongest objections, and when the Security Branch arrested an archaeologist at the University of Zululand whose research suggested that there was evidence of iron workings in the Transvaal before the arrival of Van Riebeck in 1652 the Kommandant had insisted on his release. Verkramp had protested vigorously.

'There were no black bastards in South Africa before the white man came and it's treason to say there were,' he told the Kommandant.

'I know all that,' the Kommandant replied, 'but this fellow never said there were.'

'He did. He said there were iron workings.'

'Iron workings aren't people,' the Kommandant pointed out and the archaeologist, who by this time was suffering acute symptoms of anxiety, was transferred to Fort Rapier Mental Hospital. It was there that Verkramp first met Dr von Blimenstein. As she pinned the patient's arm behind his back and frogmarched him into the hospital Luitenant Verkramp gazed at her broad shoulders and heavy buttocks and knew himself to be in love. He would visit the hospital almost daily to inquire about the archaeologist's progress and would sit in the doctor's office studying the details of her face and figure before returning to the police station like a traveller from some sexual El Dorado. There he would sit for hours constructing in his mind's eye a picture of the lovely psychiatrist out of the jigsaw fragments of his numerous visits. Each trip he would bring back another tiny hoard of intimate details to add to the outline he knew so well. Once it was her left arm. Another time the gentle swell of her stomach ridged by the constriction of a girdle or one large breast hard in the confines of her bra. Best of all, one summer day, the briefest glimpse of inner thigh, dimpled and white beneath a tight skirt. Ankles, knees, hands,

11

the occasional armpit, Verkramp knew them all with an intimacy of detail that would have surprised the doctor and then again might not have.

Now as they stood in the refreshment tent Luitenant Verkramp mentioned the change that had come over the Kommandant.

'I can't understand it,' he said, offering the doctor another cream scone. 'He's taken to dressing up in fancy clothes.' Dr von Blimenstein looked at him sharply.

'What sort of fancy clothes?' she asked.

'He's got a tweed jacket with pleated pockets and a sort of belt at the back. And he's taken to wearing strange shoes.'

'Sounds fairly normal,' Dr von Blimenstein said. 'No question of perfume or an interest in women's underwear?'

Luitenant Verkramp shook his head sadly.

'But his language has changed too. He insists on talking English and he's got a picture of the Queen of England on his desk.'

'That does sound peculiar,' said the doctor.

Verkramp was encouraged.

'It doesn't seem natural for a good Afrikaner to go around saying "Absolutely spiffing, what?" does it?'

'I'd have grave doubts about the sanity of a good Englishman who went round saying that,' said the psychiatrist. 'Does he have sudden changes of mood?'

'Yes,' said Verkramp with feeling.

'Delusions of grandeur?'

'Definitely,' said Verkramp.

'Well,' said Dr von Blimenstein, 'it does look as though your Kommandant is suffering from some sort of psychic disturbance. I should keep a close watch on him.'

By the time Police Open Day was over and Dr von Blimenstein had left, Luitenant Verkramp was in a state of mild euphoria. The notion that Kommandant van Heerden was on the verge of a breakdown opened promotion prospects. Luitenant Verkamp had begun to think that shortly he would be chief of police in Piemburg.

CHAPTER TWO

Two days later Luitenant Verkramp was sitting in his office dreaming of Dr von Blimenstein when a directive arrived from the Bureau of State Security. It was marked 'For Your Eyes Only' and had accordingly been read by several konstabels before it reached him. Verkramp read the directive through avidly. It concerned breaches of the Immorality Act by members of the South African Police and was a routine memorandum sent to all Police Stations throughout South Africa.

'You are hereby instructed to investigate cases of suspected liaison between police officers and Bantu women.' Verkramp looked 'liaison' up in the dictionary and found that it meant what he had hoped. He read on and, as he read, vistas of opportunity opened before him. 'In the light of the propaganda value afforded to enemies of South Africa by press reports of court cases involving SAP officers and Bantu women, it is of national importance that ways and means be found to combat the tendency of white policemen to consort with black women. It is also in the interests of racial harmony that transracial sexual intercourse should be prevented. Where proof of such illegal sexual activity involving members of the SAP is forthcoming, no criminal proceedings should be instituted without prior notification of the Bureau of State Security.'

By the time he had finished reading the document Luitenant Verkramp was not sure whether he was supposed to prosecute offending policemen or not. What he did know was that he had been instructed to investigate 'cases of suspected liaison' and that it was 'of national importance that ways and means be found'. The notion of doing something of national importance particularly appealed to him. Luitenant Verkramp picked up the telephone and dialled Fort Rapier Mental Hospital. He had something to ask Dr von Blimenstein.

Later the same morning the two met on what had once been the parade ground for the British garrison and which now served as an exercise area for the inmates of the hospital.

'It's the ideal spot for what I have to say,' Verkramp told the doctor as they strolled among the patients. 'No one can possibly overhear us,' a remark which gave rise in the psychiatrist's bosom to the hope that he was about to propose to her. His next remark was even more promising. 'What I have to ask you concerns . . . er . . . sex.'

Dr von Blimenstein smiled coyly and looked down at her size nine shoes. 'Go on,' she murmured as the Luitenant's Adam's apple bobbed with embarrassment.

'Of course, it's not a subject I would normally discuss with a woman,' he muttered finally. The doctor's hopes fell. 'But since you're a psychiatrist, I thought you might be able to help.'

Dr von Blimenstein looked at him coldly. This wasn't what she wanted to hear. 'Go on,' she said reverting to her professional tone of voice. 'Out with it.'

Verkramp took the plunge.

'It's like this. A lot of policemen have anti-social tendencies. They keep doing what they shouldn't do.' He stopped hurriedly. He had begun to regret ever starting the conversation.

'And what shouldn't policemen do?' There was no mistaking the note of disapproval in her voice.

'Black women,' Verkramp blurted out. 'They shouldn't do black women, should they?'

There was really no need to wait for the answer. Dr von Blimenstein's face had gone a strange mauve colour and the veins were standing out on her neck.

'Shouldn't?' she shouted furiously. Several patients scampered away towards the main block. 'Shouldn't? Do you mean to say you've brought me out here just to tell me you've been screwing coon girls?'

Luitenant Verkramp knew that he had made a terrible mistake. The doctor's voice could be heard half a mile away.

'Not me,' yelled Verkramp desperately. 'I'm not talking about me.'

Dr von Blimenstein stared at him doubtfully. 'Not you?' she asked after a pause.

'On my honour,' Verkramp assured her. 'What I meant was

14

that other police officers do and I thought you might have some ideas about how they can be stopped.'

'Why can't they be arrested and charged under the Immorality Act like everyone else?'

Verkramp shook his head. 'Well for one thing they are police officers which makes them rather difficult to catch and in any case it's important to avoid the scandal.' Dr von Blimenstein stared at him in disgust.

'Do you mean to tell me that this sort of thing goes on all the time?'

Verkramp nodded.

'In that case the punishment should be more severe,' said the doctor. 'Seven years and ten strokes isn't a sufficient deterrent. In my opinion any white man having sexual intercourse with a black woman should be castrated.'

'I quite agree,' said Verkramp enthusiastically. 'It would do them a lot of good.'

Dr von Blimenstein looked at him suspiciously but there was nothing to suggest irony in Verkramp's expression. He was staring at her with undisguised admiration. Encouraged by his frank agreement, the doctor continued.

'I feel so strongly about miscegenation that I would be quite prepared to carry out the operation myself. Is anything wrong?'

Luitenant Verkramp had suddenly turned very white. The idea of being castrated by the beautiful doctor corresponded so closely with his own masochistic fantasies that he felt quite overcome.

'No. Nothing,' he gasped, trying to rid himself of the vision of the doctor, masked and robed, approaching him on the operating table. 'It's just a bit hot out here.' Dr von Blimenstein took him by the arm.

'Why don't we continue our discussion at my cottage? It's cool down there and we can have some tea.' Luitenant Verkramp allowed himself to be led off the parade ground and down the hospital drive to the doctor's cottage. Like the rest of the hospital buildings, it dated from the turn of the century when it had been officers' quarters. Its stoep faced south and looked over the hills towards the coast and inside it was cool and dark.

While Dr von Blimenstein made tea, Liutenant Verkramp sat in the sitting-room and wondered if he had been wise to broach the subject of sex with a woman as forceful as Dr von Blimenstein.

'Why don't you take off your jacket and make yourself comfortable?' the doctor asked when she returned with the tray. Verkramp shook his head nervously. He wasn't used to having tea with ladies who asked him to take his jacket off and besides he rather doubted if his braces would go very well with the tasteful decorations in the room.

'Oh come now,' said the doctor, 'there's no need to be formal with me. I'm not going to eat you.' Coming so shortly after the news that the doctor was an advocate of castration, the idea of being eaten by her as well was too much for Verkramp. He sat down hurriedly in a chair.

'I'm perfectly all right like this,' he said, but Dr von Blimenstein wasn't convinced.

'Do you want me to take it off for you?' she asked, getting up from her own chair with a movement that disclosed more of her legs than Luitenant Verkramp had ever seen before. 'I've had lots of practice,' she smiled at him. Verkramp could well believe it. 'In the hospital.' Feeling like a weasel fascinated by a giant rabbit, Verkramp sat hypnotized in his chair as she approached.

'Stand up,' said the doctor.

Verkramp stood up. Doctor von Blimestein's fingers unbuttoned his jacket as he stood facing her and a moment later she was pushing his jacket back over his shoulders so that he could hardly move his arms. 'There we are,' she said softly, her face smiling gently close to his, 'that feels a lot more comfortable, doesn't it?'

Comfortable was hardly the word Luitenant Verkramp would have chosen to describe the sensation he was now experiencing. As her cool fingers began to undo his tie, Verkramp found himself swept from the safe remote world of sexual fantasy into an immediacy of satisfaction he had no means of controlling. With a volley of diminishing whimpers and an ecstatic release Luitenant Verkramp slumped against the doctor and was only prevented from falling by her strong arms. In the twilight of her hair he heard her murmur, 'There, there, my darling.' Luitenant Verkramp passed out.

Twenty minutes later he was sitting rigid with remorse and embarrassment wondering what to do if she asked if he wanted another cup of tea. To say 'No' would be to invite her to take the cup away for good while to say 'Yes' would still deprive him of the only means he had of hiding his lack of self-control. Dr von Blimenstein was telling him that a sense of guilt was always the cause of sexual problems. In Verkramp's opinion the argument didn't hold water but he was too preoccupied with the question of more tea or not to enter into the conversation with anything approaching fervour. Finally he decided that the best thing to do was to say 'Yes, please' and cross his legs at the same time and he had just come to this conclusion when Dr von Blimenstein noticed his empty cup. 'Would you care for some more tea?' she asked and reached out for his cup. Luitenant Verkramp's careful plan was wrecked before he realized it. He had expected her to come over and fetch his cup, not wait for it to be brought to her. Responding to the contradictory impulses towards modesty and good manners at the same time, he crossed his legs and stood up, in the process spilling the little bit of tea he had kept in his cup in case he should decide to say 'No' into his lap where it mingled with the previous evidence of his lack of *savoir-faire*. Luitenant Verkramp untangled his legs and looked down at himself with shame and embarrassment. The doctor was more practical. Picking the cup off the floor and prising the saucer from Verkramp's fingers, she hurried from the room and returned a moment later with a damp cloth. 'We mustn't let your uniform get stained, must we?' she cooed with a motherliness which reduced most of Verkramp to a delicious limpness and quite prevented him from realizing the admission of complicity in his mishap implied by the 'we' and before he knew what was happening the beautiful doctor was rubbing his fly with the damp cloth.

Luitenant Verkramp's reaction was instantaneous. Once was wicked enough but twice was more than he could bear. With a contraction that bent him almost double, he jerked himself away from the doctor's tempting hands. 'No,' he squeaked, 'not again,' and leapt for cover behind the armchair.

His reaction took Dr von Blimenstein quite by surprise.

'Not what again?' she asked, still kneeling on the floor where his flight had left her.

'Not ... What? Nothing,' said Verkramp desperately struggling to distinguish some moral landmark in the confusion of his mind.

'Not? What? Nothing?' said the doctor clambering to her feet. 'What on earth do you mean?'

Verkramp turned melodramatically away and stared out of the window.

'You shouldn't have done that,' he said.

'Done what?'

'You know,' said Verkramp.

'What did I do?' the doctor insisted. Luitenant Verkramp shook his head miserably at the hills and said nothing. 'How silly you are,' the doctor went on. 'There's nothing to be ashamed of. We get quite a few involuntary emissions every day in the hospital.'

Verkramp turned on her furiously.

'That's with lunatics,' he said, disgusted by her clinical detachment. 'Sane people don't have them.' He stopped abruptly, vaguely aware of the self-accusation.

'Of course they do,' said the doctor soothingly. 'It's only natural ... between ... passionate men and women.'

Luitenant Verkramp resisted the siren tone.

'It's not natural. It's wicked.'

Dr von Blimenstein laughed softly.

'You mustn't laugh at me,' shouted Verkramp.

'And you mustn't shout at me,' said the doctor. Verkramp wilted before the tone of authority in her voice. 'Come here,' she continued. Verkramp crossed the room nervously. Doctor von Blimenstein put her hands on his shoulders. 'Look at me,' she told him. Verkramp did as he was told. 'Do you find me attractive?' Verkramp nodded dumbly. 'I'm glad,' said the doctor and taking the astonished Luitenant's head in her hands she kissed him passionately on the mouth. 'And now I'll go and rustle up something for lunch,' she said breaking away from him and before Verkramp could say anything more she

18

was in the kitchen clattering away quite surprisingly for a woman of her size. Behind her in the kitchen doorway Luitenant Verkramp struggled with his emotions. Furious at himself, at her, and at the situation in which he found himself, he looked round for someone to blame. Sensing his dilemma Dr von Blimenstein came to his assistance.

'About the problem you mentioned,' she said, bending over seductively to get a saucepan from the cupboard under the sink, 'I think I might be able to help you after all.'

'What problem?' Verkramp asked brusquely. He'd had enough help with his problems already.

'About your men and the kaffir girls,' said the doctor.

'Oh them.' Verkramp had forgotten his original reason for coming.

'I've been thinking about it. I can see one way it might be tackled.'

'Oh really,' said Verkramp, who could think about a great many more but didn't feel up to it.

'It's really a question of psychic engineering,' the doctor continued. 'That's my term for the experiments I have been conducting here with a number of patients.'

Luitenant Verkramp perked up. He was always interested in experiments.

'I've had a number of successful cures already,' she explained, chopping a carrot up with a number of swift strokes. 'It's worked with alcoholics, transvestites and homosexuals. I can't really see any reason why it shouldn't work just as well in the case of a perversion like miscegenation.' There was no doubting Verkramp's interest now. He moved away from the kitchen doorway all attention.

'How would you go about it?' he asked eagerly.

'Well the first thing to do would be to isolate the personality factors in men with a tendency towards this sort of sexual deviation. That shouldn't be too difficult. I could work out a number of likely attributes. In fact it might be a good thing if your men were to fill in a questionnaire.'

'What? About their sex life?' Verkramp asked. He could see the sort of reception a questionnaire like that would get in the Piemburg Police Station.

'About sex and other things.'

'What other things?' Verkramp asked suspiciously.

'Oh the usual. Relations with mother. Whether the mother was the dominant figure in the home. If they were fond of their black nanny. Earliest sexual experience. Normal things like that.'

Verkramp gulped. What he had just heard sounded positively abnormal to him.

'A careful analysis of the answers should give us some lead to the sort of men who would benefit from the treatment,' Dr von Blimenstein explained.

'Do you mean to say you can tell just by answers to a questionnaire if a man wants to sleep with a kaffir?' Verkramp asked.

Dr von Blimenstein shook her head. 'Not exactly, but we'd have something to go on. After we had weeded out the likely suspects, I would interview them, in the strictest confidence, of course, and see if any were suitable for treatment.'

Verkramp was doubtful. 'I can't see anyone admitting he wanted a kaffir,' he said.

The doctor smiled. 'You would be amazed at some of the things people confess to me,' she said.

'What would you do when you'd found out?' Verkramp asked.

'First things first,' said Dr von Blimenstein, who knew the value of keeping a man in suspense. 'Let's have lunch on the stoep.' She picked up the tray and Verkramp followed her out.

By the time Luitenant Verkramp left the cottage that afternoon he had in his pocket the draft questionnaire he was to put to the men in the Piemburg Police Station but he still had no idea what form the doctor's treatment would take. All she would tell him was that she would guarantee that after a week with her no man would ever look at a black woman again. Luitenant Verkramp could well believe it.

On the other hand he had a far clearer picture of the sort of man who had transracial sexual tendencies. According to Dr von Blimenstein the signs to look for were solitariness, sudden changes of mood, pronounced feelings of sexual guilt, an unstable family background and of course an unsatisfactory sex life. As the Luitenant went through in his mind the officers and men in Piemburg one figure emerged more clearly than all the others. Luitenant Verkramp had begun to think he was about to discover the secret of the change that had come over Kommandant van Heerden.

Back in his office he read through the directive from BOSS just to make sure that he was empowered to take the action he contemplated. It was there in black and white. 'You are hereby instructed to investigate suspected cases of liaison between police officers and Bantu women.' Verkramp locked the memo away and sent for Sergeant Breitenbach.

Within the hour he had issued his instructions. 'I want him watched night and day,' he told the Security men assembled in his office. 'I want a record of everything he does, where he goes, who he meets and anything that suggests a break in his usual routine. Photograph everyone visiting his house. Put microphones in every room and tape all conversations. Tap his phone and record all his calls. Is that clear? I want the full treatment.'

Verkramp looked round the room and the men all nodded. Only Sergeant Breitenbach had any reservations.

'Isn't this a bit irregular, sir?' he asked. 'After all, the Kommandant is the commanding officer here.'

Luitenant Verkramp flushed angrily. He disliked having his orders questioned.

'I have here,' he said, brandishing the directive from BOSS, 'orders from Pretoria to carry out this investigation. Naturally,' his voice changed from authority to unction, 'I hope as I'm sure we all do that we'll be able to give Kommandant van Heerden full security clearance when we're finished but in the meantime we must carry out our orders. I need, of course, hardly remind you that the utmost secrecy must be maintained throughout this operation. All right, you may go.'

When the Security men had left, Luitenant Verkramp gave orders for the questionnaire to be xeroxed and left on his desk ready for distribution the following morning.

Next day Mrs Roussouw, whose job it was to superintend the black convicts who came from Piemburg Prison every day to do

21

the Kommandant's housework, had her work cut out answering the front-door bell to admit a succession of Municipal Officials who seemed to think there was a damaged gas pipe under the kitchen, a mains short circuit in the living-room and a leak in the water tank in the attic.

Since the house wasn't connected to the gas and the electric stove in the kitchen functioned perfectly while there were no signs of damp on the bedroom ceiling, Mrs Roussouw did her best to deter the officials who seemed determined to carry out their duties with a degree of conscientiousness and a lack of specialized knowledge she found quite astonishing.

'Shouldn't you switch off the main supply first?' she asked the man from the Electricity Board who was laying wires in the Kommandant's bedroom.

'Suppose so,' the man said and went downstairs. When ten minutes later she found the light still on in the kitchen, Mrs Roussouw took matters into her own hands and went into the cupboard under the stairs and switched the mains off herself. There was a muffled yell from the attic where the Water Board men had been relying on a handlamp connected to a plug on the landing to help them find the non-existent leak in the cistern.

'Must be the bulb,' said one of the men and clambered down the ladder to fetch another bulb from the Kommandant's bedside light. By the time he was back in the darkness of the attic the Electricity man had assured Mrs Roussouw that there was no need to cut the mains off.

'You know your own job, I suppose,' Mrs Roussouw told him rather doubtfully.

'I can assure you it's quite safe now,' the man said. Mrs Roussouw went back under the stairs and turned the supply on again. The scream that issued from the attic where the Water Board man had his fingers in the socket of the lamp was followed by an appalling rending noise from the bedroom and the sound of falling plaster. Mrs Roussouw switched the electricity off again and went upstairs.

'Whatever will the Kommandant say when he finds what a mess you've made?' she asked the leg that hung through the hole in the ceiling. An answering groan came from the attic.

'Are you all right?' Mrs Roussouw asked anxiously. The leg wriggled vigorously.

'I told you you should have cut it off,' Mrs Roussouw told the Electricity man reprovingly. In the attic the remark provoked a string of protests and the leg jerked convulsively. The Electricity man went out onto the landing.

'What's he say?' he asked peering up the ladder into the darkness.

'He says he doesn't want it cut off,' said a voice from above.

'Just as you say,' said Mrs Roussouw and went downstairs to turn the mains on again. 'Is that better?' she asked pulling the switch down. Upstairs in the Kommandant's bedroom the leg twitched violently and was still.

'You just hang on and I'll give you a shove from below,' the Electricity man said and clambered onto the bed.

Mrs Roussouw emerged from the cupboard and went upstairs again. She was getting rather puffed with all this up and down. She had just reached the landing when there was another terrible yell from the bedroom. She hurried in and found the Electricity man lying prostrate amid the plaster on the Kommandant's bed.

'What's the matter now?' she asked. The man wiped his face and looked up at the leg reproachfully.

'It's alive,' he said finally.

'That's what you think,' said a voice from the attic.

'I'm sure I don't know what to think,' Mrs Roussouw said.

'Well I do,' the Electricity man told her, sitting up on the bed. 'I think you ought to go and cut the mains supply off again. I'm not touching that leg till you do.'

Mrs Roussouw turned wearily back to the stairs.

'This is the last time,' she told the man, 'I'm not running up and downstairs any more.'

In the end with the help of the black convicts they managed to get the unconscious Water Board official down from the attic and Mrs Roussouw was persuaded to give him the kiss of life on the couch in the Kommandant's sitting-room.

'You can get those kaffirs out of here before I do,' she told the Electricity man. 'I'm not doing any kissing with them looking on. It might give them ideas.' The Electricity man shooed the convicts out and presently the Water Board official recovered enough to be taken back to the police station.

'Bungling idiots,' Verkramp snarled when they reported back to him. 'I said bug the house, not knock it to bits.'

When Kommandant van Heerden arrived home that evening it was to find his house in considerable disorder and with most of the services cut off. He tried to make himself some tea but there was no water in the tap. It took him twenty minutes to find the stopcock and another twenty to discover a spanner that fitted it. He filled his Five Minute kettle and waited half an hour for it to boil only to learn at the end of that time that the water in it was still stone cold.

'What the hell's wrong with everything?' he wondered as he filled a saucepan and put it on the stove. Twenty minutes later he was rummaging about under the stairs trying to find the fuse-box with the help of a box of matches. He had taken all the fuses out and put them back again before he realized that the main switch was off. With a sigh of relief he pulled it down to 'ON'. There was a loud bang in the fusebox and the light in the hall which had come on momentarily went out again. It took the Kommandant another half an hour to find the fuse wire and by that time he was out of matches. He gave up in disgust and went out and had dinner in a Greek café down the road.

By the time he got home again Kommandant van Heerden's temper was violent. With the help of a torch which he had bought at a garage he made his way upstairs and was appalled by the mess in his bedroom. There was a large hole in the ceiling and the bed was covered with plaster. The Kommandant sat down on the edge of the bed and shone his torch through the hole in his ceiling. Finally he turned to the phone on his bedside table and dialled the police station. He was sitting there staring out of the window wondering why it took so long for the Duty Sergeant to answer when he became aware that what looked like a shadow under the jacaranda tree across the road was smoking a cigarette. The Kommandant put the phone down and crossed to the window to take a better look. Staring into the darkness he was startled to notice another shadow

24

under another tree. He was just wondering what two shadows were doing watching his house when the phone behind him on the bed began to squeak irately. The Kommandant picked the receiver up just in time to hear the Duty Sergeant put his down. With a curse he dialled again, changed his mind and went through to the bathroom which overlooked his back garden and opened the window. A light breeze drifted in, ruffling the curtains. The Kommandant peered out and had just decided that his back garden was free of interlopers when an azalea bush lit a cigarette. In a state of considerable alarm the Kommandant scurried back to his bedroom and dialled the police station.

'I'm being watched,' he told the Duty Sergeant when the man finally picked up the phone.

'Oh really,' said the Sergeant, who was used to nutters ringing him up in the middle of the night with stories of being spied on. 'And who is watching you?'

'I don't know,' whispered the Kommandant. 'There are two men out front and another in my back garden.'

'What are you whispering for?' the Sergeant asked.

'Because I'm being watched, of course. Why else should I whisper?' the Kommandant snarled *sotto voce*.

'I've no idea,' said the Sergeant. 'I'll just get this down. You say you're being watched by two men in the front garden and one in the back. Is that correct?'

'No,' said the Kommandant who was rapidly losing patience with the Duty Sergeant.

'But you just said—'

'I said there were two men at the front of my house and one in the back garden,' the Kommandant said, trying to control his temper.

'Two ... men ... in ... front ... of ... my ... house,' said the Sergeant writing it down slowly. 'Just getting it down,' he told the Kommandant when the latter asked what the hell he thought he was doing.

'Well, you'd better hurry up,' the Kommandant shouted, losing control of himself. 'I've got a dirty great hole in the ceiling above my bed and my house has been burgled,' he went on and was rewarded for his pains by hearing the Sergeant inform somebody else at the police station that he had another nut case on the line.

'Now then, correct me if I'm wrong,' said the Sergeant before the Kommandant could reprimand him for insubordination, 'but you say there are three men watching your house, that there's a dirty great hole in your ceiling and that your house has been burgled? Is that right? You haven't left anything out?'

In his bedroom Kommandant van Heerden was on the verge of apoplexy. 'Just one thing,' he yelled into the phone, 'this is your commanding officer, Kommandant van Heerden, speaking. And I'm ordering you to send a patrol car round to my house at once.'

A sceptical silence greeted this ferocious announcement. 'Do you hear me?' shouted the Kommandant. It was clear that the Duty Sergeant didn't. He had his hand over the mouthpiece but the Kommandant could still hear him telling the konstabel on duty with him that the caller was off his head. With a slam the Kommandant replaced his receiver and wondered what to do. Finally he got to his feet and went to the window. The sinister watchers were still there. The Kommandant tiptoed to his chest of drawers and rummaged in the drawer containing his socks for his revolver. Taking it out, he made sure it was loaded and then, having decided that the hole in his ceiling made his bedroom indefensible, was tiptoeing downstairs when the phone in his bedroom began to ring. For a moment the Kommandant thought of letting it ring when the thought that it might be the Duty Sergeant ringing back to confirm his previous call sent him scurrying upstairs again. He was just in time to pick the receiver up as the ringing stopped.

Kommandant van Heerden dialled the police station.

'Have you just rung me?' he asked the Duty Sergeant.

'Depends who you are,' the Sergeant replied.

'I'm your commanding officer,' shouted the Kommandant.

The Sergeant considered the matter. 'All right,' he said finally, 'just put your phone down and we'll ring back to confirm that.'

The Kommandant looked at the receiver vindictively. 'Listen

to me,' he said, 'my number is 5488. You can confirm that and I'll hold on.'

Five minutes later patrol cars from all over Piemburg were converging on Kommandant van Heerden's house and the Duty Sergeant was wondering what he was going to say to the Kommandant in the morning.

CHAPTER THREE

Luitenant Verkramp was wondering much the same thing. News of the fiasco at the Kommandant's house reached him via Sergeant Breitenbach, who had spent the evening tapping the Kommandant's telephone and who had the presence of mind to order the watching agents to leave the area before the patrol cars arrived. Unfortunately the microphones scattered about the Kommandant's house remained and Luitenant Verkramp could imagine that their presence there would hardly improve his relations with his commanding officer if they were discovered.

'I told you this whole thing was a mistake,' Sergeant Breitenbach said while Luitenant Verkramp dressed.

Verkramp didn't agree. 'What's he making such a fuss about if he hasn't got something to hide?' he asked.

'That hole in the ceiling, for one thing,' said the Sergeant. Luitenant Verkramp couldn't see it.

'Could have happened to anyone,' he said. 'Anyway he'll blame the Water Board for it.'

'I can't see them admitting responsibility for making it, all the same,' said the Sergeant.

'The more they deny it, the more he'll believe they did,' said Verkramp, who knew something about psychology. 'Anyway I'll cook up something to explain the bugs, don't worry.'

Dismissing the Sergeant, he drove to the police station and sat up half the night concocting a memorandum to put on the Kommandant's desk in the morning.

In fact there was no need to use it. Kommandant van Heerden arrived at the police station determined to make someone pay for the damage to his property. He wasn't quite sure which of the public utilities to blame and Mrs Roussouw's explanation hadn't made the matter any clearer.

'Oh, you do look a sight,' she said when the Kommandant came down to breakfast after shaving in cold water.

'So does my bloody house,' said the Kommandant, dabbing his cheek with a styptic pencil.

'Language,' retorted Mrs Roussouw. Kommandant van Heerden regarded her bleakly.

'Perhaps you'd be good enough to explain what's been happening here,' he said. 'I came home last night to find the water cut off, a large hole in my bedroom ceiling and no electricity.'

'The Water Board man did that,' Mrs Roussouw explained. 'I had to give him the kiss of life to bring him round.'

The Kommandant shuddered at the thought.

'And what does that explain?' he asked.

'The hole in the ceiling, of course,' said Mrs Roussouw.

The Kommandant tried to visualize the sequence of events that had resulted from Mrs Roussouw's giving the Water Board man the kiss of life and his falling through the ceiling.

'In the attic?' he asked sceptically.

'Of course not, silly,' Mrs Roussouw said. 'He was looking for a hole in the cistern when I turned the electricity on . . .'

The Kommandant was too bewildered to let her continue.

'Mrs Roussouw,' he said wearily, 'am I to understand . . . oh never mind. I'll phone the Water Board when I get to the station.'

He had breakfast while Mrs Roussouw added to the confusion in his mind by explaining that the Electricity man had been responsible for the accident in the first place by leaving the current on.

'I suppose that explains the mess in here,' said the Kommandant, looking at the rubble under the sink.

'Oh, no that was the Gas man,' Mrs Roussouw said.

'But we don't use gas,' said the Kommandant.

'I know, I told him that but he said it was a leak in the mains.'

The Kommandant finished his breakfast and walked to the police station utterly perplexed. In spite of the fact that the patrol cars had been unable to find any evidence that his house had been watched, the Kommandant was certain he had been under surveillance. He even had an uneasy feeling that he was being followed to the police station but when he glanced over his shoulder at the corner there was no one in sight.

Once in his office he spent an hour on the phone haranguing the managers of the Gas, Electricity and Water Boards in an attempt to get to the bottom of the affair. It took the efforts of all three managers to convince him that their men had never been authorized to enter his house, that there was absolutely nothing the matter with his electricity or his water supply, and that there hadn't been a suspected gas leak within a mile of his house and finally that they couldn't be held responsible for the damage done to his property. The Kommandant reserved his opinion on this last point and said he would consult his lawyer. The Manager of the Water Board told him that it wasn't the business of the board to mend leaks in cisterns in any case and the Kommandant said it wasn't anybody's business to make large holes in the ceiling of his bedroom, and he certainly wasn't going to pay for the privilege of having them made.

Having raised his blood pressure to a dangerously high level in this exchange of courtesies, the Kommandant sent for the Duty Sergeant, who was dragged from his bed to explain his behaviour over the phone.

'I thought it was a hoax,' he told the Kommandant. 'It was the way you were whispering.'

The Kommandant wasn't whispering now. His voice could be heard in the cells two floors below. 'A hoax?' he yelled at the Sergeant. 'You thought it was a hoax?'

'Yes, sir, we get half a dozen every night.'

'What sort of hoaxes?' the Kommandant asked.

'People ringing up to say they're being burgled or raped or something. Mostly women.'

Kommandant van Heerden remembered when he had been a Duty Sergeant and had to agree that a lot of night calls were false alarms. He dismissed the Sergeant with a reprimand. 'Next time I call you,' he said, 'I don't want any argument.

Understand?' The Sergeant understood and was about to leave the office when the Kommandant had second thoughts. 'Where the hell do you think you're going?' the Kommandant snarled. The Sergeant said that since he'd been up all night he was thinking of going back to bed. The Kommandant had other plans for him. 'I'm putting you in charge of the investigation into the burglary at my house,' he said. 'I want a full report on who was responsible by this afternoon.'

'Yes sir,' said the Sergeant wearily and left the office. On the stairs he met Luitenant Verkramp, who was looking pretty jaded himself.

'He wants a full report by this afternoon on the break-in,' the Sergeant told Verkramp. The Luitenant sighed, went back upstairs and knocked on the Kommandant's door.

'Come in,' yelled the Kommandant. Luitenant Verkramp came in. 'What's the matter with you, Verkramp? You look as though you'd spent the night on the tiles.'

'Just an attic of colack,' spluttered Verkramp, unnerved by the Kommandant's percipience.

'A what?'

'An attack of colic,' said Verkramp trying to control his speech. 'Just a slip of the foot . . . er . . . tongue.'

'For God's sake pull yourself together Luitenant,' the Kommandant told him.

'Yes sir,' said Verkramp.

'What do you want to see me about?'

'It's about this business at your home, sir,' said Verkramp, 'I have some information which may be of interest to you.'

Kommandant van Heerden sighed. He might have guessed that Verkramp might have his grubby fingers in this particular pie. 'Well?'

Luitenant Verkramp swallowed nervously. 'We in the Security Branch,' he began, spreading the burden of responsibility as far as possible, 'have recently received information that an attempt was going to be made to bug your house.' He paused to see how the Kommandant would take the news. Kommandant van Heerden responded predictably. He sat up in his chair and stared at Verkramp in horror.

'Good God,' he said, 'you mean . . .'

'Precisely, sir,' said Verkramp. 'Acting on this information, I put your house under twenty-four hour surveillance . . .'

'You mean—'

'Exactly, sir,' Verkramp continued. 'You have probably noticed that your house has been watched.'

'That's right,' said the Kommandant, 'I saw them there last night . . .'

Verkramp nodded. 'My men, sir.'

'Across the road and in my back garden,' said the Kommandant.

'Exactly, sir,' Verkramp agreed, 'we thought they might return.'

The Kommandant was losing track of the conversation. 'Who might return?'

'The Communist saboteurs, sir.'

'Communist saboteurs? What the hell would Communist saboteurs want to do in my house?'

'Bug it, sir,' said Verkramp. 'After the failure of their attempt yesterday I thought they might return.'

Kommandant van Heerden took a firm grip on himself.

'Are you trying to tell me that all those Gas men and Water Board officials were really Communist saboteurs . . .'

'In disguise, sir. Fortunately, thanks to the efforts of my counter-agents, the attempt was foiled. One of the Communists fell through the ceiling . . .'

Kommandant van Heerden leant back in his chair satisfied. He had found the person responsible for the hole in his bedroom ceiling. 'So that was your fault?' he said.

'Entirely,' Verkramp agreed, 'and we'll see that repairs are carried out immediately.'

The news had taken a great burden off the Kommandant's mind. On the other hand he was still puzzled.

'What I don't understand is why these Communists should want to bug my house in the first place. Who are they anyway?' he asked.

'I'm afraid I can't disclose any identities yet,' Verkramp said, and fell back on the Bureau of State Security. 'Orders from BOSS.'

'Well what the hell is the point of bugging my house?' asked

31

the Kommandant, who knew better than to question orders from BOSS. 'I never say anything important there.'

Verkramp agreed. 'But they weren't to know that sir,' he said. 'In any case our information suggests that they were hoping to acquire material which would allow them to blackmail you.' He watched Kommandant van Heerden very closely to see how he would react. The Kommandant was appalled.

'God Almighty!' he gasped, and mopped his forehead with a handkerchief. Verkramp followed up his advantage swiftly.

'If they could get something on you, something sexual, anything a bit kinky.' He hesitated. The Kommandant was sweating profusely. 'They'd have you by the short hairs, wouldn't they?' Privately Kommandant van Heerden had to agree that they would but he wasn't admitting as much to Luitenant Verkramp. He raced through the catalogue of his nightly habits and came to the conclusion that there were several he would rather the world knew nothing about.

'The diabolical swine,' he muttered and looked at Verkramp with something approaching respect. The Luitenant wasn't such a fool after all. 'What are you going to do about it?' he asked.

'Two things,' said Verkramp. 'The first is to allay the suspicions of the Communists as far as possible by ignoring this affair at your house. Let them think we don't know what they are up to. Lay the blame on the Gas . . . er . . . Water Board.'

'I've done that already,' said the Kommandant.

'Good. What we have to realize is that this incident is part of a nation-wide conspiracy to undermine the morale of the South African Police. It is vital that we should do nothing premature.'

'Extraordinary,' said the Kommandant. 'Nation-wide, I had no idea there were so many Communists still at large. I thought we'd nabbed the swine years ago.'

'They spring up like dragon's teeth,' Verkramp assured him.

'I suppose they must,' said the Kommandant, who had never thought of it quite like that before. Luitenant Verkramp continued.

'After the failure of the sabotage campaign they went underground.'

'Must have done,' said the Kommandant, still obsessed with the thought of dragon's teeth.

'They've reorganized and have begun a new campaign. First to undermine our morale and secondly, when that's done, they'll start a new wave of sabotage,' Verkramp explained.

'Do you mean to tell me,' the Kommandant, 'that they are deliberately trying to obtain facts that can be used to blackmail police officers all over the country?'

'Precisely, sir,' said Verkramp. 'I have reason to believe that they are particularly interested in sexual indiscretions committed by police officers.'

The Kommandant tried to think of any sexual indiscretions he might have committed lately and rather regretfully couldn't. On the other hand he could think of thousands committed by the men under his command.

'Well,' he said finally, 'it's a good thing Konstabel Els isn't with us any more. The bugger died just in time by the sound of it.'

Verkramp smiled. 'That thought had crossed my mind,' he said. Konstabel Els' exploits in the field of transracial sexual intercourse were already a legend in the Piemburg Police Station.

'In any case I still don't see what you're going to do to stop this infernal campaign,' the Kommandant went on. 'If it isn't Els, there are still plenty of konstabels whose sex life could do with improvement.'

Luitenant Verkramp was delighted. 'My own view of the matter,' he said and took Dr von Blimestein's questionnaire out of his pocket. 'I've been working on the problem with a leading member of the psychiatric profession,' he said, 'and I think we've come up with something that may serve to indicate those officers and men most vulnerable to this form of Communist infiltration.'

'Really?' said the Kommandant, who had an idea who the leading member of the psychiatric profession might be. Luitenant Verkramp handed him the questionnaire.

'With your approval, sir,' he said, 'I'd like to have these questionnaires distributed to all the men on the station. From the answers we get it should be possible to spot any likely victims of blackmail.'

Kommandant van Heerden looked at the questionnaire, which was headed innocuously enough 'Personality Research' and marked 'Strictly Confidential'. He glanced at the first few questions and found nothing to alarm him. They seemed to be concerned with profession of father, age, and the number of brothers and sisters. Before he could get any further Verkramp was explaining that he had orders from Pretoria to carry out the investigation.

'BOSS?' asked the Kommandant.

'BOSS,' said Verkramp.

'In that case, go ahead,' said the Kommandant.

'I'll leave you to fill that one in,' said Verkramp, and left the office delighted at the turn of events. He gave orders to Sergeant Breitenbach to distribute the questionnaires and telephoned Dr von Blimenstein to let her know that everything was proceeding, if not according to plan, since he hadn't had one, at least according to opportunity. Dr von Blimenstein was delighted to hear it and before Verkramp fully realized what he was doing he found that he had invited her to have dinner with him that evening. He put the phone down astonished at his good fortune. It never crossed his mind that the pack of lies about Communist blackmailers he had told the Kommandant had no reality outside his own warped imagination. His professional task was to root out enemies of the state and it followed that enemies of the state were there to be rooted out. The exact details of their activities, if any, were of little importance to him. As he had once explained in court, it was the principle of subversion that mattered, not the particulars.

If Verkramp was satisfied with the way things were going, Kommandant van Heerden, seated at his desk with the questionnaire in front of him, wasn't. The Luitenant's story was convincing enough. The Kommandant had no doubt that Communist agitators were at work in Zululand – nothing less could explain the truculence of the Zulus in the township at the recent increase in bus fares. But that saboteurs disguised as Gas men had infiltrated his own home indicated a new phase in the campaign of subversion, and a particularly alarming one at that. The Duty Sergeant's report that the investigating team had discovered a microphone under the sink only went to prove how accurate Luitenant Verkramp's forecast had been. Ordering the Sergeant to leave the investigation to the Security Branch, the Kommandant sent a note to Verkramp which read, 'Re our discussion this morning. The presence of microphone in kitchen confirms your report. Suggest you take counteraction immediately. Van Heerden.'

With renewed confidence in the ability of his second-in-command the Kommandant decided to tackle the questionnaire Verkramp had given him. He filled in the first few questions happily enough and it was only when he had turned the page that there dawned on him the feeling that he was being led gently into a quagmire of sexual confession where every answer only dragged him deeper down.

'Did you have a black nanny?' seemed innocuous enough, and the Kommandant put 'Yes' only to find that the next question was 'Size of breasts. Large. Medium. Small.' After a moment's hesitation not unmixed with alarm he ticked 'Large,' and went on to consider 'Nipple Length. Long. Medium. Short.' 'This is a bloody funny way to fight Communism,' he thought, trying to remember the length of his nanny's teats. In the end he put 'Long' and found himself faced with 'Did black nanny tickle private parts? Often. Sometimes. Infrequently?' The Kommandant looked desperately for 'Never' and couldn't find it. In the end he ticked Infrequently and turned to the next question. 'Age at First Ejaculation, Three years, four years . . .?'

'Don't leave much to chance,' thought the Kommandant, indignantly trying to make his mind up between six years, which was quite untrue but which seemed less likely to undermine his authority than sixteen years, which was more accurate. He'd just put eight years as a compromise based on a nocturnal emission he'd had when he was ten when he saw that he'd walked into a trap. The next question was 'Age at First Wet Dream?' This time the list started at ten years. By the time he had rubbed out his answer to the previous question to make it consistent with a Wet Dream at eleven years, the Kommandant was in a thoroughly bad temper. He picked up the phone and called Verkramp's office. Sergeant Breitenbach answered the phone.

'Where's Verkramp?' the Kommandant demanded. The Sergeant said he was out, and could he help? The Kommandant said he doubted it. 'It's this damned questionnaire,' he told the Sergeant. 'Who's going to read it?'

'I think Dr von Blimenstein intends to,' the Sergeant said. 'She drew it up.'

'Did she?' snarled the Kommandant. 'Well you can tell Luitenant Verkramp that I have no intention of answering question twenty-five.'

'Which one is that?'

'It's the one that goes "How many times do you masturbate every day?"' said the Kommandant. 'You can tell Verkramp that I think it's an invasion of privacy to ask questions like that.'

'Yes, sir,' said Sergeant Breitenbach, studying the possible answers on the questionnaire, which ranged from five times to twenty-five times.

The Kommandant slammed down the phone and locking the questionnaire in his desk went out to lunch in a filthy temper. 'Dirty bitch, wanting to know things like that,' he thought as he stomped downstairs, and he was still grumbling to himself when he finished lunch in the police canteen. 'I'll be up at the Golf Club if anyone wants me,' he told the Duty Sergeant and left the police station. He spent a fruitless couple of hours trying to hit a ball down the fairway before returning to the Clubhouse with the feeling that this was not one of his days.

He ordered a double brandy from the barman and took his drink out to a table on the terrace where he could sit and watch more experienced players drive off. He was sitting there absorbing the English atmosphere and trying to rid himself of the nagging conviction that the even tenor of his life was being undermined in some mysterious way when a crunch of gravel in the Clubhouse forecourt made him glance over his shoulder. A vintage Rolls-Royce had just parked and the occupants were climbing out. For a moment the Kommandant had the extraordinary sensation that he had been transported back to the 1920s. The two men who emerged from the front seat were dressed in knickerbockers and wore hats that had been out of fashion for fifty years, while their two women companions were attired in what appeared to the Kommandant to be fancy dress with cloche hats, and carried parasols. But it was less the clothes or the immaculate vintage Rolls than the voices that affected the Kommandant so profoundly. High-pitched and languidly arrogant, they seemed to reach him like some echo from the English past and with them came a rush of certitude that all was well in the world in spite of everything. The kernel of servility which was Kommandant van Heerden's innermost self and which no amount of his own authority could ever erase quivered ecstatically within him as the group passed him without so much as a glance to indicate that they were aware of his existence. It was precisely this self-absorption to the point where it transcended self and became something immutable and absolute, a Godlike self-sufficiency, that Kommandant van Heerden had always hoped to find in the English. And here it was before him in the Piemburg Golf Club in the shape of four middle-aged men and women whose inane chatter was proof positive that there was, in spite of wars, disasters, and imminent revolution, nothing serious to worry about. The Kommandant particularly admired the elegance with which the leader of the foursome, a florid man in his fifties, clicked his fingers for the black caddie before walking over to the first tee.

'How absolutely priceless,' shrieked one of the ladies about nothing in particular as they followed.

'I've always said Boy was a glutton for punishment,' said the florid man as they passed out of earshot. The Kommandant stared after them before hurrying in to the bar to consult the barman.

'Call themselves the Dornford Yates Club,' the barman told him. 'Don't ask me why. Anyway they dress up and talk la-di-da in memory of some firm called Bury & Co which went bust some years back. Red-faced fellow is Colonel Heathcote-Kilkoon. He's the one they call Bury. The plump lady is his missus. The other bloke's Major Bloxham. Call him Boy, of all things, and he must be forty-eight if he's a day. I don't know who the thin woman is.'

'Do they live near here?' the Kommandant asked. He didn't approve of the barman's rather off-hand attitude to his betters but he desperately wanted to hear more about the foursome.

'The Colonel's got a place up near the Piltdown Hotel but

they seem to spend most of their time on a farm in the Underville district. It's got a queer name like White Woman or something. I've heard they have some pretty queer goings-on up there, too.'

The Kommandant ordered another brandy and took it out to his table on the terrace to wait for the party to return. Presently he was joined by the barman who stood in the doorway looking bored.

'Has the Colonel been a member here long?' the Kommandant asked.

'A couple of years,' the barman said, 'since they all came down from Rhodesia or Kenya or somewhere. Seem to have plenty of spending money too.'

Aware that the man was looking at him rather curiously, the Kommandant finished his drink and strolled over to inspect the vintage Rolls-Royce.

'1925 Silver Ghost,' said the barman who had followed him over. 'Nice condition.'

The Kommandant grunted. He was beginning to tire of the barman's company. He moved round the other side of the car, only to find the barman at his elbow.

'You after them for something?' the man asked conspiratorially.

'What the hell makes you think that?' the Kommandant asked.

'Just wondered,' said the barman, and with some remark about a nod being as good as a wink which the Kommandant didn't understand, the man went back into the Clubhouse. Left to himself, the Kommandant finished his inspection of the car and was just turning away when he caught sight of something on the back seat that stopped him in his tracks. It was a book and from its back cover there stared impassively the portrait of a man. High cheek bones, slightly hooded eyelids, impeccably straight nose and a trimmed moustache, the face looked past the Kommandant into a bright and assured future. Peering through the window, Kommandant van Heerden gazed at the portrait and as he gazed knew with a certainty that passed all understanding that he was on the brink of a new phase of discovery in his search for the heart of an English gentleman. There before him on the back seat of the Rolls was portrayed with an exactitude he would never have believed possible the face of the man he wanted to be. The book was *As Other Men Are* by Dornford Yates. The Kommandant took out his notebook and wrote the title down.

By the time Colonel Heathcote-Kilkoon and his party returned to the Clubhouse, the Kommandant had left and was making his way to the Public Library in the certain knowledge that he was about to learn, from the works of Dornford Yates, the secret of that enigma which had puzzled him for so long, how to be an English gentleman.

By the time Luitenant Verkramp left the police station that evening and returned to his flat to change he was a supremely happy man. The ease with which he had allayed the Kommandant's suspicions, the results he was getting from the questionnaires, the prospects of spending the evening in the company of Dr von Blimenstein all contributed to the Luitenant's sense of well-being. Above all, the fact that the Kommandant's house was still bugged and that he would be able to lie in bed and listen to every movement the Kommandant was indiscreet enough to make in his home lent a piquancy to Verkramp's sense of achievement. Like the Kommandant, Luitenant Verkramp felt himself on the brink of a discovery that would change his whole life and transform him from merely second-in-command into a position of authority more suited to his ability. As he waited for his bath water to run, Luitenant Verkramp adjusted the receiver in his bedroom and checked the tape recorder connected to it. Before long he could make out the Kommandant shuffling about his house and opening and shutting cupboards. Satisfied that his listening device was functioning properly, Verkramp switched it off and went and had his bath. He had just finished and was climbing out when the front-door bell rang.

'Damn,' said Verkramp grabbing a towel and wondering who the hell was visiting him at this inconvenient moment. He went out into the hall trailing drops of bath water as he went, opened the door irritably and was amazed to see Dr von Blimenstein standing on the landing. 'I don't want . . .' said Verkramp, reacting automatically to the sound of his doorbell at inconvenient moments before he realized who his visitor was.

'Don't you, darling?' said Dr von Blimenstein loudly and opened her musquash coat to disclose a tight-fitting dress of some extremely shiny material. 'Are you sure you don't . . .'

'For hell's sake,' Verkramp said, looking wildly round. He was conscious that his neighbours were extremely respectable people and that Dr von Blimenstein, for all her education and professional standing as a psychiatrist, was not at the best of times overly worried about observing the social niceties. And now, with a bath towel round his middle and the doctor with whatever it was she had round her middle and top and bottom, was not the best of times. 'Come in quick,' he squawked. Somewhat disappointed by the reception he had given her, Dr von Blimenstein drew her coat around her and entered the flat. Verkramp hurriedly shut the door and scurried past her into the safety of his bathroom. 'I wasn't expecting you,' he shouted softly. 'I was coming up to the hospital to collect you.'

'I couldn't wait to see you,' the doctor shouted back, 'and I thought I'd give you a little surprise.'

'You did that all right,' Verkramp muttered, desperately searching for a sock that had hidden itself somewhere in the bathroom.

'I didn't quite catch that. You'll have to speak up.'

Verkramp found the sock under the washbasin. 'I said you did give me a surprise.' He hit his head on the washbasin straightening up and ended with a curse.

'You're not angry with me coming like this?' the doctor inquired. In the bathroom Verkramp sat on the edge of the bath and pulled his sock on. It was wet.

'No, of course not. Come whenever you like,' he said sourly.

'You do mean that, don't you? I mean I wouldn't like you to think I was being . . . well . . . intruding,' the doctor continued while Verkramp, still protesting his delight that she should visit him as often as possible, discovered that all the clothes he had carefully laid out on the lavatory seat had got wet, thanks to her precipitate arrival. By the time he emerged Luitenant Verkramp was feeling distinctly clammy, and quite unprepared for the sight that met his eyes. Doctor von Blimenstein had taken off her musquash coat and was lying provocatively on his sofa in a bright red dress which clung to her body with an intimacy of contour which astonished Verkramp and made him wonder how she had ever got into it.

'Do you like it?' the doctor inquired stretching voluptuously. Verkramp swallowed and said that he did, very much. 'It's the new wet look in stretch nylon.' Verkramp found himself staring at her breasts hypnotically and with the terrible realization that he was committed to an evening spent in public with a woman who was wearing what amounted to a semi-transparent scarlet bodystocking. Luitenant Verkramp's reputation for sober and God-fearing living was something he had always been proud of and as a devout member of the Verwoerd Street Dutch Reformed Church he was shocked by the doctor's outfit. As he drove up to the Piltdown Hotel the only consolation he could find was that the beastly garment was so tight she wouldn't be able to dance in it. Luitenant Verkramp didn't dance. He thought it was sinful.

At the Hotel the Commissionaire opened the car door and Verkramp's sense of social inadequacy, already heightened by the knowledge that his Volkswagen was parked next to a Cadillac, was increased by the man's manner.

'I want the brassière,' Verkramp said.

'The what, sir?' said the Commissionaire with his eye on Dr von Blimenstein's bosom.

'The brassière,' said Verkramp.

'You won't find one here, sir,' the Commissionaire said. Dr von Blimenstein came to the rescue.

'The brasserie,' she said.

'Oh you mean the grill room,' the Commissionaire said and, still finding it difficult to believe the evidence of his senses, directed them to the Colour Bar. Verkramp was delighted to find the lights low so that he could sit hidden from public view in a high-backed booth in a corner. Besides, Dr von Blimenstein had come to the rescue and had ordered dry martinis from the wine waiter, who had been looking superciliously at Verkramp's efforts to find something vaguely familiar in the wine list. After three martinis Verkramp was feeling decidedly better.

Dr von Blimenstein was telling him about aversion therapy.

'It's quite straightforward,' she said. 'The patient is tied to a bed while slides of his particular perversion are projected on a screen. For instance, if you're dealing with a homosexual, you show him slides of nude men.'

'Really,' said Verkramp. 'How very interesting. What do you do then?'

'At the very moment you show him the picture, you also administer an electric shock.'

Verkramp was fascinated. 'And that cures him?' he asked.

'In the end the patient shows signs of anxiety every time a slide is shown,' said the doctor.

'I can well believe it,' said Verkramp, whose own experiments with electric shock treatment had resulted in much the same anxiety on the part of his prisoners.

'The process has to be kept up for six days to be really effective,' Dr von Blimenstein continued, 'but you'd be surprised at the number of cures we have achieved by this method.'

Verkramp said he wouldn't be in the least surprised. While they ate, Dr von Blimenstein explained that a modified form of aversion therapy was what she had in mind for treating cases of miscegenation among policemen in Piemburg. Verkramp, whose mind was cloudy with gin and wine, tried to think what she meant. 'I don't quite see . . .' he began.

'Nude black women,' said the doctor, smiling across her plank steak. 'Project slides of nude black women on the screen and administer an electric shock at the same time.' Verkramp looked at her with open admiration.

'Brilliant,' he said. 'Marvellous. You're a genius.' Dr von Blimenstein simpered. 'It's not my original idea,' she said modestly, 'but I suppose you could say that I have adapted it to South African needs.'

'It's a breakthrough,' said Verkramp. '*The* breakthrough one might say.'

'One likes to think so,' murmured the doctor.

'A toast,' said Verkramp raising his glass, 'I drink to your success.'

Dr von Blimenstein raised her glass. 'To our success, darling, to our success.' They drank and as they drank it seemed to Verkramp that for the first time in his life he was really happy. He was dining in a smart hotel with a lovely woman with whose help he was about to make history. No longer would the danger of South Africa becoming a country of coloureds haunt the minds of White South Africa's leaders. With Dr von Blimenstein at his side, Verkramp would set up clinics throughout the republic where white perverts could be cured of their sexual lusts for black women by aversion therapy. He leant across the table towards her entrancing breasts and took her hand.

'I love you,' he said simply.

'I love you too,' murmured the doctor, gazing back at him with an intensity almost predatory. Verkramp looked nervously round the restaurant and was relieved to find that no one was watching them.

'In a nice way, of course,' he said after a pause.

Dr von Blimenstein smiled. 'Love isn't nice, darling,' she said. 'It's dark and violent and passionate and cruel.'

'Yes ... well ...' said Verkramp who had never looked at love in this light before. 'What I meant was that love is pure. My love, that is.'

In Dr von Blimenstein's eyes a flame seemed to flicker and die down. 'Love is desire,' she said. Beneath the nylon sheath her breasts bulged onto the table, imminent with a motherly menace that Verkramp found disturbing. He shifted his narrow legs under the table and tried to think of something to say.

'I want you,' whispered the doctor, emphasizing her need by digging her crimson fingernails into the palm of Verkramp's hand. 'I want you desperately.' Luitenant Verkramp shuddered involuntarily. Beneath the table Dr von Blimenstein's ample knees closed firmly on his leg. 'I want you,' she repeated and Verkramp, who had begun to think that he was having dinner with a volcano on heat, found himself saying, 'Isn't it time we went?' before he realized the interpretation the doctor was likely to put on his sudden desire to leave the relative safety of the restaurant.

As they went out to the car, Dr von Blimenstein put her arm through Verkramp's and held him close to her. He opened the

43

car door for her and with a wheeze of nylon the doctor slid into her seat. Verkramp, whose previous sense of social inadequacy had been quite replaced by a feeling of sexual inadequacy in the face of the doctor's open intimation of desire, climbed in hesitantly beside her.

'You don't understand,' he said, starting the car, 'I don't want to do anything that would spoil the beauty of this evening.' In the darkness Dr von Blimenstein's hand reached out and squeezed his leg.

'You mustn't feel guilty,' she murmured. Verkramp put the car into reverse with a jerk.

'I respect you too much,' he said.

Dr von Blimstein's musquash coat heaved softly as she leant her head on his shoulder. A heavy perfume wafted across Verkramp's face. 'You're such a shy boy,' she said.

Verkramp drove out of the hotel grounds onto the Piemburg road. Far below them the lights of the city flickered and went out. It was midnight.

Verkramp drove slowly down the hill, partly because he was afraid of being booked for drunken driving but more importantly because he was terrified by the prospect that awaited him when they got back to his flat. Twice Dr von Blimenstein insisted they stop the car and twice Verkramp found himself wrapped in her arms while her lips searched for and found his own thin mouth. 'Relax, darling,' she told him as Verkramp squirmed with a feverish mixture of refusal and consent which satisfied both his own conscience and Dr von Blimenstein's belief that he was responding. 'Sex has to be learnt.' Verkramp had no need to be told.

He started the car again and drove on while Dr von Blimenstein explained that it was quite normal for a man to be afraid of sex. By the time they reached Verkramp's flat the euphoria that had followed the doctor's explanation of how she was going to cure the miscegenating policemen had quite left him. The strange mixture of animal passion and clinical objectivity with which the doctor discussed sex had aroused in the Luitenant an aversion for the subject that no electric shocks were needed to reinforce.

'Well, that was a very nice evening,' he said hopefully, parking next to the doctor's car, but Dr von Blimenstein had no intention of leaving so soon.

'You're going to ask me up for a nightcap?' she asked and, when Verkramp hesitated, went on, 'In any case I seem to have left my handbag in your flat so I'll have to come up for a bit.'

Verkramp led the way upstairs quietly. 'I don't want to disturb the neighbours,' he explained in a whisper. In a voice that seemed calculated to wake the dead, Dr von Blimenstein said she'd be as quiet as a mouse and followed this up by trying to kiss him while he was fumbling for his key. Once inside she took off her coat and sat on the divan with a display of leg that went some way to reawakening the desire which her conversation had quenched. Her hair spilled over the cushions and she raised her arms to him. Verkramp said he'd make some coffee and went through to the kitchen. When he came back Dr von Blimenstein had turned the main light off and a reading lamp in one corner on and was fiddling with his radio. 'Just trying to get some music,' she said. Above the divan the loudspeaker crackled. Verkramp put the coffee cups down and turned to attend to the radio but Dr von Blimenstein was no longer interested in music. She stood before him with the same gentle smile Verkramp had seen on her face the day he had first met her at the hospital and before he could escape the lovely doctor had pinned him to the divan with that expertise Verkramp had once so much admired. As her lips silenced his weak protest Luitenant Verkramp lost all sense of guilt. He was helpless in her arms and there was nothing he could do.

CHAPTER FOUR

Kommandant van Heerden emerged from the Piemburg Public Library clutching his copy of *As Other Men Are* with a sense of anticipation he had last experienced as a boy when he swopped comics outside the cinema on Saturday mornings. He hurried through the street, occasionally glancing at the cover with a cartouche on the front and with the portrait of the great author on the back. Each time he looked at the face with its slightly hooded eyelids and brisk moustache he was filled with that sense of social hierarchy for which his soul hankered. All the doubts about the existence of good and evil which twenty-five years as an officer in the South African Police had naturally inflicted on him vanished before the assurance that radiated from that portrait. Not that Kommandant van Heerden had ever for a moment had reason to doubt the existence of evil. It was the lack of its opposite that he found so spiritually debilitating, and since the Kommandant was not given to anything approaching conceptual thought, the goodness he sought had to be seen to be believed. Better still it had to be personified in some socially acceptable form and here at last, breathing an arrogance that brooked no question, the face that looked past him from the jacket of *As Other Men Are* was proof positive that all those values like chivalry and courage, to which Kommandant van Heerden paid so much private tribute, still existed in the world.

Once home and ensconced in an armchair with a pot of tea made and a cup by his side, he opened the book and began to read. 'Eve Malory Carew tilted her sweet pretty chin,' he read, and as he read the world of sordid crime, of murder and fraud, burglary and assault, cowardice and deception, with which his profession brought him into daily contact, disappeared, to be replaced by a new world in which lovely ladies and magnificent men moved with an ease and assurance and wit towards inevitably happy endings. As he followed the adventures of Jeremy Broke and Captain Toby Rage, not to mention Oliver Pauncefote and Simon Beaulieu, the Kommandant knew that he had come home. Luitenant Verkramp, Sergeant Breitenbach and the six hundred men under his command were happily forgotten as the hours passed and the Kommandant, his tea stone cold, read on. Occasionally he would read some particularly moving passage aloud to savour the words more fully. At one o'clock in the morning he glanced at his watch and was amazed that time had passed so unnoticeably. Still, there was no need to get up early in the morning and he had come to another stirring episode.

'The pearls that George gave me sprawl, pale and indignant

by my side,' he read aloud in what he vainly imagined was an adequate impersonation of a female voice, 'I've taken them off. I don't want his pearls about me; I want your arms.'

While Kommandant van Heerden was finding it a wonderful relief to escape from the real world of sordid experience into one of pure fantasy, Luitenant Verkramp was doing just the opposite. Now that the sexual fantasies he had entertained about Dr von Blimenstein through many sleepless nights seemed all too likely to be fulfilled in reality, Verkramp found the prospect unbearable. For one thing, the attractions which an absent and imagined Dr von Blimenstein had held had quite disappeared, to be replaced by the awareness that she was a heavily built woman with enormous breasts and muscular legs whose sexual needs he had no desire whatsoever to satisfy. And for another, the walls of his apartment were so constructed as to allow the sounds in one flat to be clearly heard in another. To add to his worries, the doctor was drunk.

In a foolish attempt to induce in her the feminine equivalent of whisky droop, Verkramp had plied her with Scotch from a bottle he kept for special occasions and had been horrified not only by the doctor's capacity for hard liquor but also by the fact that the damned stuff seemed to act as an aphrodisiac. Deciding to try to reverse the process, he went through to the kitchen to make some more black coffee. He had just lit the stove when an eruption of noise from the living-room sent him scurrying back. Dr von Blimenstein had switched on his tape recorder.

'I want an old-fashioned house with an old-fashioned fence and an old-fashioned millionaire,' cried Eartha Kitt.

Dr von Blimenstein accompanying her was more modest in her demands. 'I want to be loved by you, just you and nobody else but you,' she crooned in a voice several decibels above the legal limit.

'For heaven's sake,' said Verkramp, trying to edge past her to the tape recorder, 'you'll wake the neighbourhood.'

In the flat above, the creak of bedsprings suggested that Verkramp's neighbours were taking notice of the doctor's demand even if he wasn't.

'I want to be loved by you alone, boo boopy doop,' Dr von Blimenstein continued, clasping Verkramp in her arms. In the background Miss Kitt added to his embarrassment by announcing to the world her desire for oil wells and Verkramp's own predilection for coloured singers.

'Whasso wrong with love, baby?' asked the doctor, managing to combine whimsy with sex in a manner Verkramp found particularly irritating.

'Yes,' he said placatorily, trying to escape from her embrace, 'If you—'

'Were the only girl in the world and I was the only boy,' bawled the doctor.

'For God's sake,' squawked Verkramp, appalled at the prospect.

'Well, you're not,' came a voice from the flat upstairs. 'You've got me to consider.'

Spurred on by this support Verkramp squeezed out of the doctor's arms and fell back on the divan.

'Give me, give me what I long for,' sang the doctor, changing her tune.

'Some fucking sleep,' yelled the man upstairs, evidently sickened by the doctor's erratic repertoire.

In the flat next door, where a lecturer in Religious Instruction lived with his wife, someone banged on the wall.

Scrambling off the divan, Verkramp hurled himself at the tape recorder.

'Let me turn that coon girl off,' he shouted. Miss Kitt was on about diamonds now.

'Leave the coon girls alone. You've turned me on,' screamed Dr von Blimenstein, tackling Verkramp by the legs and bringing him down with a crash. Squatting on top of him she pressed herself against him with an urgency that inserted the bobble of her garter belt into his mouth, and fumbled with his trouser buttons. With a revulsion that sprang from his ignorance of female anatomy, Verkramp spat the thing out only to find himself facing an even more disgusting prospect. With his horizon bounded obscenely by thighs, garter belts and those portions of the doctor which figured so largely in his fantasies but which on closer acquaintance had quite lost their charm, Verkramp fought desperately for air.

It was at this juncture that Kommandant van Heerden unwittingly chose to intervene. Enormously amplified by Verkramp's electronic equipment, the Kommandant's falsetto voice added its peculiar charm to Miss Kitt's contralto, and Dr von Blimenstein's insistent commands to Verkramp to lie still.

'Simon,' squeaked the Kommandant, oblivious of the effect he was having half a mile away, 'that last night here we buried our love alive, our glorious, blessed passion, we buried alive.'

'Whazzat?' asked Dr von Blimenstein who had ignored all Verkramp's previous entreaties in her drunken frenzy.

'Let me go,' screamed Verkramp, to whom the Kommandant's mention of burying alive seemed particularly relevant.

'Somone's being murdered in there,' squealed the Religious Instructor's wife next door.

'I must have been mad. I suppose I thought it'd die,' continued the Kommandant.

'Whazzat?' shrieked Dr von Blimenstein again, drunkenly trying to distinguish between Verkramp's frantic screams and the Kommandant's impassioned confession, a process of decoding made no less difficult by Eartha Kitt impersonating a Turk.

On the landing the man from the flat above was threatening to break the door down.

At the centre of this maelstrom of noise and movement Luitenant Verkramp stared lividly into the vermilion flounces of Dr von Blimenstein's elaborate panties and then, overcome by the hysterical fear that he was about to be castrated, took the bit between his teeth.

With a scream that could be heard half a mile away and which had the effect of stopping the Kommandant reading aloud, Dr von Blimenstein shot forward across the room, dragging the demented Verkramp inextricably entangled in her garter belt behind.

To Luitenant Verkramp the next few minutes were a foretaste of hell. Behind him the man from the flat above, by now convinced beyond doubt that he was privy to some hideous crime, hurled himself against the door. In front Dr von Blimenstein, equally convinced that she had at last aroused her lover's sexual appetite but anxious that it should express itself in a more orthodox fashion, hurled herself onto her back. As the door burst open, Verkramp peered up through the torn vermilion flounces with all the *Weltschmerz* of a decapitated Rhode Island Red. In the doorway the man from upstairs was standing dumbfounded at the spectacle.

'Now, darling, now,' screamed Dr von Blimenstein writhing ecstatically. Verkramp scrambled furiously to his feet.

'How dare you break in?' he yelled, desperately trying to convert his embarrassment into justified rage. From the floor Dr von Blimenstein intervened more effectively.

'Coitus interruptus,' she shouted, 'coitus interruptus!' Verkramp seized on the phrase, which sounded vaguely medical to him.

'She's an epileptic,' he explained as the doctor continued to twitch. 'She's from Fort Rapier.'

'Christ,' said the man, now thoroughly embarrassed himself. The Religious Instructor's wife pushed her way into the room.

'There, there,' she said to the doctor, 'It's all right. We're here.'

In the confusion Verkramp slunk away and locked himself in his bathroom. He sat there, white with humiliation and disgust, until the ambulance arrived to take the doctor back to the hospital. In the living-room Dr von Blimenstein was still shouting drunkenly about erogenous zones and the emotional hazards of interrupted coition.

When everyone had left, Verkramp emerged from the bathroom and surveyed the mess in his living-room with a jaundiced eye. The only consolation he could find for the evening's horror was the knowledge that his suspicions about the Kommandant had been confirmed. Verkramp tried to remember what that ghastly falsetto voice had said. It was something about burying someone alive. It seemed highly unlikely somehow but Luitenant Verkramp's whole evening had been calculated to induce in him the suspicion that the most respectable people were capable of the most bizarre acts. Of one thing he was absolutely certain – he never wanted to set eyes on Dr von Blimenstein again.

Kommandant van Heerden, arriving at his office next morning freshly imbued with the determination to behave like a gentleman, felt much the same. Dr von Blimenstein's questionnaire had aroused a storm of protest in the Piemburg Police Station.

'It's part of a campaign to stop the spread of Communism,' the Kommandant explained to Sergeant de Kok, who had been deputed to express the men's sense of grievance.

'What's the size of a kaffir's teats got to do with the spread of Communism?' the Sergeant wanted to know. Kommandant van Heerden agreed that the connection did seem rather obscure.

'You'd better ask Luitenant Verkramp about it,' he said. 'It's his affair, not mine. As far as I'm concerned no one need answer the beastly thing. I certainly don't intend to.'

'Yes, sir. Thank you, sir,' said the Sergeant and went off to cancel Verkramp's orders.

In the afternoon the Kommandant returned to the Golf Club in the hope of catching a glimpse of the foursome who called themselves the Dornford Yates Club. He hit a few balls into the woods for the look of the thing and returned to the Clubhouse quite shortly. As he approached the stoep, he was delighted to see the vintage Rolls steal noiselessly down the drive from the main road and park overlooking the course. Mrs Heathcote-Kilkoon was driving. She was wearing a blue sweater and skirt and matching gloves. For a moment she sat in the car and then climbed out and walked round the bonnet with a wistfulness that touched the Kommandant to the quick.

'Excuse me,' she called to him, leaning on the radiator with a gesture of elegance the Kommandant had seen only in the more expensive women's magazines, 'but I wonder if you could help me.'

Kommandant van Heerden's pulse rate went up abruptly. He said he would be honoured to help her.

'I'm such a fool,' continued Mrs Heathcote-Kilkoon, 'and I know absolutely nothing about cars. I wonder if you could just

51

have a look at it and tell me if anything's wrong.'

With a gallantry that belied his utter ignorance of motor cars in general and vintage Rolls-Royces in particular, the Kommandant fumbled with the catches of the bonnet and was presently greasily engaged in looking for anything that might indicate why the car had so fortuitously ceased to function at the top of the Golf Club drive. Behind him Mrs Heathcote-Kilkoon urged him on with an indulgent smile and the idle chatter of a fascinating woman.

'I feel so helpless when it comes to machinery,' she murmured as the Kommandant, who shared her feelings, poked his finger into a carburettor hopefully. It didn't get very far, which he judged to be a good sign. Presently, when he had inspected the fan-belt and the dip-stick, which more or less exhausted his automotive know-how, he gave up the unequal task.

'I'm so sorry,' he said, 'but I can't see anything obviously wrong.'

'Perhaps I'm just out of petrol,' smiled Mrs Heathcote-Kilkoon. Kommandant van Heerden looked at the petrol gauge and found it registered Empty.

'That's right,' he said. Mrs Heathcote-Kilkoon breathed her apologies. 'And you've been to so much trouble too,' she murmured but Kommandant van Heerden was too happy to feel that he had been to any trouble at all.

'My pleasure,' he said blushing, and was about to go and get the grease off his hands when Mrs Heathcote-Kilkoon stopped him.

'You've been so good,' she said, 'I must buy you a drink.'

The Kommandant tried to say there was no need but she wouldn't hear of it. 'I'll telephone the garage for some petrol,' she told him, 'and then I'll join you on the verandah.'

Presently the Kommandant found himself sipping a cool drink while Mrs Heathcote-Kilkoon, sucking hers through a straw, asked him about his work.

'It must be so absolutely fascinating to be a detective,' she said. 'My husband's retired you know.'

'I didn't know,' said the Kommandant.

'Of course he still dabbles in stocks and shares,' she went on, 'but it isn't the same thing, is it?'

The Kommandant said he didn't suppose it was though he wasn't quite sure as what. While Mrs Heathcote-Kilkoon chattered on the Kommandant drank in the details of her dress, the crocodile-skin shoes, the matching handbag, the discreet pearls, and marvelled at her excellence of taste. Even the way she crossed her legs had about it a demureness Kommandant van Heerden found irresistible.

'Are your people from this part of the world?' Mrs Heathcote-Kilkoon inquired presently.

'My father had a farm in the Karoo,' the Kommandant told her. 'He used to keep goats.' He was conscious that it sounded a fairly humble occupation but from what he knew of the English they held landowners in high esteem. Mrs Heathcote-Kilkoon sighed.

'How I adore the countryside,' she said. 'That's one reason why we came to Zululand. My husband retired to Umtali after the war, you know, and we loved it up there but somehow the climate affected him and we came down here. We chose Piemburg because we both adore the atmosphere. So gorgeously *fin de siècle*, don't you think?'

The Kommandant, who didn't know what *fin de siècle* meant, said that he liked Piemburg because it reminded him of the good old days.

'You're so right,' said Mrs Heathcote-Kilkoon. 'My husband and I are absolute addicts of nostalgia. If only we could put the clock back. The elegance, the charm, the gallantry of those dear dead days beyond recall,' She sighed and the Kommandant, feeling that for once in his life he had met with a kindred spirit, sighed with her. Presently when the barman reported that the garage had put the petrol in the Rolls, the Kommandant stood up.

'I mustn't keep you,' he said politely.

'It was sweet of you to help,' Mrs Heathcote-Kilkoon said and held out her gloved hand. The Kommandant took it and with a sudden impulse that sprang from page forty-nine of *As Other Men Are* pressed it to his lips. 'Your servant,' he murmured.

He was gone before Mrs Heathcote-Kilkoon could say anything and was soon driving down into Piemburg feeling strangely elated. That evening he took *Berry & Co* from the library and went home to draw fresh inspiration from its pages.

'Where've you been?' Colonel Heathcote-Kilkoon asked when his wife arrived home.

'You'll never believe it but I've been talking with a real hairy-back. Not one of your slick ones but the genuine article. Absolutely out of the Ark. You'll never believe this but he actually kissed my hand when we parted.'

'How disgusting,' said the Colonel, and went off down the garden to look at his azaleas. If there was one thing he detested after white ants and cheeky kaffirs, it was Afrikaners. In the living-room Major Bloxham was reading *Country Life*.

'I suppose they can't all be swine,' he said graciously when Mrs Heathcote-Kilkoon told him about the Kommandant, 'though for the life of me I can't remember meeting one who wasn't. I knew a fellow called Botha once in Kenya. Never washed. Does your friend wash?'

Mrs Heathcote-Kilkoon snorted and went upstairs for a rest before dinner. Lying there in the still of the late afternoon listening to the gentle swirl of the lawn sprinkler, she felt a vague regret for the life she had once led. Born in Croydon, she had come from Selsdon Road via service in the Women's Auxiliary Air Force to Nairobi where her suburban background had served to earn her a commission and a husband with money. From those carefree days she had gradually descended the dark continent, swept southward on the ebb tide of Empire and acquiring with each new latitude those exquisite pretensions Kommandant van Heerden so much admired. Now she was tired. The affectations which had been so necessary in Nairobi for any sort of social life were wasted in Piemburg, whose atmosphere was by comparison wholly lower-middle-class. She was still depressed when she dressed for dinner that night.

'What's the use of going on pretending we are what we're not when no one even cares that we aren't?' she asked plaintively. Colonel Heathcote-Kilkoon looked at her with disapproval.

'Got to keep up a good front,' he barked.

'Stiff upper lip, old girl,' said Major Bloxham, whose grandmother had kept a winkle stand in Brighton. 'Can't let the side down.'

But Mrs Heathcote-Kilkoon no longer knew which side she was on. The world to which she had been born was gone and with it the social aspirations that made life bearable. The world she had made by dint of affectation was going. After scolding the Zulu waiter for serving the soup from the wrong side, Mrs Heathcote-Kilkoon rose from the table and took her coffee into the garden. There, soundlessly pacing the lawn under the lucid night sky, she thought about the Kommandant. 'There's something so real about him,' she murmured to herself. Over their port Colonel Heathcote-Kilkoon and the Major were discussing the Battle for Normandy. There was nothing real about them. Even the port was Australian.

CHAPTER FIVE

In the following days Kommandant van Heerden, oblivious of the interest that was being focused on him both by Luitenant Verkramp and Mrs Heathcote-Kilkoon, continued his literary pilgrimage with increased fervour. Every morning, closely shadowed by the Security men detailed by Verkramp to watch him, he would visit the Piemburg Library for a fresh volume of Dornford Yates and every evening return to his bugged home to devote himself to its study. When finally he went to bed he would lie in the darkness repeating to himself his adaptation of Coué's famous formula, 'Every day and in every way, I am becoming Berrier and Berrier,' a form of auto-suggestion that had little observable effect on the Kommandant himself but drove the eavesdropping Verkramp frantic.

'What the hell does it all mean?' he asked Sergeant Breitenbach as they listened to the tape-recording of these nocturnal efforts at self-improvement.

'A berry is a sort of fruit,' said the Sergeant without much conviction.

'It's also something you do when you want to get rid of bodies,' said Verkramp, whose own taste was more funereal, 'but why the devil does he repeat it over and over again?'

'Sounds like a sort of prayer,' Sergeant Breitenbach said. 'I had an aunt who got religious mania. She used to say her prayers all the time . . .' but Luitenant Verkramp didn't want to hear about Sergeant Breitenbach's aunt.

'I want a close watch kept on him all the time,' he said, 'and the moment he starts doing anything suspicious like buying a spade let me know.'

'Why don't you ask that headshrinker of yours . . .' the Sergeant asked, and was startled by the vehemence of Verkramp's reply. He left the office with the distinct impression that if there was one thing Luitenant Verkramp didn't want, need or wish for, it was Dr von Blimenstein.

Left to himself Verkramp tried to concentrate his mind on the problem of Kommandant van Heerden by looking through the reports of his movements.

'Went to Library. Went to police station. Went to Golf Club. Went home.' The regularity of these innocent activities was disheartening and yet hidden within this routine there lay the secret of the Kommandant's terrible assurance and awful smile. Even the news that his house was being bugged by Communists had shaken it only momentarily and as far as Verkramp could judge the Kommandant had entirely forgotten the affair. True, he had banned Dr von Blimenstein's questionnaire but, now that Verkramp had first-hand knowledge of the doctor's sexual behaviour, he had to admit that it was a wise decision. With what amounted to, literally, hindsight Luitenant Verkramp realized that he had been on the verge of disclosing the sexual habits of every policeman in Piemburg to a woman with vested interests in the subject. He shuddered to think what use she would have put that information to and turned his attention to the question of miscegenating policemen. It was obvious that he would have to tackle that problem without outside help and after trying to remember what Dr von Blimenstein had told him about the technique he went off to the Public Library, partly to see if there were any books there on aversion therapy but also because the Library figured so frequently in Kommandant van Heerden's itinerary. An hour later, clutching a copy of *Fact & Fiction in Psychology* by H. J. Eysenck, he returned to the police station satisfied that he had got hold of the definitive work on aversion therapy but still no nearer any understanding of the change that had come over the Kommandant. His inquiries about the Kommandant's reading habits, unconvincingly prefaced by the remark that he was thinking of buying him a book for Christmas, had elicited no more than that Kommandant van Heerden was fond of romantic novels which wasn't very helpful.

On the other hand Dr Eysenck was. By skilful use of the index Luitenant Verkramp managed to avoid having to read those portions of the book which taxed his intellectual stamina and instead concentrated on descriptions and cures effected by apomorphine and electric shock treatment. He was particularly interested in the case of the Cross Dressing Truck Driver and the case of the Corseted Engineer both of whom had come to see the error of their ways thanks in the case of the former to injections of apomorphine and of the latter to electric shocks. The treatment seemed quite simple and Verkramp had no doubt that he would be able to administer it if only he was given the opportunity. Certainly there was no difficulty about electric shock machines. Piemburg Police Station was littered with the things and Verkramp felt sure the police surgeon would be able to supply apomorphine. The main obstacle lay in the presence of Kommandant van Heerden, whose opposition to all innovations had proved such a handicap to Luitenant Verkramp in the past. 'If only the old fool would take a holiday,' Verkramp thought as he turned to the case of the Impotent Accountant only to learn to his disappointment that the man had been cured without recourse to apomorphine or electric shocks. The Case of the Prams and Handbags was much more interesting.

While Verkramp tried to forget Dr von Blimenstein by immersing himself in the study of abnormal psychology, the doctor, unaware of the fatal impact her sexuality had had on Verkramp's regard for her, tried desperately to remember the full details of their night together. All she could recall was arriving at Casualty Department of Piemburg Hospital classified according to the ambulance driver as an epileptic. When that misunderstanding had been cleared up she had been diagnosed as blind drunk and could vaguely remember having her stomach pumped out before being bundled into a taxi and sent back to Fort Rapier where her appearance had led to an unpleasant interview with the Hospital Principal the following morning. Since then she had telephoned Verkramp several times only to find that his line seemed to be permanently engaged. In the end she gave up and decided that it was unladylike to pursue him. 'He'll come back to me in due course,' she said smugly. 'He won't be able to keep away.' Every night after her bath she admired Verkramp's teeth marks in the mirror and slept with her torn vermilion panties under the pillow as proof of the Luitenant's devotion to her. 'Strong oral needs,' she thought happily, and her breasts heaved in anticipation.

Mrs Heathcote-Kilkoon was too much of a lady to have any doubts about the propriety of pursuing her acquaintance with Kommandant van Heerden. Every afternoon the vintage Rolls would steal down the drive of the golf course and Mrs Heathcote-Kilkoon would play a round of very good golf until the Kommandant arrived. Then she would save him the embarrassment of displaying his ineptness with a golf club by engaging him in conversation.

'You must think I'm absolutely frightful,' she murmured one afternoon as they sat on the verandah.

The Kommandant said he didn't think anything of the sort.

'I suppose it's because I've had so little experience of the real world,' she continued, 'that I find it so fascinating to meet a man with so much *je ne sais quoi*.'

'Oh, I don't know about that,' said the Kommandant modestly. Mrs Heathcote-Kilkoon wagged a gloved finger at him.

'And witty too,' she said though the Kommandant couldn't imagine what she was talking about. 'One somehow never expects a man in a position of responsibility to have a sense of humour and being the Kommandant of Police in a town the size of Piemburg must be an awesome responsibility. There must be nights when you simply can't get to sleep for worry.'

The Kommandant could think of several nights recently when he couldn't sleep but he wasn't prepared to admit it.

'When I go to bed,' he said, 'I go to sleep. I don't worry.' Mrs Heathcote-Kilkoon looked at him with admiration.

'How I envy you,' she said, 'I suffer terribly from insomnia. I lie awake thinking about how things have changed in my life-time and remembering the good old days in Kenya before those awful Mau-Mau came along and spoilt everything. Now look what a horrible mess the blacks have made of the country. Why they've even stopped the races at Thomson's Falls.' She sighed and the Kommandant commiserated with her.

'You should try reading in bed,' he suggested. 'Some people find that helps.'

'But what?' Mrs Heathcote-Kilkoon asked in a tone which suggested she had read everything there was to read.

'Dornford Yates,' said the Kommandant promptly and was delighted to find Mrs Heathcote-Kilkoon staring at him in as-tonishment. It was precisely the effect he had hoped for.

'You too?' she gasped. 'Are you a fan?'

The Kommandant nodded.

'Isn't he marvellous?' Mrs Heathcote-Kilkoon continued breathlessly, 'Isn't he absolutely brilliant? My husband and I are devoted to him. Absolutely devoted. That's one of the reasons we went to live in Umtali. Just to be near him. Just to breathe the same air he breathed and to know that we were living in the same town as the great man. It was a wonderful experience. Really wonderful.' She paused in her recital of the literary amenities of Umtali long enough for the Kommandant to say that he was surprised Dornford Yates had lived in Rho-desia. 'I've always pictured him in England,' he said, con-veniently forgetting that always in this case meant a week.

'He came out during the war,' Mrs Heathcote-Kilkoon explained, 'and then went back to the house at Eaux Bonnes in the Pyrenees afterwards, the House That Berry Built you know but the French were so horrid and everything so terribly changed that he couldn't stand it and settled in Umtali till his death.'

The Kommandant said he was sorry he had died and that he would like to have known him.

'It was a great privilege,' Mrs Heathcote-Kilkoon agreed sadly. 'A very great privilege to know a man who has enriched the English language.' She paused in memory for a moment before continuing. 'How extraordinary that you should find him so wonderful. I mean I don't want to ... well ... I always thought he appealed only to the English and to find a true Afrikaner who likes him ...' she trailed off, evidently afraid of offending him. Kommandant van Heerden assured her that Dornford Yates was the sort of Englishman Afrikaners most admired.

'Really,' said Mrs Heathcote-Kilkoon, 'you do amaze me. He'd have loved to hear you say that. He had such a loathing for foreigners himself.'

'I can understand that too,' said the Kommandant. 'They're not very nice people.'

By the time they parted Mrs Heathcote-Kilkoon had said that the Kommandant must meet her husband and the Kommandant had said he would be honoured to.

'You must come and stay at White Ladies,' Mrs Heathcote-Kilkoon said as the Kommandant opened the door of the Rolls for her.

'Which white lady's?' the Kommandant inquired. Mrs Heathcote-Kilkoon reached out a gloved hand and tweaked his ear.

'Naughty,' she said delightfully, 'naughty, witty man,' and drove off leaving the Kommandant wondering what he had said to merit the charming rebuke.

'You've done what?' Colonel Heathcote-Kilkoon asked apoplectically when she told him that she had invited the Kommandant to stay. 'At White Ladies? A bloody Boer? I won't hear of it. My God, you'll be asking Indians or niggers next. I don't care what you say, I'm not having the swine in my house.'

Mrs Heathcote-Kilkoon turned to Major Bloxham. 'You explain, Boy, he'll listen to you,' and took herself to her room with a migraine.

Major Bloxham found the Colonel among his azaleas and was disheartened by his florid complexion.

'You ought to take it easy, old chap,' he said. 'Blood pressure and all that.'

'What do you expect when that damned woman tells me she's invited some blue-based baboon to come and stay at White Ladies?' the Colonel snarled, gesticulating horridly with his pruning shears.

'A bit much,' said the Major placatorily.

'A bit? It's a damned sight too much if you ask me. Not that anyone does round here. Sponging swine,' and he disappeared into a bush leaving the Major rather hurt by the ambiguity of the remark.

'Seems he's a fan of the Master,' said the Major addressing himself to a large blossom.

'Hm,' snorted the Colonel who had transferred his attentions to a rhododendron, 'I've heard that tale before. Says that to get his foot in the door and before you know what's happened the whole damned club is full of 'em.'

Major Bloxham said there was something to be said for that point of view but that the Kommandant sounded quite genuine. The Colonel disagreed.

'Used to wave a white flag and shoot our officers down,' he shouted. 'Can't trust a Boer further than you can see him.'

'But . . .' said the Major trying to keep track of the Colonel's physical whereabouts while staying with his train of thought.

'But me no buts,' shouted the Colonel from a hydrangea. 'The man's a scoundrel. Got coloured blood too. All Afrikaners have a touch of the tar. A known fact. Not having a nigger in my house.' His voice distant in the shrubbery rumbled on to the insistent click of the secateurs and Major Bloxham turned back towards the house. Mrs Heathcote-Kilkoon, her migraine quite recovered, was drinking a sundowner on the stoep.

'Intransigent, my dear,' said the Major treading warily past the chihuahua that lay at her feet. 'Utterly intransigent.' Proud of his use of such a diplomatically polysyllabic communique the Major poured himself a double whisky. It was going to be a long hard evening.

'Cub hunting season,' said the Colonel over avocado pears at dinner. 'Look forward to that.'

'Fox in good form?' asked the Major.

'Harbinger's been keeping him in trim,' said the Colonel, 'been taking him for a ten-mile trot every morning. Good man, Harbinger, knows his job.'

'Damn fine whipper-in,' said the Major, 'Harbinger.'

At the far end of the polished mahogany table Mrs Heathcote-Kilkoon gouged her avocado resentfully.

'Harbinger's a convict,' she said presently. 'You got him from the prison at Weezen.'

'Poacher turned gamekeeper,' said the Colonel, who disliked his wife's new habit of intruding a sense of reality into his world of reassuring artifice. 'Make the best sort, you know. Good with dogs too.'

'Hounds,' said Mrs Heathcote-Kilkoon reprovingly. 'Hounds, dear, never dogs.'

Opposite her the Colonel turned a deeper shade of puce.

'After all,' continued Mrs Heathcote-Kilkoon before the Colonel could think of a suitable reply, 'if we are going to pretend we're county and that we've ridden to hounds for countless generations, we might as well do it properly.'

Colonel Heathcote-Kilkoon regarded his wife venomously. 'You forget yourself, my dear,' he said at last.

'How right you are,' Mrs Heathcote-Kilkoon answered, 'I have forgotten myself. I think we all have.' She rose from the table and left the room.

'Extraordinary behaviour,' said the Colonel. 'Can't think what's come over the woman. Used to be perfectly normal.'

'Perhaps it's the heat,' suggested the Major.

'Heat?' said the Colonel.

'The weather,' Major Bloxham explained hurriedly. 'Hot weather makes people irritable, don't you know.'

'Hot as hell in Nairobi. Never bothered her there. Can't see why it should give her the habdabs here.'

They finished their meal in silence and the Colonel took his coffee through to his study where he listened to the stock-market report on the radio. Gold shares were up, he noted thankfully. He would ring his broker in the morning and tell him to sell West Driefontein. Then switching the radio off he went to the bookshelf and took down a copy of *Berry & Co.* and settled down to read it for the eighty-third time. Presently, unable to concentrate, he laid the book aside and went out on to the stoep where Major Bloxham was sitting in the darkness with a glass of whisky looking out at the lights of the city far below.

'What are you doing, Boy?' asked the Colonel with something akin to affection in his voice.

'Trying to remember what winkles taste like,' said the Major. 'Such a long time since I had them.'

'Prefer oysters meself,' said the Colonel. They sat together in silence for some time. In the distance some Zulus were singing.

'Bad business,' the Colonel said, breaking the silence. 'Can't have Daphne upset. Can't have this damned fellow either. Don't know what to do.'

'Don't suppose we can,' agreed the Major. 'Pity we can't put him off somehow.'

'Put him off?'

'Tell him we've got foot-and-mouth or something,' said the Major whose career was littered with dubious excuses. Colonel Heathcote-Kilkoon considered the idea and rejected it.

'Wouldn't wash,' he said finally.

'Never do. Boers,' said the Major.

'Foot-and-mouth.'

'Oh.'

There was a long pause while they stared into the night.

'Bad business,' said the Colonel in the end and went off to bed. Major Bloxham sat on thinking about shellfish.

In her room Mrs Heathcote-Kilkoon lay under one sheet unable to sleep and listened to the Zulus' singing and the occasional murmur of voices from the stoep with increasing bitterness. 'They'll humiliate him if he comes,' she thought, recalling the miseries of her youth when napkins had been serviettes and lunch dinner. It was the thought of the humiliation she would suffer by proxy as the Kommandant fumbled for the fish fork for the meat course that finally decided Mrs Heathcote-Kilkoon. She switched on the light and sat at her writing table and wrote a note on mauve deckle-edged paper to the Kommandant.

'You're going to town, Boy?' she asked the Major next morning at breakfast. 'Pop this into the police station will you?' She slid the envelope across the table to him.

'Right you are,' said Major Bloxham. He hadn't intended going to Piemburg but his position in the household demanded just this sort of sacrifice. 'Putting him off?'

'Certainly not,' Mrs Heathcote-Kilkoon said looking coldly at her husband. 'Compromising. It's the English art or so I've been led to believe. I've said we're full up and . . .'

'Damned good show, my dear,' interrupted the Colonel.

'And I've asked him if he would mind putting up at the hotel instead. He can have lunch and dinner with us and I trust you'll have the decency to treat him properly if he accepts.'

'Seems a fair arrangement to me,' said the Colonel.

'Very fair,' the Major agreed.

'It's the least I can do,' said Mrs Heathcote-Kilkoon, 'in the circumstances. I've told him you'll foot the bill.'

She got up and went into the kitchen to vent her irritation on the black servants.

At Piemburg Police Station Kommandant van Heerden was busy making arrangements for his holiday. He had bought a map of the Weezen district, a trout rod and flies, a pair of stout walking boots, a deerstalker hat, a twelve-bore shotgun, some waders, and a pocket book called *Etiquette for Everyman*. Thus accoutred he felt confident that his stay with the Heathcote-Kilkoons would give him valuable experience in the art of behaving like an English gentleman.

He had even gone to the trouble of buying two pairs of pyjamas and some new socks because his old ones had mended holes in them. Having acquired the outward vestiges of Englishness, the Kommandant had practised saying 'Frightfully' and 'Absolutely' in what he hoped was an authentic accent. When it was dark he went into his garden with the trout rod and practised casting flies into a bucket of water on the lawn without ever managing to land a fly in the bucket but decapitating several dozen dahlias in the attempt.

'Practising what?' Luitenant Verkramp asked incredulously when his men reported this new activity to him.

'Fishing from a bucket,' the Security men told him.

'He's off his rocker,' Verkramp said.

'Keeps muttering to himself too. Repeats "Fascinating" and "Pleased to make your acquaintance, sir" over and over again.'

'I know that,' said Verkramp who had listened in to the Kommandant's monologue on his radio.

'Here's a list of all the things he's bought,' said another Security man. Verkramp looked down the list of waders and deerstalkers and boots, completely mystified.

'What's all this about him meeting some woman at the Golf Club?' he asked. He had never given up his original idea that the Kommandant was engaged in some sort of illicit love affair.

'Chats her up every day,' the Security men told him. 'Plump little thing with dyed hair aged about fifty-five. Drives an old Rolls.'

Verkramp gave orders to his men to find out all they could about Mrs Heathcote-Kilkoon and went back to his study of *Fact & Fiction in Psychology*. He had no sooner started than his phone rang with a message that the Kommandant wanted to see him. Verkramp put the book away and went along the passage to the Kommandant's office.

'Ah, Verkramp,' said the Kommandant, 'I'm taking a fortnight's leave as from Friday and I'm leaving you in charge here.' Luitenant Verkramp was delighted.

'Sorry to hear that, sir,' he said diplomatically. 'We'll miss you.' The Kommandant looked up unpleasantly. He didn't for one moment believe that Verkramp would miss him, particularly when he had been left in command.

'How are you getting on in the search for those Communists?' he asked.

'Communists?' said Verkramp, puzzled for a moment. 'Oh well it's a long business sir. Results take a long time.'

'They must do,' said the Kommandant feeling that he had punctured Verkramp's irritating complacency a bit. 'Well, while I'm away I expect you to concentrate on routine crime and the maintenance of law and order. I don't want to find that rapes, burglaries and murders have gone up in my absence. Understand?'

'Yes sir,' said Verkramp. The Kommandant dismissed him and Verkramp went back to his office in high spirits. The opportunity he had been waiting for had arrived at long last. He sat down at his desk and considered the manifold possibilities offered by his new authority.

'A fortnight,' he thought. 'A fortnight in which to show what I can really do.' It wasn't long but Luitenant Verkramp had no intention of wasting time. There were two things he had particularly in mind. With the Kommandant out of the way he would put into effect Plan Red Rout. Crossing to his safe he took out the folder in which all the details of the operation were kept. Months before he had drawn up the plan in secret. It was time to put it into practice. By the time Kommandant van Heerden returned from his holiday, Luitenant Verkramp was certain that he would have uncovered the network of saboteurs he was convinced was operating in Piemburg.

During the course of the morning Verkramp made a number of phone calls and in various firms throughout the city employees who didn't normally receive phone calls during working hours were called to the phone. In each case the procedure was the same.

'The mamba is striking,' said Verkramp.

'The cobra has struck,' said the secret agent. Designed as an infallible method of communicating the order to his agents to meet him at their prearranged rendezvous, it had its disadvantages.

'What was all that about?' the girl in agent 745396's office asked when he put down the phone after what could hardly be called a prolonged conversation.

'Nothing,' agent 745396 replied hastily.

'You said "The cobra has struck,"' said the girl, 'I distinctly heard you. What cobra's struck? That's what I want to know.'

All over Piemburg Verkramp's system of code words aroused interest and speculation in the offices where his secret agents worked.

*   *   *

That afternoon Luitenant Verkramp, disguised as a motor mechanic and driving a breakdown truck, left town for the first of his appointments, and half an hour later ten miles out on the Vlockfontein road was bending over the engine of 745396's car pretending to mend a broken distributor to lend verisimilitude to his disguise while giving 745396 his instructions.

'Get yourself fired,' Verkramp told the agent.

'Done that already,' said 745396 who had taken the afternoon off without permission.

'Good,' said Verkramp wondering how the hell he was going to get the distributor together again. 'I want you to work full-time from now on.'

'Doing what?'

'Infiltrating the revolutionary movement in Zululand.'

'Where do I start?' 745396 asked.

'Start hanging about Florian's café and the Colonial Bar. Plenty of students and Commies go there. The University canteen is another place where subversives gather,' Verkramp explained.

'I know all that,' said 745396. 'Last time I went there I got chucked out on my ear.'

'The last time you went there you hadn't blown anything up,' said Verkramp. 'This time you won't just say you're a saboteur, you'll be able to prove it.'

'How?'

Verkramp led the way round to the cab of his breakdown truck and handed the agent a packet. 'Gelignite and fuses,' he explained. 'On Saturday night blow the transformer on the Durban road. Put it there at eleven and get back into town before it goes up. It's got a fifteen-minute fuse.'

745396 looked at him in astonishment. 'Jesus wept,' he said, 'you really mean it?'

'Of course I do,' snapped Verkramp, 'I've given the matter a lot of thought and it's obviously the only way to infiltrate the sabotage movement. No one's going to doubt the dedication to the Communist party of a man who's blown up a transformer.'

'I don't suppose they are,' 745396 agreed nervously. 'What happens if I get arrested?'

'You won't be,' Verkramp said.

'That's what you told me when I had to pass those messages in the men's lavatory in the Market Square,' said 745396, 'and I got nabbed for soliciting.'

'That was different. Uniformed branch got you that time.'

'Uniformed branch could get me this time,' said 745396. 'You never know.'

'I'm in charge of the uniformed branch from now on. I'm Kommandant from Friday,' Verkram explained. 'And anyway who paid your fine?'

'You did,' 745396 admitted, 'but I got the publicity. You want to try working in an office where everyone thinks you make a habit of soliciting old men in public lavatories. It took me months to live that down and I had to move my lodgings five times.'

'We've all got to make sacrifices for a White South Africa,' said Verkramp, 'which reminds me. I want you to move your digs every few days. That's what real saboteurs do and you've got to be really convincing this time.'

'All right, so I blow the transformer. What then?'

'Do as I say. Mingle with the students and the lefties and let it be known you're a saboteur. You'll soon find the swine letting you in on their plans.'

745396 was doubtful. 'How do I prove I blew the transformer?' he asked. Verkramp considered the problem.

'You've got a point there,' he agreed, 'I suppose if you could show them some gelignite it would do the trick.'

'Fine,' said 745396 sarcastically, 'and where do I get gelly from? I don't keep the stuff handy you know.'

'The police armoury,' said Verkramp, 'I'll have a key cut and you can take some out when you need it.'

'What do I do when I've found the real saboteurs?' 745396 asked.

'Get them to blow something up and inform me before they do so that we can nab the bastards,' said Verkramp, and having arranged to drop the key of the police armoury at an arranged spot, he handed over 500 rand from Security Branch funds for expenses and left 745396 to fix the distributor he had taken to bits.

'Remember to get them to blow something up before we arrest them,' Verkramp told the agent before he left. 'It's important that we have proof of sabotage so we can hang the swine. I don't want any conspiracy trials this time. I want proof of terrorism.'

He drove off to his next rendezvous and during the course of the next two days twelve secret agents had left their jobs and had been given targets round Piemburg to destroy. Twelve keys for the police armoury had been cut and Verkramp felt confident that he was about to strike a blow for freedom and Western Civilization in Piemburg which would significantly advance his career.

Back in his office Luitenant Verkramp checked the scheme and memorized all the details carefully before burning the file on Operation Red Rout as an added precaution against a security leak. He was particularly proud of his system of secret agents whom he had recruited separately over the years and paid out of the funds allocated by BOSS for informers. Each agent used a *nom de guerre* and was known to Verkramp only by his number so that there was nothing to connect him with BOSS. The method by which the agents reported back to him was similarly devious and consisted of coded messages placed in 'drops' where they were collected by Verkramp's security men. Each day of the week had a different code and a different 'drop' which ensured that Verkramp's men never met his agents, of whose existence they were only vaguely aware. The fact that the system was complex and that there were seven codes and seven drops for each agent and that there were twelve agents would have meant that there was an enormous amount of work being done had it not been for lack of Communist and subversive activity in Piemburg to be reported. In the past Verkramp had been lucky to receive more than one coded message per week, and that inevitably of no value. Now it would be different and he looked forward to an influx of information.

Having initiated Operation Red Rout, Luitenant Verkramp considered his second campaign, that against miscegenating policemen, which he had code-named White Wash. Out of defence to Dr Eysenck he had decided to try apomorphine injections as well as electric shock and sent Sergeant Breitenbach to a wholesale chemist with an order for one hundred hypodermic syringes and two gallons of apomorphine.

'Two gallons?' asked the chemist incredulously. 'Are you sure you've got this right?'

'Quite sure,' said Sergeant Breitenbach.

'And a hundred hypodermics?' asked the chemist, who still couldn't believe his ears.

'That's what I said,' insisted the Sergeant.

'I know that's what you said but it doesn't seem possible,' the chemist told him. 'What in God's name are you going to do with two gallons?'

Sergeant Breitenbach had been briefed by Verkramp.

'It's for curing alcoholics,' he said.

'Dear God,' said the chemist, 'I didn't know there was that number of alcoholics in the country.'

'It makes them sick,' the Sergeant explained.

'You can say that again,' muttered the chemist. 'With two gallons you could probably kill them all off too. Probably block the sewage system into the bargain. Anyway I can't supply it.'

'Why not?'

'Well for one thing I haven't got two gallons and wouldn't know where to get it and for another you need a doctor's prescription and I doubt if any doctor in his right mind would prescribe two gallons of apomorphine anyway.'

Sergeant Breitenbach reported his refusal to Luitenant Verkramp.

'Need a doctor's prescription,' he said.

'You can get one from the police surgeon,' Verkramp told him and the Sergeant went down to the police morgue where the surgeon was performing an autopsy on an African who had been beaten to death during questioning.

'Natural causes,' he wrote on the death certificate before attending to Sergeant Breitenbach.

'There's a limit to what I'm prepared to do,' said the surgeon with a sudden display of professional ethics. 'I've got my Hippocratic oath to consider and I'm not issuing prescriptions for two gallons. A thousand cc is the most I'll do and if Verkramp

70

wants anything more out of them he'll have to tickle their throats with a feather.'

'Is that enough?'

'At 3cc a dose you should get 330 pukes,' said the surgeon. 'Don't overdo it though. I've got my work cut out signing death certificates as it is.'

'Stingy old bastard,' said Verkramp when Sergeant Breitenbach returned from the chemist with twenty hypodermics and 1000cc of apomorphine. 'The next thing we need is slides of kaffir girls in the raw. You can get the police photographer to take those as soon as the Kommandant leaves on Friday.'

While his deputy was making these preparations for Kommandant van Heerden's holiday, the Kommandant was adjusting himself to the change of plans occasioned by Mrs Heathcote-Kilkoon's letter. He was just passing the desk in the police station when Major Bloxham arrived.

'A letter for Kommandant van Heerden,' said the Major.

Kommandant van Heerden turned back. 'That's me,' he said. 'Pleased to make your acquaintance,' and shook the Major's hand vigorously.

'Bloxham, Major,' said the Major nervously. Police stations always had this effect on him.

The Kommandant opened the mauve envelope and glanced at the letter.

'Hunting season. Always the same,' said the Major, by way of explanation, and alarmed by the suffusion of blood to the Kommandant's face. 'Damned awkward. Sorry.'

Kommandant van Heerden stuffed the letter hurriedly into his pocket.

'Yes. Well. Hm,' he said awkwardly.

'Any message?'

'No. Yes. I'll stay at the hotel,' said the Kommandant and was about to shake hands again. But Major Bloxham had already left the police station and was getting his breath back in the street. The Kommandant went upstairs to his office and read the letter again in a state of considerable agitation. It was hardly the sort of letter he had expected to receive from Mrs. Heathcote-Kilkoon.

71

'Darling Van,' he read, 'I feel so terrible writing to you like this but I'm sure you'll understand. Aren't husbands a frightful bore? It's just that Henry's being awkward and I would so love to have you but I think it would be better for all our sakes if you stayed at the hotel. It's this wretched club thing of his and he's so stubborn and anyway I'm sure you'll be more comfortble there and you can come and eat with us. Please say you will and don't be angry, Your loving Daphne.' It was heavily scented.

Unaccustomed as he was to receiving perfumed letters on mauve deckle-edged paper from other men's wives, the Kommandant found the contents quite bewildering. What Mrs Heathcote-Kilkoon meant by calling him Darling Van and describing her husband as a dreadful bore he could only surmise, but he was hardly surprised that Henry was being awkward. Given half an inkling that his wife was writing letters like this, the Colonel had every right to be awkward and the Kommandant, recalling the Major's enigmatic remark about the hunting season being always the same, shuddered.

On the other hand the notion that he found favour in Mrs Heathcote-Kilkoon's eyes, and if the letter was anything to go by there wasn't much doubt about that, appealed to the chivalrous instincts of the Kommandant. Of course, he wouldn't be angry. Circumspect certainly but not angry. After consulting *Etiquette for Everyman* to see what it had to say about replying to amorous letters from married women and finding it of little use, the Kommandant began to draft a reply. As he couldn't decide for ten minutes whether to use Dearest, My Dear, or simply Dear the letter took some considerable time to write and in its final form read, 'Dearest Daphne, Kommandant van Heerden has pleasure in accepting Colonel & Mrs Heathcote-Kilkoon's kind invitation to stay at the hotel. He also has pleasure in accepting your invitation to dinner. Yours affectionately, Van,' which the Kommandant thought was a nice blend of informal and formal and unlikely to offend anyone. He sent it up by police messenger to the Heathcote-Kilkoons' house at Piltdown. Then he turned his attention to the map and planned his route to Weezen. Lying at the foot of the Aardvark mountains, the little town had something of a reputation as a health resort – had once in fact been something of a spa – but in recent years had been forgotten like Piemburg itself and replaced as a holiday centre by the skyscrapers and motels along the coast.

CHAPTER SIX

On Friday morning the Kommandant was up early and on the road to Weezen. He had packed his fishing rod and the paraphernalia he had acquired for his holiday in the boot of his car the night before and was wearing his Norfolk jacket and brown brogues. As he drove up the long hill out of Piemburg he looked down at the red tin roofs without regret. It was a long time since he had permitted himself a holiday and he was look-ing forward to learning at first hand how the British aristocracy really lived on their country estates. As the sun rose the Kommandant turned off the national road at Leopard's River and was presently bucketing over the corrugations of the dirt road towards the mountains. Around him the countryside varied according to the race of its occupants, being gentle undulating grassland in the white areas and, down by the Voetsak River which was part of Pondoland and therefore a black area, badly eroded scrub country where goats climbed the lower branches of the trees to gnaw at the leaves. The Kommandant practised being British by smiling at the Africans by the side of the road but got little response and after a while gave it up. At Sjambok he stopped for morning coffee which he asked for in English instead of his usual Afrikaans and was delighted when the Indian waiter diplomatically asked him if he was an over-seas visitor.

He left Sjambok in high spirits and an hour later was thread-ing the pass over Rooi Nek. At the top he stopped and got out of the car to look at the countryside which had figured recently so much in his imagination. The reality exceeded his expec-tations. Weezen lay on a rolling upland of gentle hills and meadows through which streams meandered to a lazy river glinting in the distance. Here and there a wood darkened a hillside or bordered the river to add a darker green to the landscape, or a grove of trees sheltered a farmhouse. In the distance the mountains rose in a great crescent above the rolling plateau and above them again a sky of impeccable blue darkened towards the meridian. To Kommandant van Heerden, emerging from the dusty dryness of the Rooi Nek pass, the countryside before him spoke of the shires of England. 'It's just like a picture on a biscuit-tin,' he murmured ecstatically, 'only more real,' before climbing back into the hot seat of his car and driving on down the curving dirt road into Weezen.

Here again his hopes were more than realized. The little town, hardly more than a village, was unspoilt. A stone-built church with a lych-gate, a colonial baronial town hall with rusting metal gargoyles, and a row of shops with an arcade looked onto a square in the centre of which Queen Victoria sat plumply staring with evident distaste over a kaffir who was lying asleep on a bench in the garden at her feet. Whatever else had changed in South Africa since her Diamond Jubilee it was clear that Weezen hadn't and the Kommandant, for whom the British Empire still retained its magic, rejoiced in the fact. 'No pot-smoking long-hairs lounging about juke boxes here,' he thought happily, stopping the car and entering a trading store which smelt of sacks and polish. He asked a tall gaunt man the way to the hotel.

'Bar or bed?' the man asked with a taciturnity the Kommandant felt was wholly authentic.

'Bed,' said the Kommandant.

'That'll be Willow Water,' the man told him. 'Half a mile on. There's a sign.'

The Kommandant went out and drove on. 'Willow Water Guest Farm,' said a sign and the Kommandant turned in down a narrow drive lined with blue gums to a low stucco building which looked less like an hotel than an abandoned pumping station of a defunct waterworks. The Kommandant stopped his car uncertainly on the mossy forecourt and looked at the building without enthusiasm. Whatever it was it wasn't what he had expected. Above the doorway he could just make out the faded inscription Weezen Spa and Philosophical Society, made pointillist by the suckers of some long-since decayed creeper. He got out and climbed the steps to the little terrace and peered through the revolving door into the interior vaguely aware that several large flies, trapped in the door, were buzzing insistently. Neither their presence nor what he could see of the foyer suggested that the place was much frequented. The Kommandant pushed through the revolving door and leaving the flies trapped on the other side stood looking around him at the white-tiled hall. Light from a glass dome in the roof illuminated what appeared to be the inquiry desk in a niche at the far end and the Kommandant crossed to it and banged the brass bell that stood there on the marble top. 'I've come to the wrong place,' he thought looking uneasily at a plaque above a doorway which said Thermal Douche No 1, and he was about to make his way back to town when a door slammed somewhere in the distance to be followed by the sound of slippers shuffling along the corridor and an elderly man appeared.

'Is this the Weezen Hotel?' the Kommandant asked.

'Don't serve drinks,' said the old man.

'I don't want a drink,' said the Kommandant, 'I'm supposed to be staying at the Weezen Hotel. A room has been booked for me by Mrs Heathcote-Kilkoon if this is the right place.'

The old man shuffled round the marble-topped desk and rooted under it for a book.

'Sign here,' he said putting the book in front of the Kommandant. 'Name, address, age, occupation and disease.' Kommandant van Heerden looked at the register with growing alarm.

'I'm sure I've come to the wrong place,' he said.

'Only hotel in Weezen you can stay in,' the old man told him. 'If you want a drink you'll have to go into town. We haven't a licence.'

The Kommandant sighed and signed the register.

'There's nothing wrong with me,' he said when he got to Disease.

'Put Obesity,' said the old man. 'Got to have something. Any next of kin?'

'I've got a second cousin in Wakkerstrom,' the Kommandant said unhappily.

75

'That'll do,' said the old man. 'You can have Colonic Irrigation No 6.'

'For God's sake,' said the Kommandant, 'I don't need Colonic Irrigation. There's absolutely nothing the matter with me.'

'Throat and Nose 4 is vacant too but you don't have the same view,' said the old man shuffling off down the corridor. Reluctantly the Kommandant followed him past rooms whose enamel plaques ranged from Galvanic Therapy No 8 to Inhalation No 12. At the far end of the corridor the old man stopped outside Colonic Irrigation No 6 and unlocked the door.

'Mind the cold tap,' he said. 'It's a bit hot.'

The Kommandant followed him into the room and looked round. A white-painted bed of the sort he had last seen in hospital stood in one corner with a wardrobe whose mirror was mottled and stained. More to the point and entirely confirming the plaque on the door was a series of glazed troughs, tubs and pans which stood at the far end of the room together with a maze of brass taps and tubes whose purpose the Kommandant had no wish to explore. To add to the clinical inhospitality of the room the walls were covered in white tiles.

'Gets the sun in the morning,' said the old man. 'And the view is lovely.'

'I daresay,' said the Kommandant looking at the frosted glass windows. 'What's that smell?'

'Sulphur in the water,' the old man said. 'Want to have a look at Nose and Throat?'

'I think I'd better,' said the Kommandant. They went out into the corridor and down a side passage.

'Much better take Colonic Irrigation,' the old man told him, ushering the Kommandant into a small dark room which, while it contained less sinister equipment, emanated an even stronger smell of sulphur. Kommandant van Heerden shook his head.

'I'll have the first room,' he said, unable to bring himself to use words which might lead to misunderstanding. 'I'm only staying,' he explained as they went back. 'Visiting the district.'

76

'Well if there's anything I can do, let me know,' said the old man. 'Lunch will be in the Pump Room in half an hour,' and shuffled off leaving the Kommandant sitting on the edge of his bed surveying his room with a deep sense of disappointment. Presently he got up and went to look for someone to carry his things in. In the end he had to do it himself and arranged his bags and fishing rods as best he could to obscure the taps and tubes that so disturbed him. Then he opened the window and standing on one of the pans looked out. As the old man had said the view was lovely. Below him weedy paths led down beside what had once been a lawn to the river which was bordered, not, as the signpost had suggested, by willows, but by some trees with which the Kommandant was unfamiliar. But it was not the immediate vicinity that held his attention, not even the enormous drainpipe partially disguised as a rockery that ran, doubtless carrying tons of hideous effluent, down to the river, but the mountains. Seen from the head of Rooi Nek they had looked impressive. From Colonic Irrigation No 6 they were majestic. Their lower slopes clothed in the raiment of wattle and thorn and gum, they rose imperiously through meadows where goats munched precariously among the boulders to scree and krantz and the vacant sky.

'Must be baboons up there,' thought the Kommandant poetically and clambering down from his own eminence which was, he noted, manufactured by Fisons & Sons of Hartlepool, makers of Glazed Sanitary ware, went in search of the dining-room and lunch.

He found it in the Pump Room, a large room with a miniature marble fountain in the centre which gurgled incessantly and from which emanated the smell the Kommandant found so unusual in his room. Here, blending with the odour of boiled cabbage from the kitchen, it was less mineral than vegetable and the Kommandant seated himself near a window overlooking the terrace. There were three other tables occupied in the room which had clearly been designed to hold a hundred. Two elderly ladies with suspiciously short hair conversed in whispers in one corner while a man whom the Kommandant took to be a salesman sat at a table near the fountain.

Nobody said anything to him and the Kommandant, having

ordered his lunch from the coloured waitress, tried to enter into a conversation with the salesman.

'You come here often?' he asked above the gurgle of the fountain.

'Flatulence. They're stones,' said the young man, indicating the two ladies in the corner.

'Really,' said the Kommandant.

'Your first time here?' asked the man.

The Kommandant nodded.

'Grows on you,' said the man. Not wishing to hear, the Kommandant finished his meal in silence and went out into the foyer to look for the telephone.

'You'll have to go into the village for that,' the old man told him.

'Where do the Heathcote-Kilkoons live?'

'Oh them,' said the old man with a sniff. 'Can't phone them. They're too snooty for that. Offered a party line, they were and turned it down. Not sharing a line with anyone they aren't. Want their privacy, they do. And if what they say is true, they need it.' He disappeared into a room marked Manipulation leaving the Kommandant with no alternative but to drive to town and ask the way to the Heathcote-Kilkoons' there.

In Piemburg Kommandant van Heerden's absence had already brought changes. Luitenant Verkramp arrived early and ensconced himself in the Kommandant's office.

'The following men to report to me at once,' he told Sergeant Breitenbach and handed him a list he had drawn up of ten konstabels whose moral delinquency in the matter of miscegenation was notorious. 'And have the cells cleared on the top floor. A bed in each one and the wall whitewashed.'

When the men presented themselves, Verkramp interviewed them one by one.

'Konstabel van Heynigen,' he told the first man, 'you have been sleeping with black women. Don't deny it. You have.'

Konstable van Heynigen looked dumfounded.

'Well, sir—' he began but Verkramp cut him short.

'Good,' he snapped, 'I'm glad you've made a clean breast of

78

it. Now, you are going to have a course of treatment that will cure you of this disease.'

Konstabel van Heynigen had never considered raping black women as a disease. He'd always thought of it as one of the perks in an underpaid job.

'Do you agree that this treatment will benefit you?' Verkramp asked with a sternness that excluded any possibility of contradiction. 'Good. Just sign here,' and he thrust a typewritten form before the astonished konstabel and pushed a ballpoint pen into his hand. Konstabel van Heynigen signed.

'Thank you. Next one,' said Verkramp.

By the end of an hour the Luitenant had treated all ten konstabels to the same swift process and had ten signed statements agreeing to aversion therapy as a cure for the disease of miscegenation.

'This is going so well,' Verkramp told Sergeant Breitenbach, 'we might as well get every man on the station to sign one.' The Sergeant gave his qualified consent.

'I think we should exclude the non-commissioned officers, don't you, sir?' he said.

Verkramp considered the matter. 'I suppose so,' he agreed grudgingly. 'We'll need someone to administer the drugs and shocks.'

While the Sergeant gave orders for all konstabels to sign the consent forms when they came on duty, Verkramp went upstairs to inspect the cells which had been cleared for treatment.

In each cell a bed had been placed facing the wall which had been whitewashed and beside the bed on a table stood a slide projector. All that was needed were the slides. Verkramp went back to his office and sent for Sergeant Breitenbach.

'Take a couple of vans out to the township and bring back a hundred coon girls,' he ordered. 'Try and pick attractive ones. Bring them back here and have the photographer photograph them in the raw.'

Sergeant Breitenbach went downstairs and drove out to Adamville, the black township outside Piemburg, to carry out what appeared on the surface to be a fairly straightforward order. In practice it turned out to be rather difficult. By the time his men had dragged a dozen young black women from their homes and locked them in the pick-up van, an angry crowd had gathered and the township was in an uproar.

'We want our women back,' yelled the crowd.

'Let us out,' screamed the girls in the van. Sergeant Breitenbach tried to explain.

'We only want to photograph them without their clothes on,' he said. 'It's to stop white policemen sleeping with Bantu women.'

As an explanation it was obviously unconvincing. The crowd evidently thought that photographing black women in the nude would have the opposite effect.

'Stop raping our women,' shouted the Africans.

'That's what we're trying to do,' said the Sergeant through a loudhailer but his words had no effect. The news that the police intended raping the girls spread like wildfire through the township. As the stones began to land round the police vans, Sergeant Breitenbach ordered his men to cock their Sten guns and gave the order to retreat.

'Typical,' said Verkramp when the Sergeant reported the incident. 'Try to help them and what do they do. Bloody riot. I tell you, kaffirs are thick. Plain stupid.'

'Do you want me to try and get some more?' the Sergeant asked.

'Of course. Ten isn't enough,' said Verkramp. 'Photograph this lot and take them back. When they see these girls haven't been raped the crowd will quieten down.'

'Yes sir,' said the Sergeant doubtfully.

He went down to the basement and supervised the police photographer who was having some difficulty getting the girls to stand still. In the end the Sergeant had to take out his revolver to threaten to shoot the girls unless they cooperated.

His second visit to the township was even less successful than the first. Wisely taking the precaution of convoying the pick-up vans with four Saracen armoured cars and several lorry loads of armed policemen, he still ran into trouble.

Addressing the incensed crowd Sergeant Breitenbach ordered the girls to be released.

'As you can see they haven't been hurt,' he shouted. Naked and bruised, the girls poured out of the vans.

'He said he'd shoot us,' one of them screamed.

In the riot that followed this announcement and the attempt to secure another ninety girls for the same treatment, the police shot four Africans dead and wounded a dozen more. Sergeant Breitenbach left the scene of carnage with twenty-five more women and a nasty cut over his left eye where he had been hit by a stone.

'Fuck the bastards,' he said as the convoy left, a comment that had unfortunate results for the twenty-five women in the vans who were photographed and duly fucked in the police station before being released to make their own way home. That evening Acting Kommandant Verkramp announced to the press that four Africans had been killed in a tribal fight in the township.

As soon as the colour transparencies were ready, Verkramp and Sergeant Breitenbach went to the top floor where the ten konstabels were waiting in some trepidation for the treatment to begin. The arrival of the hypodermics and the shock machines had done nothing to improve their morale.

'Men,' said Verkramp as they stood in the corridor, 'today you are about to take part in an experiment which may alter the course of history. As you know, we Whites in South Africa are threatened by millions of blacks and if we are to survive and maintain our purity of race as God intended we must learn not only to fight with guns and bullets but we must fight a moral battle too. We must cleanse our hearts and minds of impure thoughts. That is what this course of treatment is intended to do. Now, we all have a natural aversion for kaffirs. It's part of our nature to feel disgust for them. The course of treatment which you have volunteered for will reinforce that feeling of disgust. That is why it is called aversion therapy. By the end of your treatment the sight of a black woman will make you sick and you will be conditioned to avoid all contact with them. You won't want to sleep with them. You won't want to touch them. You won't want to have them in your home as servants. You won't want them washing your clothes. You won't want them in the streets. You won't want them anywhere in South Africa . . .'

As Luitenant Verkramp's voice went higher and higher with the catalogue of things the konstabels wouldn't want, Sergeant Breitenbach coughed nervously. He had had a tiring day and the cut on his forehead was throbbing painfully and he knew that the one thing he didn't want was a demented and hysterical Acting Kommandant.

'Isn't it about time we started, sir?' he said nudging Verkramp. The Luitenant stopped.

'Yes,' he said. 'Let the experiment begin.'

The volunteers went into their cells where they were made to take off their clothes and get into the strait-jackets which were laid out like pyjamas on the beds. There was some trouble on this score and it required the assistance of several non-commissioned officers to get one or two of the larger men into them. Finally, however, the ten konstabels were strapped down and Verkramp filled the first hypodermic with apomorphine.

Sergeant Breitenbach watched him with growing alarm.

'The surgeon said not to overdo it,' he whispered. 'He said you could kill someone. Only 3cc.'

'You're not getting cold feet are you, Sergeant?' Verkramp asked. On the bed the volunteer regarded the needle with bulging eyes.

'I've changed my mind,' he shouted desperately.

'No, you haven't,' said Verkramp. 'We're going to do that for you.'

'Shouldn't we try it on a kaffir first?' Sergeant Breitenbach asked. 'I mean it isn't going to look very good if one of these men dies, is it?'

Verkramp thought for a moment. 'I suppose you're right,' he agreed finally. They went down to the cells on the ground floor and injected several African suspects with varying amounts of apomorphine. The results entirely confirmed Sergeant Breitenbach's worst fears. As the third black went into a coma, Verkramp looked puzzled.

'Potent stuff,' he said.

'Wouldn't it be better to stick to the electric shock machines?' the Sergeant asked.

'I suppose so,' said Verkramp sadly. He'd been looking forward to sticking needles in the volunteers. Ordering the Sergeant to send for the police surgeon to sign the death certificates, the Luitenant went back to the top floor and reassured the five volunteers who had been selected for apomorphine treatment that they needn't worry.

'You're going to have electric shocks instead,' he told them and switched on the projector. At the end of the cell a naked black woman appeared on the wall. As each volunteer had an erection, Verkramp shook his head.

'Disgusting,' he muttered attaching the terminal of the shock machine to the glans penis with a piece of surgical tape. 'Now then,' he told the Sergeant who sat beside the bed, 'every time you change the slide, give him an electric shock like this.' Verkramp wound the handle of the generator vigorously and the konstabel on the bed jerked convulsively and screamed. Verkramp examined the man's penis and was impressed. 'You can see it works,' he said and changed the slide.

Going from cell to cell, Luitenant Verkramp explained the technique and supervised the experiment. As erections followed the slides and contractions followed the shocks to be followed by more slides, more erections, more shocks and more contractions, the Luitenant's enthusiasm grew.

Sergeant Breitenbach, returning from the morgue, was less sanguine.

'You can hear them screaming in the street,' he shouted in Verkramp's ear as the corridor echoed to the shrieks of the volunteers.

'So what?' said Verkramp. 'We're making history.'

'Making a horrible din too,' said the Sergeant.

To Verkramp the screams were like music. It was as though he were conducting some great symphony in which the seasons, spring, summer, autumn and winter, were celebrated in a welter of screams and shocks and slides, erections and contractions, each of which he could summon forth or dismiss at will.

Presently he sent for a camp bed and lay down in the corridor to get some rest. 'I'm exorcizing the devil,' he thought and, dreaming of a world cleansed of sexual lust, fell asleep.

83

When he awoke he was surprised how quiet it was. He got up and found the volunteers asleep and the Sergeants smoking in the lavatory.

'What the hell do you mean by stopping the treatment?' he shouted. 'It's got to be continuous if it's to work at all. It's called reinforcement.'

'You'll need reinforcements if you want to go on,' said one Sergeant mutinously.

'What's the matter with you?' asked Verkramp angrily.

The Sergeants looked shamefaced.

'It's a delicate matter,' Sergeant de Kok told him finally.

'What is?'

'Well we've been in there all night looking at slides of naked ladies . . .'

'Coon girls not ladies,' snarled Verkramp.

'And . . .' the Sergeant hesitated.

'And what?'

'We've got lover's balls,' said the Sergeant bluntly.

Luitenant Verkramp was appalled.

'Lover's balls,' he shouted. 'You've got lover's balls from looking at naked coon girls? You stand there and admit you . . .' Verkramp was speechless with disgust.

'It's only natural,' said the Sergeant.

'Natural?' screamed Verkramp. 'It's downright unnatural. Where the hell is this country going to if men in your positions of authority can't control your sexual instincts? Now you listen to me. As Kommandant of this station I'm ordering you to continue the treatment. Any man refusing to do his duty will be put on the list for the next batch of volunteers.'

The Sergeants straightened their uniforms and hobbled back to the cells and a moment later the screams that were proof of their devotion to duty began again. In the morning the shift was changed and fresh non-commissioned officers took their place. Throughout the day Luitenant Verkramp went upstairs to see how they were getting on.

He had just visited one cell and was about to leave when he became aware that there was something vaguely wrong with the picture projected on the wall. He looked at it and saw it was a view of the Kruger National Park.

'Like it?' asked the Sergeant. Luitenant Verkramp stared dumbfounded at the slide. 'The next one is even better.'

The Sergeant pressed the switch and the slide changed to a close-up of a giraffe. On the bed the volunteer jerked convulsively from the electric shock. Luitenant Verkramp couldn't believe his eyes.

'Where the hell did you get those slides?' he demanded. The Sergeant looked up brightly.

'They're my holiday shots from last summer. We went to the game reserve.' He changed the slide and a herd of zebra appeared on the wall. The patient jerked with them too.

'You're supposed to be showing slides of naked black women,' Verkramp yelled, 'not fucking animals in the game reserve!'

The Sergeant was unabashed.

'I just thought they'd make a change,' he explained, 'and besides it's the first time I've had a chance to show them. We haven't got a slide projector at home.'

On the bed the patient was screaming that he couldn't stand any more.

'No more hippos, please,' he moaned. 'Dear God no more hippos. I swear I'll never touch another hippo again.'

'See what you've been and done,' said Verkramp frantically to the Sergeant. 'Do you realize what you've done? You've conditioned him to loathe animals. He won't be able to take his kids to the Zoo without becoming a nervous wreck.'

'Oh dear,' said the Sergeant, 'I am sorry. He'll have to give up fishing too in that case.'

Verkramp confiscated all the slides of the game reserve and the Durban Aquarium and told the Sergeant to show only slides of naked black women. After that he made a point of checking the slides in each cell and came across one other discrepancy. Sergeant Bischoff had included a slide of an unattractive white woman in a bathing costume among the naked blacks.

'Who the hell is this old bag?' Verkramp asked when he found the slide.

'You shouldn't have said that,' said Sergeant Bischoff looking hurt.

'Why not?' yelled Verkramp.

'That's my wife,' said the Sergeant. Verkramp could see that he had made a mistake.

'Listen,' he said, 'it's not nice to put her in with a whole lot of kaffir girls.'

'I know that,' said the Sergeant, 'I just thought it might help.'

'Help?'

'Help my marriage,' the Sergeant explained. 'She's a bit ... well, a bit flirtatious and I just thought I'd make sure one man didn't look at her again.'

Verkramp looked at the slide. 'I shouldn't have thought you need have bothered,' he said and gave orders that Mrs Bischoff wasn't to appear at a mixed gathering again.

Finally having ensured that everything was proceeding according to plan, he went down to the Kommandant's office and tried to think what else he could do to make his tenure of office a memorable one. The next step, as far as he could see, would come in the evening when his agents began work in the field.

CHAPTER SEVEN

By the time he had driven into Weezen after lunch and found it was early closing day, the Kommandant had begun to think that he was never going to find the Heathcote-Kilkoons's house. His earlier impression that time stood still in the little town was entirely reinforced by the absence of anyone in the streets in the afternoon. He wandered round looking for the Post Office only to find it shut, tried the store he had been to in the morning with equal lack of success and finally sat down in the shadow of Queen Victoria and contemplated the dusty cannas in the ornamental garden. A thin yellow dog sitting on the verandah of the store scratched itself lethargically and recalled the Kommandant to his new role. 'Mad dogs and Englishmen go out in the mid-day sun,' he thought to cheer himself up and wondered what a genuine Englishman who found himself in a strange town at this time of the day would have done.

'Gone fishing,' he imagined and with the uneasy feeling that he was being observed rather critically which resulted subliminally from the great Queen above him, he got up and drove back to the hotel.

There too the sense of inanition with which the old building was so imbued was even more marked now. The two flies were still trapped in the revolving door but they no longer buzzed. Kommandant van Heerden went down the corridor to his room and collected his rod. Then after some confusion in the revolving door, which refused to take both his rod and his basket at the same time, he was out and threading his way down the weedy paths to the river. At the foot of the enormous drainpipe he hesitated, looked to see which way the river flowed, and went upstream on the grounds that he didn't want to catch fish that had grown fat on its discharge. He had some difficulty in finding a spot which wasn't encumbered with branches and presently settled down to casting his most promising-looking fly, a large red-winged affair, onto the water. Nothing stirred beneath the surface of the river but the Kommandant was well content. He was doing what an English gentleman would do on a hot summer afternoon, and knowing how ineffectual Englishmen were in other matters he doubted if they caught anything when fishing. As time slowly passed the Kommandant's mind, somnolent in the heat, pondered gently. With something remotely akin to insight he saw himself, a plump middle-aged man standing in unfamiliar clothes on the bank of an unknown river fishing for nothing in particular. It seemed a strange thing to do yet restful and in some curious way fulfilling. Piemburg and the police station seemed very far away and insignificant. He no longer cared what happened there. He was away from it, away in the mountains, being, if not himself, at least something equivalent and he was just considering what this admiration for things English meant when a voice interrupted him.

'Oh, never fly conceals a hook!' said the voice and the Kommandant turned to find the salesman with flatulence standing watching him.

'It does as a matter of fact,' said the Kommandant who thought the remark was rather foolish.

'A quote, a quote,' said the man. 'I'm afraid I'm rather given to them. It's not a particularly sociable habit but one that arises from my profession.'

'Really,' said the Kommandant non-committally, not being sure what a quote was. He wound in his line and was disconcerted to find that his fly had disappeared.

'I see I was right after all,' said the man. 'Squamous, omnipotent and kind.'

'I beg your pardon,' said the Kommandant.

'Just another quote,' said the man. 'Perhaps I ought to introduce myself. Mulpurgo. I lecture in English at the University of Zululand.'

'Van Heerden, Kommandant South African Police, Piemburg,' said the Kommandant and was startled by the effect his announcement had on Mr Mulpurgo. He had gone quite pale and was looking decidedly alarmed.

'Is anything wrong?' asked the Kommandant.

'No,' said Mr Mulpurgo shakily. 'Nothing at all. It's just that . . . well I had no idea you were . . . well . . Kommandant van Heerden.'

'You've heard about me then?' the Kommandant asked.

Mr Mulpurgo nodded. It was perfectly clear that he had. The Kommandant dismantled his rod.

'I don't suppose I'll catch anything now,' he said. 'Too late.'

'Evening is the best time,' said Mr Mulpurgo looking at him curiously.

'Is it? That's interesting,' the Kommandant said as they strolled back along the river bank. 'This is my first try at fishing. Are you a keen fisherman? You seem to know a lot about it.'

'My associations are purely literary,' Mr Mulpurgo confessed, 'I'm doing my thesis on "Heaven".'

Kommandant van Heerden was astonished.

'Isn't that a very difficult subject?' he asked.

Mr Mulpurgo smiled. 'It's a poem about fish by Rupert Brooke,' he explained.

'Oh is that what it is?' said the Kommandant who, while he'd never heard of Rupert Brooke, was always interested in hearing about English literature. 'This man Brooke is an English poet?'

Mr Mulpurgo said he was.

'He died in the First World War,' he explained and the Kommandant said he was sorry to hear it, 'The thing is' continued the English lecturer, 'that I believe that while it's possible to interpret the poem quite simply as an allegory of the human condition, *la condition humaine*, if you understand me, it has also a deeper relevance in terms of the psycho-alchemical process of transformation as discovered by Jung.'

The Kommandant nodded. He didn't understand a word that Mr Mulpurgo was saying but he felt privileged to hear it all the same. Encouraged by this acquiescence the lecturer warmed to his task.

'For instance the lines "One may not doubt that, somehow, good, Shall come of water and of mud" clearly indicate that the poet's intention is to introduce the concept of the philosopher's stone and its origin in the *prima materia* without in any way diverting the reader's attention from the poem's superficially humorous tone.'

They came to the enormous drain and Mr Mulpurgo helped the Kommandant with his basket. The evident alarm with which he had greeted the Kommandant's introduction had given way to nervous garrulity in the face of his friendly if uncomprehending interest.

'It's the individuation *motif* without a doubt,' he went on as they walked up the path to the hotel. ' "Paradisal grubs", "Unfading moths", "And the worm that never dies" all clearly point to that.'

'I suppose they must do,' said the Kommandant as they parted in the foyer. He went down the corridor to Colonic Irrigation No 6 feeling vaguely elated. He had spent the afternoon in an authentic English fashion, fishing and engaged in intellectual conversation. It was an auspicious start to his holiday and went some way to compensate for the disappointment he had felt on his arrival at the hotel. To celebrate the occasion he decided on a bath before dinner and spent some time searching for a bathroom before returning to his room and washing himself all over in the basin that looked most suited to that purpose and least likely to have been used for any other. As the old man had warned, the cold water was hot. The Kommandant tried the hot tap but that was just as hot and in the end he sprayed himself with warm water from a tube that was clearly too large to have been used as an enema but which left him smelling distinctly odd all the same. Then he sat on the bed and read a chapter of *Berry & Co.* before going to dinner. He found it difficult to concentrate because whichever way he sat he was still faced by his stained reflection in the wardrobe mirror which made him feel that there was someone with him in the room all the time. To avoid the compulsive introspection this induced he lay back on the bed and tried to imagine what Mr Mulpurgo had been talking about. It had meant nothing at the time and even less now but the phrase 'And the worm that never dies' stuck in his mind relentlessly. It seemed unlikely somehow but remembering that worms could break in half and still go on living separate existences, he supposed it was possible that when one end was mortally ill, the other end could dissociate itself from its partner's death and go on living. Perhaps that was what was meant by terminal. It was a word he'd never understood. He'd have to ask Mr Mulpurgo, who was evidently a highly educated man.

But when he went to the Pump Room for dinner, Mr Mulpurgo wasn't there. The two ladies at the far end of the room were his only companions and since their whispered conversation was made inaudible by the gurgling of the marble fountain the Kommandant ate his dinner in what amounted to silence and watched the sky darken behind the Aardvarkberg. Tomorrow he would find the address of the Heathcote-Kilkoons and let them know he had arrived.

Seventy miles away in Piemburg the evening which had begun so uneventfully took on a new animation towards midnight. The twelve violent explosions that rocked the city within minutes of one another at eleven-thirty were so strategically placed that they confirmed entirely Luitenant Verkramp's contention that a well-organized conspiracy of sabotage and subversion existed. As the last bomb brightened the horizon, Piemburg retreated still further into that obscurity for which it was so famous. Bereft of electricity, telephones, radio mast, and with road and rail links to the outside world severed by the explosive zeal of his secret agents, the tiny metropolis' tenuous hold on the twentieth century petered out.

From the roof of the police station where he was taking the air, Verkramp found the transformation quite spectacular. One moment Piemburg had been a delicate web of street lights and neon signs, the next it had merged indistinguishably with the rolling hills of Zululand. As the distant rumble from Empire View announced that the radio tower had ceased to be such a large blot on the landscape, Verkramp left the roof and hurried down the stairs to the cells where the only people in the city who would have actively canvassed for electricity cuts were still receiving their jolts from the hand-cranked generators in the darkness. The consolation for the volunteers was the disappearance of the naked black women as the projectors went out.

In the confusion Luitenant Verkramp remained disconcertingly calm.

'It's all right,' he shouted. 'There is nothing to be alarmed about, just continue the experiment using ordinary photographs.' He went from cell to cell distributing torches which he had kept handy for just such an eventuality as this. Sergeant Breitenbach was as usual less unperturbed.

'Don't you think it's more important to investigate the cause of the power failure?' he asked. 'It sounded to me like there were a whole lot of explosions.'

'Twelve,' said Verkramp emphatically, 'I counted them.'

'Twelve bloody great explosions in the middle of the night and you aren't worried?' said the Sergeant with astonishment. Luitenant Verkramp refused to be flustered.

'I've been expecting this for some time,' he said truthfully.

'Expecting what?'

'The sabotage movement has begun again,' he said going downstairs to his office. Behind him Sergeant Breitenbach, still literally and metaphorically in the dark, tried to follow him. By the time he reached the Kommandant's office, he found Verkramp checking a list of names by the light of an emergency lamp. It crossed the Sergeant's mind that Verkramp was remarkably well prepared for the crisis that seemed to have caught the rest of the city unawares.

'I want the following people detained at once,' Verkramp told him.

'Aren't you going to check on what's been going on first?' Sergeant Breitenbach asked. 'I mean you don't even know for sure that those explosions were made by bombs.'

Luitenant Verkramp looked up sternly.

'I've had enough experience of sabotage to know a bomb when I hear one,' he said. Sergeant Breitenbach decided not to argue. Instead he studied the list of names Verkramp had handed him and was horrified by what he saw. If Verkramp were right and the city had been disrupted by a series of bomb attacks, the consequences to public life in Piemburg would be mild by comparison with the chaos that would ensue if the men on the list were arrested. Clergymen, councillors, bank managers, lawyers, even the Mayor himself appeared to be the object of Verkramp's suspicions. Sergeant Breitenbach put the list down hurriedly. He didn't want anything to do with it.

'Don't you think you're being a bit hasty?' he asked nervously.

Luitenant Verkramp clearly didn't. 'If I am right, and I am, the city has been subjected to a premeditated campaign of sabotage. These men are all well-known—'

'You can say that again,' muttered the Sergeant.

'—opponents of the Government,' continued the Acting Kommandant. 'Many of them were Horticulturalists.'

'Horticulturalists?' asked the Sergeant who couldn't see anything wrong with being a horticulturalist. He was one himself in a small way.

'The Horticulturalists,' Verkramp explained, 'were a secret organization of wealthy farmers and businessmen who were planning to take Zululand out of the Union at the time of the Republic referendum. They were prepared to use force. Some were officers in the Piemburg Mounted Rifles and they were going to use weapons from the military arsenal.'

'But that was ten years ago,' Sergeant Brietenbach pointed out.

'Men like that don't change their opinions,' said Verkramp sententiously. 'Will you ever forgive the British for what they did to our women and children in the concentration camps?'

'No,' said the Sergeant, who hadn't had any women or children in concentration camps in the Boer war but who knew the right answer.

'Exactly,' said Verkramp. 'Well, these swine are no different and they'll never forgive us for taking Zululand out of the British Empire. They hate us. Don't you understand how the British hate us?'

'Yes,' said the Sergeant hastily. He could see that Verkramp was working himself up into a state again and he preferred to be out of the way when it came. 'You're probably right.'

'Right?' shouted Verkramp. 'I'm always right.'

'Yes,' said the Sergeant even more hastily.

'So what do they do, these Horticulturalists? Go underground for a time, then gang up with Communists and Liberalists to overthrow our glorious Afrikaner republic. These bomb attacks are the first sign that their campaign has started. Well, I'm not going to sit back and let them get away with it. I'll have those bastards in prison and squeeze the truth out of them before they can do any real harm.'

Sergeant Breitenbach waited until the seizure had run its course before demurring once again.

'Don't you think it would be safer to tell Kommandant van Heerden first? Then he can carry the can if there is a balls-up.'

Luitenant Verkramp wouldn't hear of it. 'Half the trouble in this town is due to the way the old fool treats the English,' he snapped. 'He's too bloody soft with them. Sometimes I think he prefers them to his own people.'

Sergeant Breitenbach said he didn't know about that. All he knew was that the Kommandant's grandfather had been shot by the British after the Battle of Paardeberg which was more than could be said for Verkramp's. His grandfather had sold horses to the British army and had been practically a khaki Boer but the Sergeant was too discreet to mention the fact now. Instead he picked up the list again.

'Where are we going to put them all?' he asked. 'The cells on the top floor are being used for your kaffirboetje cure and the ones in the basement are all full.'

'Take them down to the prison,' Verkramp told him, 'and see

that they're kept in isolation. I don't want them cooking up any stories.'

Half an hour later the homes of thirty-six of Piemburg's most influential citizens had been raided by armed police, and angry frightened men had been hustled in their pyjamas into pick-up vans. One or two put up a desperate resistance in the mistaken belief that the Zulus had risen and had come to massacre them in their beds, a misunderstanding that arose from the total black-out into which Verkramp's agents had plunged the city. Four policemen were wounded in these battles and a local coal merchant shot his wife to save her from being raped by the black hordes before the situation was clarified.

By dawn the arrests had all been made though one or two mistakes remained to be rectified. The man torn from the arms of the lady Mayoress turned out to be not the civic dignitary himself but a neighbour he had asked to help with his election. When the Mayor was finally apprehended he was under the impression that he was being arrested for corruption in high places. 'This is disgraceful,' he shouted as he was bundled into the pick-up van. 'You have no right to pry into my private wife. I am your ewected representative,' a protest that did nothing to effect his release but went some way to explain the presence of the neighbour in his wife's bed.

In the morning after a few hours sleep Luitenant Verkramp and Sergeant Breitenbach toured the installations which had been destroyed by the saboteurs. Once again the Acting Kommandant's grasp of the situation astonished Sergeant Breitenbach. Verkramp seemed to know exactly where to go without being told. As they surveyed the remains of the transformer on the Durban Road, the Sergeant asked him what he was going to do now.

'Nothing,' said Verkramp to his amazement. 'In a few days' time we'll be in a position to arrest the whole Communist organization in Zululand.'

'But what about all the people we arrested last night?'

'They will be interrogated and the evidence they give will help to reveal their co-conspirators,' Verkramp explained.

Sergeant Breitenbach shook his head in bewilderment.

'I hope to hell you know what you're doing,' was all he said.

They drove back via the prison where Verkramp gave instructions to the teams of Security Policemen who were to conduct the interrogation round the clock.

'The usual routine,' he told them. 'Keep them standing up. No sleep. Rough them up a bit to start with. Explain they'll be tried under the Terrorist Act and have to prove their innocence. No right to a lawyer. Can be detained indefinitely and incommunicado. Any questions?'

'Any, sir?' asked one of the men.

'You heard me,' snapped Verkramp, 'I said, "Any questions?" ' The men looked at him dumbly and Verkramp dismissed them and they filed off to begin their arduous duties. Luitenant Verkramp went to see Governor Schnapps to apologize for the temporary inconvenience he was causing in the prison. When he returned to the wing in which the detainees were being interrogated Luitenant Verkramp found that his orders were being obeyed to the letter.

'Who won Test Series in 1948?' shouted Sergeant Scheepers at the manager of Barclays Bank.

'I don't know,' squealed the manager who had been twice kicked in the scrotum for his failure to follow cricket.

Verkramp asked the Sergeant to come out into the corridor.

'What do you want to know that for?' he asked.

'Seems a fairly easy question,' said the Sergeant.

'I suppose it does,' said Verkramp. He went to the next cell where the Dean of Piemburg had avoided a similar fate by knowing the road distance between Johannesburg and Capetown, the age of the Prime Minister, and what the initials USA stood for.

'You said "Any questions",' the Security man explained when Verkramp demanded the reason for the quiz game.

'You dumb bastard,' Verkramp yelled, 'I said "Any questions?" not "Any questions." What do I have to do? Spell it out for you?'

'Yes sir,' said the man. Verkramp called the teams together and briefed them more explicitly.

'What we need is proof that these men have been conspiring to overthrow the government by force,' he explained, and got the Security men to write it down. 'Secondly that they have been actively inciting the blacks to rebel.' The men wrote that down too. 'Thirdly that they have been receiving money from overseas. Fourthly that they are all Communists or communist sympathizers. Is that quite clear?'

Sergeant Scheepers asked if he could tell the Mayor that one of the aldermen had said he was a cuckold.

'Of course,' Verkramp said. 'Tell him that the Alderman is prepared to give evidence to that effect. Get them started giving evidence against one another and we'll soon get to the root of this affair.'

The men went back to the cells with their list of questions and the interrogations began again. Having satisfied himself that his men were keeping to the point, Luitenant Verkramp returned to the police station to see if there were any messages from his secret agents. He was rather disappointed to find that none had arrived but he supposed it was too early to expect any concrete results.

Instead he decided to test the effectiveness of the aversion therapy on the volunteers on the top floor who were still screaming rhythmically. He sent for Sergeant Breitenbach and ordered him to bring a coon girl from the cells.

The Sergeant went away and returned with what he evidently thought was a suitable subject. She was fifty-eight if she was a day and hadn't been a beauty at half her age. Luitenant Verkramp was horrified.

'I said "Girl" not "Old bag",' he shouted. 'Take her away and get a proper girl.'

Sergeant Breitenbach went back downstairs with the old woman wondering why it was that you called a black man of seventy or eighty a boy but you couldn't call a woman of the same age a girl. It didn't seem to make sense. In the end he found a very large black girl and told her to come up with him to the top floor. Ten minutes and eight konstabels later, one of whom had a broken nose and another complained he couldn't find his testicles, they managed to get the girl up to the top floor only to find that Verkramp was still not satisfied.

'Do you really think that any sane man would find that attractive?' he asked pointing to the unconscious and battered

96

body that the konstabels were trying to keep on its feet and off theirs. 'What I want is a nice kaffir girl that any man would find attractive.'

'Well, you go and get one then,' Sergeant Breitenbach told him. 'You just go down to the cells and tell a nice attractive black girl that the policemen on the top floor want her and see what happens.'

'The trouble with you, Sergeant,' Verkramp said as they went down for the third time, 'is that you don't understand psychology. If you want people to do things for you, you mustn't frighten them. That's particularly true with blacks. You must use persuasion.' He stopped outside a cell door. The Sergeant unlocked it and the large black girl was pitched inside. Verkramp stepped over her body and looked at the women cringing against the wall.

'Now then, there's no need to be frightened,' he told them. 'Which one of you girls would like to come upstairs and see some pictures? They are pretty pictures.' There was no great rush of volunteers. Verkramp tried again.

'No one is going to hurt you. You needn't be afraid.'

There was still no response apart from a moan from the girl on the floor. Verkramp's sickly smile faded.

'Grab the bitch,' he yelled at the konstabels and the next moment a thin black girl was being hustled upstairs.

'You see what I mean about psychology,' Luitenant Verkramp said to the Sergeant as they followed her up. Sergeant Breitenbach still had his doubts.

'I notice you didn't pick a big one,' he said.

On the top floor the girl had her clothes stripped off her by several willing konstabels whom Verkramp put down on his list for treatment and was then paraded before the volunteers in the nude. Luitenant Verkramp was delighted by their lack of positive reaction.

'Not an erection from one of them,' he said. 'That's scientific proof that the treatment works.'

Sergeant Breitenbach was, as usual, more sceptical.

'They haven't had any sleep for two days,' he said. 'If you brought Marilyn Monroe in here in the raw, I don't suppose you'd get much response.'

Verkramp looked at him disapprovingly. 'Peeping Thomas,' he said.

'I don't see what that has to do with it,' said the Sergeant. 'All I'm saying is that if you want to be really scientific you should bring a white girl up and try her on them.' Luitenant Verkramp was furious.

'What a disgusting suggestion,' he said. 'I wouldn't dream of subjecting a white girl to such a revolting ordeal.'

He gave orders for the treatment to be continued for at least another two days.

'Two more days of this and I'll be dead,' moaned one of the volunteers.

'Better dead than a black in your bed,' said Verkramp and went back to his office to draw up the plans for the mass treatment of the other five hundred and ninety men under his temporary command.

At Florian's café Verkramp's secret agents were making remarkable headway in their search for members of the sabotage movement. After years of frustration in which they had mingled in liberal circles but had been unable to find anyone remotely connected with the Communist party or prepared to admit that they approved of violence, they had suddenly met quite a number. 745396 had discovered 628461 who seemed to know something about the explosion at the telephone exchange and 628461 had gained the very definite impression that 745396 wasn't unconnected with the destruction of the transformer on the Durban Road. Likewise 885974 had bumped into 378550 at the University Canteen and was sounding him out about his part in the disappearance of the radio mast, while hinting that he could tell 378550 something about the bomb that had destroyed the railway bridge. All over Piemburg Verkramp's agents had something to report in the way of progress and busied themselves encoding messages and moving digs as instructed. By the following day the conviction that each agent held that he was onto something big grew when 745396 and 628461, who had arranged to meet at the University Canteen, found a sympathetic audience in 885974 and 378550, who had been so successful there the previous day they had decided to return. As the coalescence of conspirators continued Verkramp was kept busy trying to decode the messages. This complex process was made even more difficult because he had no idea on which day the message had been sent. 378550's message had been deposited at the foot of a tree in the park which was the correct drop for Sunday but after working at it for two hours using the code for that day Verkramp had managed to turn 'hdfpkymwrqazxtivbnkon' which was designed to be difficult to understand into 'car dog wormsel sag infrequent banal out plunge crate', which wasn't. He tried Saturday's code and got 'dahlia chrysanthemum fertilizer decorative foxglove dwarf autumn bloom shady'. Cursing himself for the limited vocabulary provided by page 33 of the Piemburg Bulb Catalogue which he had chosen as the codebook for Saturday on account of its easy availability, Verkramp turned wearily to Friday's codebook and finally came up with the deciphered message that Agent 378550 had carried out instructions and was proceeding to new lodgings. After six hours hard labour Verkramp felt his efforts merited something more interesting than that. He tried 885974's message and was glad to find it came out correctly first time and contained the reassuring information that the agent had made contact with several suspected saboteurs but was having difficulty in reaching the drop as he was being followed.

885974's experience was not confined to him alone. In their attempts to find where the other saboteurs lived Verkramp's secret agents were trailing one another all over Piemburg or being tailed. As a result they were covering an enormous mileage every day and were too tired when they finally got home to sit down and encode the messages he expected. Then again they had to move lodgings every day on his orders and this required finding new ones so that all in all the sense of disorientation already induced by the multiple identities their work demanded became more pronounced as the days went by. By Monday 628461 wasn't sure who he was or where he lived or even what day of the week it was. He was even more uncertain where 745396 lived. Having tailed him successfully for fifteen miles up and down the sidestreets of Piemburg he wasn't altogether surprised when 745396 gave up the attempt to shake him off and returned to a lodging house on Bishoff Avenue only to find that he had left there two days before. In the end he slept on a bench in the park and 628461, who had several large blisters from all this walking, turned to go back to his digs when he became aware that someone was following him. He stepped up his limp and the footsteps behind him did the same. 628461 gave up the struggle. He no longer cared if he was followed home. 'I'll move in the morning anyway,' he decided and climbed the stairs to his room in the Lansdowne Boarding House. Behind him 378550 went back to his digs and spent the night encoding a message for Luitenant Verkramp giving the address of a suspected saboteur. Since he started it at ten-thirty on Monday and finished it at two a.m. on Tuesday Verkramp had even more difficulty than usual making out what it meant. According to Monday's codebook it read 'Suggest raid on infestation wood but pollute in the', while Tuesday's ran 'Chariot Pharoah withal Lansdowne Boarding House for Frederick Smith.' By the time Luitenant Verkramp had decided that there was no sense in 'Chariot Pharoah withal infestation wood but pollute in the' there was no point in raiding the Lansdowne Boarding House, Frederick Smith had registered at the YMCA as Piet Retief.

If Luitenant Verkramp was having difficulties in the communications field much the same could be said of both Mrs Heathcoat-Kilkoon and Kommandant van Heerden.

'Are you sure he's not there?' Mrs Heathcoat-Kilkoon asked the Major, whom she had sent on his daily outing into Weezen to tell the Kommandant that they were expecting him to lunch.

'Absolutely certain,' said Major Bloxham. 'I sat in the bar for nearly an hour and there was no sign of the fellow. Asked the barman if he'd seen him. Hadn't.'

'I think it's most peculiar,' said Mrs Heathcote-Kilkoon. 'His card definitely said he would stay at the hotel.'

'Damned peculiar card, if you ask me,' said the Colonel. 'Dearest Daphne, Kommandant van Heerden has pleasure—'

'I thought it was a very amusing card,' Mrs Heathcote-

Kilkoon interrupted him. 'It shows what a sense of humour the Kommandant has.'

'Didn't strike me as having a sense of humour,' said the Major who had not got over his encounter with the Kommandant.

'Personally I think we should be thankful for small mercies,' said the Colonel. 'It doesn't look as if the swine is coming after all.' He went out to the yard at the back of the house where Harbinger was grooming a large black horse. 'Everything ready for tomorrow, Harbinger? Fox fit?'

'Took him for a run this morning,' said Harbinger, a thin man with eyes close together and short hair. 'He went quite quick.'

'Fine, fine,' said the Colonel. 'Well we'll get off early.' In the house Mrs Heathcote-Kilkoon was still puzzled.

'Are you sure you went to the right hotel?' she asked the Major.

'I went to the store and asked for the hotel,' the Major insisted. 'The fellow tried to sell me a bed. Seemed to think that's what I wanted.'

'It sounds most peculiar,' said Mrs Heathcote-Kilkoon.

'I said I didn't want a bed,' said the Major. 'He sent me across the road to the hotel in the end.'

'And they hadn't heard of him?'

'Didn't know anything about any Kommandant van Heerden.'

'Perhaps he'll turn up tomorrow,' said Mrs Heathcote-Kilkoon wistfully.

CHAPTER EIGHT

Unaware of the portentous events that were taking place in Piemburg, Kommandant van Heerden nevertheless spent a restless first night in his room at Weezen Spa. For one thing the strong smell of sulphur irritated his olfactory nerve and for another one of the many taps in his room insisted on dripping

101

irregularly. The Kommandant tried to get rid of the sulphurous smell by spraying the room with the deodorant he'd bought to avoid giving bodily offence to Mrs Heathcote-Kilkoon. The resulting pot-pourri was rather nastier than the sulphur alone and in any case it made his eyes water. He got up and opened the window to let the smell out only to find that he had let a mosquito in. He shut the window again and switching on the light killed the mosquito with a slipper. He got back into bed and the tap dripped. He got out again and tightened all six taps and got back into bed. This time he was about to get to sleep when a dull rumble in the pipes suggested an air lock. There wasn't anything he could do in the way of major plumbing so he lay and listened to it while watching the moon rise mistily through the frosted glass window. In the early hours he finally slept to be awakened by a coloured maid at half past seven bringing him a cup of tea. The Kommandant sat up and drank some tea. He had already swallowed some before he realized how horrible it tasted. For a moment the thought that he had been the victim of a poison attempt crossed his mind before he realized that the taste was due to the ubiquitous sulphur. He got out of bed and began brushing his teeth with water that tasted vile. Thoroughly fed up, he washed and dressed and went to the pump room for breakfast.

'Fruit juice,' he ordered when the waitress asked him what he wanted. He ordered a second glass when she brought the first and swilling the grapefruit juice round his mouth managed to eradicate some of the taste of sulphur.

'Boiled eggs or fried,' the waitress asked. The Kommandant said fried on the ground that they were less likely to be tainted. When the old man came in and asked if everything was all right, the Kommandant took the opportunity of asking him if it was possible to have some fresh water.

'Fresh?' said the old man. 'The water here is as fresh as mother nature can make it. Hot springs under here. Comes straight from the bowels of the earth.'

'I can well believe it,' said the Kommandant.

Presently he was joined by Mr Mulpurgo who sat at his usual table by the fountain.

'Good morning,' said the Kommandant cheerily and was

a little hurt by the rather chilly 'Morning' he got back. The Kommandant tried again.

'How's the flatulence this morning?' he asked sympathetically.

Mr Mulpurgo ordered corn flakes, bacon and eggs, toast and marmalade before replying.

'Flatulence?'

'You said yesterday you came here for flatulence,' said the Kommandant.

'Oh,' said Mr Mulpurgo in the tone of one who didn't want to be reminded what he had said yesterday. 'Much better, thank you.'

The Kommandant refused the waitress' offer of coffee and ordered a third fruit juice.

'I've been thinking about that worm you spoke of yesterday, the one that never dies,' he said as Mr Mulpurgo attempted to get the rind off a soggy piece of bacon. 'Is it true that worms don't die?'

Mr Mulpurgo looked at him distrustfully. 'My own impression is that worms are not immune from the consequences of mortality,' he said finally, 'and that they shuffle off this mortal coil at their own equivalent of three-score years and ten.' He concentrated on his bacon and eggs and left the Kommandant to consider whether worms could shuffle off anything. He wondered what a mortal coil was. It sounded like a piece of radio equipment.

'But you mentioned one that didn't,' he said after giving the matter some thought.

'Didn't what?'

'Die.'

'I was speaking metaphorically,' Mr Mulpurgo said. 'I was talking about rebirth.' Like a reluctant Ancient Mariner prodded into action by the Kommandant's insistent curiosity Mr Mulpurgo found himself embarking on a lengthy disquisition that had been no part of his plans for the morning. He had intended working quietly in his room on his thesis. Instead an hour later he found himself strolling beside the river expounding his belief that the study of literature added a new dimension to the life of the reader. Beside him Kommandant van Heerden lumbered along occasionally recognizing a phrase which was not wholly unfamiliar but for the most part merely lost in admiration for the intellectual excellence of his companion. He had no idea what 'aesthetic awareness' or 'extended sensibilities' were though 'emotional anaemia' did suggest a lack of iron, but these were all minor problems beside the major one which was that Mr Mulpurgo for all his divagations seemed to be saying that a man could be born again through the study of literature. That at least the Kommandant discerned and the message coming from such an obviously well-informed source brought him fresh hope that he would one day achieve the transformation he so desired.

'You don't think heart transplants are any good then?' he asked when Mr Mulpurgo paused for breath. The devotee of Rupert Brooke looked at him suspiciously. Not for the first time Mr Mulpurgo had the feeling that he was having his leg pulled, but Kommandant van Heerden's face was alight with a grotesque innocence which was quite disarming.

Mr Mulpurgo chose to assume that in his own quaint way the Kommandant was reviving the arguments in favour of science put forward by C. P. Snow in his famous debate with F. R. Leavis. If he wasn't, Mr Mulpurgo couldn't imagine what he was talking about.

'Science deals only with the externals,' he said. 'What we need is to change man's nature from within.'

'I should have thought heart transplants did that very well,' said the Kommandant.

'Heart transplants don't alter man's nature in the least,' said Mr Mulpurgo who was finding the Kommandant's train of thought no less incomprehensible than the Kommandant had found his. What organ transplants had to do with extended sensibilities he couldn't begin to think. He decided to change the topic of conversation before it became too inconsequential.

'Do you know these mountains well?' he asked.

The Kommandant said he didn't personally but that his great-great-grandfather had crossed them in the Great Trek.

'Did he settle in Zululand?' Mr Mulpurgo asked.

'He was murdered there,' said the Kommandant. Mr Mulpurgo was sorry to hear it.

'By Dingaan,' continued the Kommandant. 'My great-great-grandmother was one of the few women to survive the massacre at Blaauwkrans River. The Zulu impis swept down without warning and hacked them all to death.'

'A dreadful business,' Mr Mulpurgo murmured. His own family history was less chequered. He couldn't remember his great-great-grandmother but he felt fairly certain she hadn't been massacred by anyone.

'That's one reason we don't trust the kaffirs,' the Kommandant continued.

'There's no chance of that happening again,' Mr Mulpurgo said.

'You never can tell with kaffirs,' said the Kommandant. 'The leopard doesn't change its spots.'

Mr Mulpurgo's liberal leanings forced him to protest.

'Come now, you don't mean to say that you think today's Africans are savages,' he said mildly. 'I know some highly educated ones.'

'Blacks are savages,' insisted the Kommandant vehemently, 'and the more educated they are the more dangerous they get.'

Mr Mulpurgo sighed.

'Such a beautiful country,' he said. 'It seems such a shame that people of different races can't live amicably together in it.'

Kommandant van Heerden looked at him curiously.

'It's part of my job to see that people of different races don't live together,' he said by way of a warning. 'You take my advice and put the idea out of your mind. I wouldn't like to see a nice young fellow like you going to prison.'

Mr Mulpurgo stopped and began to hiccup. 'I wasn't suggesting,' he began but the Kommandant stopped him.

'I wasn't suggesting you were,' he said kindly. 'All of us have these ideas once in a while but it's best to forget them. If you want some black tail go up to Lourenço Marques. The Portuguese let you have it quite legally, you know. Some nice girls too, I can tell you.' Mr Mulpurgo stopped hiccuping but he still stared at the Kommandant very nervously. Life at the University of Zululand had never prepared him for an encounter such as this.

'You see,' continued the Kommandant as they resumed their walk, 'we know all about you intellectuals and your talk about education for the kaffirs and equality. Oh we keep an eye on you, you needn't worry.'

Mr Mulpurgo was not reassured. He knew perfectly well that the police kept an eye on the university. There had been too many raids to think otherwise. He began to wonder if the Kommandant had deliberately sought him out to question him. The notion brought on another attack of hiccups.

'There's only one real question in this country,' continued the Kommandant, quite unaware of the effect he was having on his companion, 'and that is who works for who. Do I work for a kaffir or does he work for me? What do you say to that?'

Mr Mulpurgo tried to say that it was a pity people couldn't work together cooperatively but he was hiccuping too much to be wholly coherent.

'Well I'm not working down some gold mine to make some black bastard rich,' said the Kommandant ignoring what he supposed was an acute attack of flatulence, 'and I'm not having a kaffir tell me to wash his car. It's dog eat dog and I'm the bigger dog. That's what you intellectuals forget.'

With this simple statement of his philosophy the Kommandant decided it was time to turn back.

'I've got to go and find where my friends live,' he said.

They walked back in silence for some time, Mr Mulpurgo mulling over the Kommandant's Spencerian view of society while the Kommandant, ignoring what he had just said about leopards and their spots, wondered if he could become an Englishman by reading books.

'How do you go about studying your poem?' he asked presently.

Mr Mulpurgo returned to the topic of his thesis with some relief.

'The main thing is to keep notes,' he explained. 'I make references and cross-references and keep them on file. For instance Brooke uses the image of smell frequently. It's there in "Lust", in "Second Best", and of course in "Dawn".'

'It's there all the time,' said the Kommandant. 'It's the water, there's sulphur in it.'

'Sulphur?' said Mr Mulpurgo absentmindedly. 'Yes, you get that in "The Last Beatitude". "And fling new sulphur on the sin incarnadined."'

'I don't know about that,' said the Kommandant uneasily, 'but they certainly put some in my tea this morning.'

By the time they reached the hotel Mr Mulpurgo had come to the conclusion that the Kommandant had no professional interest in him after all. He had recited 'Heaven' to him twice and explained what 'fish fly replete' meant and was beginning to feel that the Kommandant was quite a kind man in spite of his earlier utterances.

'I must say you have unusual interests for a policeman,' he said condescendingly as they climbed the steps to the terrace, 'I had gained quite a different impression from the newspapers.'

Kommandant van Heerden smiled darkly.

'They say a lot of lies about me in the papers,' he said. 'You mustn't believe all you hear.'

'Not as black as you're painted, eh?' said Mr Mulpurgo.

The Kommandant stopped in his tracks.

'Who said anything about me being black?' he demanded lividly.

'No one. No one,' said Mr Mulpurgo appalled at his *faux pas*. 'It was purely a figure of speech.'

But Kommandant van Heerden wasn't listening. 'I'm as white as the next man,' he yelled, 'and if I hear anyone say any different I'll rip the balls off the swine. Do you hear me? I'll castrate the bugger. Don't let me hear you saying such a thing again,' and he hurled himself through the revolving doors with a violence that propelled the two flies quite involuntarily into the open air. Behind him Mr Mulpurgo leant against the balustrade and tried to stop hiccuping. When the door finally stopped revolving he pulled himself together and went shakily down the corridor to his room.

Having collected his keys from his room Kommandant van Heerden went out to his car. He was still inwardly raging at the insult to his ancestry.

'I'm as white as the next man,' he muttered pushing blindly past a Zulu gardener who was weeding a flower-bed. He got into his car and drove furiously into Weezen. He was still in a foul temper when he parked in the dusty square and went up the steps into the trading store. There were several farmers waiting to be served. The Kommandant ignored them and spoke to the gaunt man behind the counter.

'Know where the Heathcote-Kilkoons live?' he asked.

The gaunt man ignored his question and went on attending to his customer.

'I said do you know where the Heathcote-Kilkoons live?' the Kommandant said again.

'Heard you the first time,' the man told him, and was silent.

'Well?'

'I'm serving,' said the gaunt man. There were murmurs from the farmers but the Kommandant was in too irritable a mood to worry.

'I asked a civil question,' he insisted.

'In an uncivil fashion,' the man told him. 'If you want answers you wait your turn and ask decently.'

'Do you know who I am?' the Kommandant asked angrily.

'No,' said the man, 'and I don't care. I know where you are though. On my premises and you can get the hell off them.'

The Kommandant looked wildly round. All the men in the store were staring at him unpleasantly. He turned and lumbered out onto the verandah. Behind him someone laughed and he thought he caught the words 'Bloody hairy-back.' No one had called him a hairy-back for a very long time. First a black and now a baboon. He stood for a moment controlling himself with an effort before turning back into the shop.

He stood in the doorway with the sunlit square behind him, a squat silhouette. The men inside stared at him.

'My name is van Heerden,' said the Kommandant in a low and terrible voice, 'I am Kommandant of Police in Piemburg. You will remember me.' It was an announcement that would have caused alarm anywhere else in Zululand. Here it failed hopelessly.

'This is Little England,' said the gaunt man. 'Voetsak.'

The Kommandant turned and went. He had been told to

voetsak like a dog. It was an insult he would never forget. He went blindly down the steps into the street and stood with clenched teeth squinting malevolently at the great Queen whose homely arrogance had no appeal for him now. He, Kommandant van Heerden, whose ancestors had manhandled their wagons over the Aardvark Mountains, who had fought the Zulus at Blood River, and the British at Spion Kop, had been told to voetsak like a kaffir dog by men whose kinfolk had scuttled from India and Egypt and Kenya at the first hint of trouble.

'Stupid old bitch,' said the Kommandant to the statue and turned away to look for the post office. As he walked his rage slowly subsided to be replaced by a puzzled wonder at the arrogance of the English. 'Little England,' the gaunt man had said as if he had been proud of its being so little. To Kommandant van Heerden there was no sense in it. He stomped along the sidewalk brooding on the malfeasance of chance that had given him the power to rule without the assurance that was power's natural concomitant. In some strange way he recognized the right of the storekeeper to treat him like a dog no matter what awesome credentials he presented. 'I'm just Boeremense,' he thought with sudden self-pity and saw himself alone in an alien world unattached to any true community but outspanned temporarily among strange hostile tribes. The English had Home, that cold yet hospitable island in the North to which they could always turn. The blacks had Africa, the vast continent from which no law or rule could ever utterly remove them. But he, an Afrikaner, had only will and power and cunning between him and oblivion. No home but here. No time but now. With a fresh fear at his own inconsequence the Kommandant turned down a side street to the Post Office.

At White Ladies Mrs Heathcote-Kilkoon, idly turning the pages of a month-old *Illustrated London News* in an impractical attempt to relieve her boredom, told Major Bloxham to make her a dry Martini.

'You would think he'd let us know he wasn't coming,' she said petulantly. 'I mean it's only common courtesy to send a postcard.'

'What do you expect from a pig but a grunt?' said the Major. 'Can't make silk purses out of sows' ears.'

'I suppose you're right,' Mrs Heathcote-Kilkoon murmured, 'I see Princess Anne's been chosen Sportswoman of the Year.'

'Wonder she accepted,' said the Major. 'Seems a common sort of thing to be.'

'Oh I don't know,' said Mrs Heathcote-Kilkoon. 'They even knight jockeys these days.'

After lunch Mrs Heathcote-Kilkoon insisted on going for a drive and the Colonel who was expecting a telegram from his stockbroker drove them into Weezen and then over to the Sani Pass Hotel for tea.

The Kommandant, who had finally found their address at the Post Office, discovered the house empty when he visited it in the afternoon. He had recovered his temper though not his confidence and he was therefore not altogether surprised at the lack of welcome afforded by the empty house and the ancient Zulu butler who answered the door when he rang.

'Master gone,' the butler said and the Kommandant turned back to his car with the feeling that this was not a lucky day for him. He stood looking round at the house and garden before getting back into his car, and tried to absorb some of the amour-propre which was so evident in the atmosphere.

Well-trimmed lawns and disciplined herbaceous borders, carefully labelled rose bushes and a bush clipped to the replica of a chicken, all was ordered agreeably. Even the fruit trees in the orchard looked as though they'd been given short back and sides by a regimental barber. Against a wall a vine grew symmetrically, while the house with its stone walls and shuttered windows suggested a cosy opulence in its com- bination of garrison Georgian and art nouveau. On a flagstaff the Union Jack hung limply in the hot summer air and the Kommandant, forgetting his fury of the morning, was glad to see it there. It was, he supposed, because the Heathcote-Kil- koons were real Englishers not the descendants of settlers that the place was so trim and redolent of disciplined assurance. He got into his car and drove to the hotel. He spent the rest of the afternoon fishing the river with no better luck than he had had previously but recovering from the emotional upsets of the morning. Once again the strange sense of self-awareness, of seeing himself from a distance, came over him and with it came a sense of calm acceptance of himself not as he was but as he might remotely be in other, better circumstances. When the sun faded over the Aardvarks he dismantled his rod and walked back to the hotel through the swift dusk. Somewhere near him someone hiccupped but the Kommandant ignored the overture. He'd seen enough of Mr Mulpurgo for one day. He had dinner and went early to bed with a new novel by Dornford Yates. It was called *Perishable Goods*.

In Piemburg Operation White Wash was about to move into a new phase. Luitenant Verkramp had tested his ten volunteers once again in a live situation and was satisfied that the experiment had been wholly successful. Confronted with black women the volunteers had all demonstrated an entirely convincing aversion for them and Verkramp was ready to move to phase two. Sergeant Breitenbach's enthusiasm for the project was as usual less marked.

'Two hundred at a time in the drill hall?' he asked incredulously. 'Two hundred konstabels strapped to chairs and wired up in the drill hall?'

'One sergeant to operate the projector and administer the electric shocks,' Verkramp said. 'Won't be any difficulty about that.'

'There'll be a hell of a difficulty getting two hundred sane men to sit there in the first place,' said the Sergeant, 'and anyway it's impossible. Those generators aren't big enough to shock two hundred men.'

'We'll use the mains,' said Verkramp.

Sergeant Breitenbach stared at him with bulging eyes.

'You'll use what?'

'The mains,' said Verkramp. 'With a transformer of course.'

'Of course,' said the Sergeant with an insane laugh, 'a transformer off the mains. And what happens if something goes wrong?'

'Nothing is going to go wrong,' said Verkramp, but Sergeant

Breitenbach wasn't listening. He was visualizing a drill hall filled with the corpses of two hundred konstabels electrocuted while being shown slides of naked black women. Quite apart from the public outcry he would almost certainly be lynched by the widows.

'I'm not having any part of this,' he said emphatically. 'You can keep it.' He turned to leave the office but the Acting Kommandant called him back.

'Sergeant Breitenbach, what we are doing is for the ultimate good of the white race in South Africa,' Verkramp said solemnly. 'Are you prepared to sacrifice the future of your country simply because you are afraid to take a risk?'

'Yes,' said Sergeant Breitenbach who couldn't see how the electrocution of two hundred policemen could possibly benefit South Africa.

Luitenant Verkramp adopted a more practical line of reasoning.

'In any case there will be fuses to prevent accidental overloading,' he said.

'15 Amp I suppose,' said the Sergeant caustically.

'Something of the sort,' said Verkramp airily. 'I'll leave the details to the police electrician.'

'More likely the mortician,' said the Sergeant, whose knowledge of power points was somewhat less limited. 'In any case you'll never get the men to submit to the ordeal. I'm not forcing any man to risk getting himself electrocuted.'

Luitenant Verkramp smiled.

'No need for force,' he said. 'They've all signed the necessary forms.'

'It's one thing to sign a form. It's another to allow someone to give you electric shocks. And what about the electricity? Where are you going to get that from? It's all been cut off since the sabotage.'

Luitenant Verkramp dialled the manager of the Electricity Board. While he waited he showed Sergeant Breitenbach the forms the men had signed. 'Read the small print at the bottom,' he told him.

'Can't without my glasses,' the Sergeant told him. Verkramp snatched the form back and read it aloud.

'I admit freely and of my own volition that I have had sexual intercourse with Bantu women and am in need of treatment,' he said before being interrupted by a horrified squawk from the telephone receiver. The manager of the Electricity Board was on the line.

'You do what?' yelled the manager, appalled at the confession he had just been privy to.

'Not me,' Verkramp tried to explain.

'I heard you quite distinctly,' the manager shouted back. 'You said "I admit freely and of my own volition that I have had sexual intercourse with Bantu women." Deny that if you can.'

'All right, I did say it . . .' Verkramp began but the manager was too incensed to let him continue.

'What did I say? You can't deny it. This is an outrage. You ring me up to tell me that you sleep with kaffir girls. I've a good mind to ring the police.'

'This is the police,' said Verkramp.

'Good God, the whole world's gone mad,' shouted the manager.

'I was just reading a prisoner's confession out loud,' Verkramp explained.

'Over the phone?' asked the manager. 'And why to me of all people? I've got enough trouble on my hands without that sort of filth.'

Sergeant Breitenbach left Verkramp to sort the thing out with the Electricity Board. The tempo of events since Verkramp had taken over was so rapid the Sergeant was beginning to feel totally confused.

Much the same could be said of the state of mind of Verkramp's secret agents. Lack of sleep, the need to move their lodgings, the incessant following and being followed that was so much a part of their duties, had left them utterly exhausted and with what little hold on reality they had ever possessed badly impaired. The one sure thing they all knew was that they had been ordered to get the real saboteurs to blow something up. In Florian's café they sat round a table and worked to this end.

745396 suggested the petrol storage tanks in the railway yard as a suitable target. 628461 was in favour of the gasworks. 885974, not to be outdone, recommended the sewage disposal plant on the grounds that the ensuing epidemic would benefit the cause of world Communism, and all the others had their own favourite targets. By the time they had argued the pros and cons of each suggestion no one was clear what target had finally been selected and the air of mutual suspicion had been exacerbated by 885974 who had accused 745396 of being a police spy in the belief that this would add credibility to his own claim to be a genuine saboteur. Accusations and counter-accusations were exchanged and when the group finally left Florian's café to go their none too separate ways, each agent was determined to prove himself to the others by a demonstration of zeal for sabotage. That night Piemburg experienced a second wave of bombings.

At ten the petrol storage tanks exploded and set light to a goods train in the railway yard. At ten-thirty the gasometer exploded with a roar that blew the windows out in several neighbouring streets. As the fire brigade rushed in different directions the sewage disposal plant erupted. All over the previously darkened city fires broke out. In an attempt to prevent a further spread of the flames in the railway yard the goods train was moved down the line and in the process set fire to four tool sheds in the gardens it passed and started a grass fire which spread to a field of sugar cane. By morning Piemburg's fire-fighting force was exhausted and a dark smudge of smoke hung ominously over the city.

Sergeant Breitenbach arrived at the police station with his face covered in sticking plaster. He had been looking out of his bedroom window when the gasometer exploded. He found Verkramp desperately trying to decode several messages from his agents which he hoped would give him some lead to the new outbreak of violence. So far all he had learnt was that the petrol tanks were due to be sabotaged by a man who called himself Jack Jones who lived at the Outspan Hotel. By the time Verkramp had received and deciphered the message both the petrol tanks and Jack Jones had vanished. The manager of the Outspan hotel said he had checked out two days ago.

'What are you doing?' Sergeant Breitenbach asked as he entered the office. The Acting Kommandant stuffed the messages hurriedly into a drawer in his desk.

'Nothing,' he said nervously. 'Nothing at all.'

Sergeant Breitenbach eyed the handbook on Animal Husbandry which was the codebook for the day and wondered if Verkramp was thinking of taking up farming. In the light of the catastrophes which were taking place under his command it seemed wise of Verkramp to be thinking about retiring.

'Well?' said Verkramp, annoyed that he had been interrupted. 'What is it?'

'Isn't it about time you did something about these saboteurs? Things are getting out of hand,' said the Sergeant.

Verkramp stirred uneasily in his chair. He had the feeling that his authority was being impugned.

'I can see you got out of bed on the wrong side this morning,' he said.

'I didn't get out at all,' said the Sergeant, 'I was blown out. By the sewage disposal works.'

Verkramp smiled.

'I thought you'd cut your face shaving,' he said.

'That was the gasometer,' Sergeant Breitenbach told him. 'I was looking out the window when it blew up.'

'Through. Not out of,' said Verkramp pedantically.

'Through what?'

'Through the window. If you had been looking out the window you wouldn't have been hit by flying glass. It's really very important for a police officer to get his facts right.'

Sergeant Breitenbach pointed out that he was lucky to be still alive.

'A miss is as good as a mile,' said Verkramp.

'Half a mile,' said the Sergeant.

'Half a mile?'

'I live half a mile from the gasometer since you want the facts right,' said the Sergeant. 'What it must have been like for the people living next door to it I can't think.'

Luitenant Verkramp stood up and strode across to the window and stared out. Something about the way he was standing reminded the Sergeant of a film he had seen about a

115

general on the eve of a battle. Verkramp had one hand behind his back and the other tucked into his tunic.

'I am about to strike a blow at the root of all this evil,' he said dramatically before turning and fixing an intense look on the Sergeant. 'Have you ever looked evil in the face?'

Sergeant Breitenbach, remembering the gasometer, said he had.

'Then you'll know what I am talking about,' said Verkramp enigmatically and sat down.

'Where do you think we should start looking?' the Sergeant asked.

'In the heart of man,' said Verkramp.

'In where?' said the Sergeant.

'In the heart of man. In his soul. In the innermost regions of his nature.'

'For saboteurs?' asked Sergeant Breitenbach.

'For evil,' said Verkramp. He handed the Sergeant a long list of names. 'I want these men to report to the Drill Hall immediately. Everything is ready. The chairs have been wired and the projector and the screen have been installed. Here is a list of the Sergeants who will administer the treatment.'

Sergeant Breitenbach stared maniacally at his commanding officer.

'You've gone mad,' he said finally. 'You must have gone out of your mind. We've got the biggest wave of bombings this country has seen, with petrol tanks and gasometers going up and radio masts coming down and all you can think about is stopping people going to bed with coons. You're fucking loony.' The Sergeant stopped, stunned by the accuracy of his last remark. Before he could draw any further conclusions from it, Luitenant Verkramp was on his feet.

'Sergeant Breitenbach,' he screamed, and the Sergeant shrank at his fury, 'are you refusing to obey an order?' A demonic hopefulness in Verkramp's tone frightened the Sergeant.

'No, sir. Not an order,' he said. The sacrosanct word recalled him to his uncritical senses. 'Law and order have to be maintained at all times.'

Luitenant Verkramp was mollified.

'Precisely,' he said. 'Well I'm the law round this town and I give the orders. My orders are that you start the treatment of aversion therapy at once. The sooner we have a truly Christian and incorruptible police force the sooner we will be able to eradicate the evil of which these bombings are merely the symptom. It's no use treating the mere manifestations of evil, Sergeant, unless we first cleanse the body politic and that, God willing, is what I intend to do. What has happened in Piemburg should be a lesson to us all. That smoke out there is a sign from Heaven of God's anger. Let us all see to it that we incur no more.'

'Yes sir. I sincerely hope so, sir,' said Sergeant Breitenbach. 'Any special precautions you want taken in case we do, sir? Any guards on the remaining public installations?'

'No need, Sergeant,' said Verkramp loftily, 'I have the matter in hand.'

'Very good, sir,' said Sergeant Breitenbach and left the room to carry out his orders. Twenty minutes later he was facing near-mutiny in the drill hall as two hundred konstabels, already alarmed at the deteriorating situation in the city, refused to allow themselves to be strapped to the chairs wired to a large transformer. Quite a few had already said they would rather stand trial for sleeping with kaffir girls and take their chance of getting ten strokes with a heavy cane and do seven years hard labour than run the risk of electrocution. Finally he telephoned Luitenant Verkramp, and explained the dilemma. Verkramp said he'd be down in five minutes.

He arrived to find the men milling about rebelliously in the Drill Hall.

'Outside,' he ordered briskly and turned to Sergeant Breitenbach. 'Assemble these men in platoons under their sergeants.'

Two hundred konstabels lined up obediently on the parade ground. Luitenant Verkramp addressed them.

'Men,' he said. 'Men of the South African Police, you have been brought here to test your steadfast loyalty to your country and your race. The enemies of South Africa have been using black women to seduce you from the path of duty. Now is your chance to prove that you are worthy of the great trust the

117

white women of South Africa have placed in you. Your wives and mothers, your sisters and daughters look to you in this great moment of trial to prove yourself loyal fathers and husbands. The test that you have now to pass will prove that loyalty. You will singly come in to the Drill Hall and be shown certain pictures. Those of you who do not respond to them will return immediately to the police station. Those of you who fail will assemble here on the parade ground to await instructions. In the meantime Sergeant Breitenbach will give the rest of you drill practice. Carry on, Sergeant.'

As the konstabels marched and countermarched up and down the hot parade ground they watched the men who were called singly disappear into the drill hall. It was quite clear that they all passed the test. None returned to the parade ground. As the last man passed through the door, Sergeant Breitenbach followed him in curious to see what had happened. In front of him the last konstabel was seized by four sergeants, had sticking plaster swiftly clapped over his mouth and was strapped to the last empty chair. Two hundred silent konstabels glared frantically at their Acting Kommandant. The lights were switched off and the projector on. On the vast screen at the end of the hall, naked as the day she was born and forty times as large, there appeared the brilliantly coloured image of a gigantic black woman. Luitenant Verkramp mounted the stage and stood in front of the screen, partially obscuring the woman's sexual organs and with an aura of pubic hairs sprouting round his head. With a nauseating realism Verkramp opened his mouth, his face livid with projected labia.

'This is for your own good,' he said. 'By the time you leave this hall your transracial sexual tendencies will have been eradicated for ever. You will have been cleansed of the lusts of the flesh. Start the treatment.' Below him two hundred konstabels jerked in their seats with a uniformity of movement that had been noticeably lacking in their drill.

As they drove back to the police station, Sergeant Breitenbach complimented Verkramp on his cunning.

'It's all a question of psychology,' said Verkramp smugly. 'Divide and rule.'

CHAPTER NINE

At Fort Rapier Mental Hospital Dr von Blimenstein was unaware of the effect her advice about aversion therapy was having on the lives of Piemburg's policemen. She still thought about Verkramp and wondered why he hadn't contacted her but the outbreak of sabotage suggested an explanation which did something to satisfy her vanity. 'He's too busy, poor lamb,' she thought and found an outlet for her sense of disappointment by trying to cope with the influx of patients suffering from acute anxiety following the bombings. A great many were suffering from Bloodbath Phobia, and were obsessed by the belief that they were going to be chopped to pieces one morning by the black servant next door. Dr von Blimenstein was not immune to the infection, which was endemic among South African Whites, but she did her best to calm the fears of her new patients.

'Why the servant next-door?' she asked a particularly disturbed woman who wouldn't even allow a black orderly into her room at the hospital to empty the chamber pot but preferred to do it herself, an action so extraordinarily menial for a white woman that it was a clear symptom of insanity.

'Because that's what my kitchen boy told me,' the woman said through her tears.

'Your kitchen boy said the servants next-door would come and kill you?' Dr von Blimenstein asked patiently.

The woman struggled to control herself.

'I said to him, "Joseph, you wouldn't kill your missus, would you?" and he said, "No missus, the boy next-door would kill you and I'd kill his missus for him." You see they've got it all worked out. We're going to be massacred in our beds when they bring the tea in at seven o'clock in the morning.'

'You don't think it might be wise to give up morning tea?' the doctor asked but the woman wouldn't hear of it.

'I don't think I could get through the day without my morning cup of tea,' she said. Dr von Blimenstein refrained from pointing out that there was a logical inconsistency between this assertion and her previous remarks about being cut up. Instead she wrote out her usual prescription in such cases and sent her to see the Gunnery Instructor.

'Occupational therapy,' she explained to the woman who was presently happily engaged in firing a ·38 revolver into targets painted to look like black servants holding tea trays in one hand and pangas in the other.

Dr von Blimenstein's next patient suffered from Blackcock Fever which was even more frequent than Bloodbath Phobia.

'They've got such big ones,' she mumbled to the doctor when asked what the trouble was.

'Big whats?' Dr von Blimenstein asked although she could recognize the symptoms immediately.

'You know. Hoohas,' the woman muttered indistinctly.

'Hoohas?'

'Whatsits.'

'Whatsits?' said the doctor who believed that part of the cure consisted in getting the patient to express her fears openly. In front of her the woman went bright pink.

'Their wibbledy wands,' she said frantically trying to make herself understood.

'I'm afraid you'll have to make yourself clearer, my dear,' said Dr von Blimenstein, 'I've no idea what you're trying to tell me.'

The woman screwed up her courage. 'They've got long pork swords,' she said finally. Dr von Blimenstein wrote it down repeating each word. 'They ... have ... long ... pork ... swords.' She looked up. 'And what is a pork sword?' she asked brightly. The patient looked at her wildly.

'You mean to say you don't know?' she asked.

Dr von Blimenstein shook her head. 'I've no idea,' she lied.

'You're not married?' the woman asked. The doctor shook her head again. 'Well in that case I'm not telling you. You'll find out on your wedding night.' She relapsed into a stubborn silence.

'Shall we start again?' Dr von Blimenstein asked. 'A pork sword is a wibbledy wand is a whatsit is a hoo ha, is that right?'

'Oh for God's sake,' shouted the woman appalled at the catalogue of sexual euphemisms. 'I'm talking about their knobs.'

'Is a knob,' said the doctor and wrote it down. In front of her the woman squirmed with embarrassment.

'What do you want me to do? Spell it out for you?' she yelled.

'Please do,' said the doctor, 'I think we should get this matter straight.' The patient shuddered.

'Pee, Are, Eye, See, Kay, spells prick,' she screamed. She seemed to think it was the definitive term.

'You mean penis, don't you, dear?' Dr von Blimenstein asked.

'Yes,' screamed the patient hysterically, 'I mean penis, prick, pork sword, knob, the lot. What's it matter what you call it? They've all got huge ones.'

'Who have?'

'Kaffirs have. They're eighteen inches long and three inches thick and they've got foreskins like umbrellas and they—'

'Now, hold it a moment,' Dr von Blimenstein said as the woman became more hysterical. Coming on top of her previous embarrassment the suggestion was more than the woman could take.

'Hold it?' she screamed. 'Hold it? I couldn't bear to look at it let alone hold the beastly thing.'

Dr von Blimenstein leant across the desk.

'That's not what I meant,' she said. 'You're taking this thing too far.'

'Far?' shrieked the woman. 'I'll say it's far. It's far farther than I can take it. It's instant hysterectomy. It's . . .'

'You've got to try to see this—'

'I don't want to see it. That's the whole point. I'm terrified of seeing it.'

'In proportion,' shouted the doctor authoritatively.

'In proportion to what?' the woman shouted. 'In proportion to my creamy way I suppose. Well I tell you I can't take it.'

'No one is asking you to,' said the doctor. 'In the first place—'

'In the first place? In the first place? Don't tell me they'd try the second.' The patient was on her feet now.

Dr von Blimenstein left her chair and pushed the patient back into her seat.

'We mustn't let our imaginations run away with us,' she said soothingly. 'You're quite safe here with me. Now then,' she continued when the woman had calmed down, 'if we are to do any good you've got to realize that penises are merely symptoms. It's the thing behind them we've got to look for.'

The woman stared wildly round the room. 'That's not difficult,' she said. 'They're all over the place.'

Dr von Blimenstein hastened to explain. 'What I mean is the deep-seated . . . Now what's the matter?' The woman had slumped to the floor. When she came round again the doctor revised her approach.

'I'm not going to say anything,' she explained, 'and I just want you to tell me what you think.'

The woman calmed down and pondered.

'They hang weights on the end to make them longer,' she said finally.

'Do they really?' said the doctor. 'That's very interesting.'

'It's not. It's disgusting.'

Dr von Blimenstein agreed that it was also disgusting.

'They walk about with half-bricks tied to the end with bits of string,' the woman continued. 'Under their trousers of course.'

'I should hope so,' said Dr von Blimenstein.

'They put butter on too to make them grow. They think butter helps.'

'I should have thought it would have made it difficult to keep the brick on,' said Dr von Blimenstein more practically. 'The string would slip off, wouldn't it?'

The patient considered the problem.

'They tie the string on first,' she said finally.

'That seems perfectly logical,' said the psychiatrist. 'Is there anything else you'd like to tell me? Your married life is quite satisfactory?'

'Well,' said the woman doubtfully, 'it could be worse if you see what I mean.' Dr von Blimenstein nodded sympathetically.

'I think we can cure your phobia,' she said making some

notes. 'Now the course of treatment I'm prescribing is a little unusual at first sight but you'll soon get the hang of it. First of all what we do is this. We get you used to the idea of holding quite a small penis, a small white one and then . . .'

'You get me used to doing what?' the woman asked in amazement and with a look that suggested she thought the doctor was insane.

'Holding small white penises.'

'You must be mad,' shouted the woman, 'I wouldn't dream of such a thing. I'm a respectable married woman and if you think I'm going to . . .' She began to weep hysterically.

Dr von Blimenstein leant across the desk reassuringly.

'All right,' she said. 'We'll cut out the penises to begin with.'

'God Almighty,' shouted the woman, 'and I thought I needed treatment.'

Dr von Blimenstein calmed her. 'I mean we'll leave them out,' she said. 'We'll start with pencils. Have you any rooted objection to holding a pencil?'

'Of course not,' said the woman. 'Why the hell should I mind holding a pencil?'

'Or a ball-point pen?' Dr von Blimenstein watched the woman's face for any sign of hesitancy.

'Ball-points are fine with me. So are fountain pens,' said the patient.

'How about a banana?'

'You want me to hold it or eat it?' the woman inquired.

'Just hold it.'

'That's no problem.'

'A banana and two plums?'

The woman looked at her critically. 'I'll hold a fruit salad if you think it'll do me any good though what the hell you think you're getting at is beyond me.'

In the end Dr von Blimenstein began treatment by accustoming the patient to hold a vegetable marrow until it ceased to provoke any symptoms of anxiety.

While the Doctor wrestled with the psychological problems of her patients and Verkramp served his God by casting out devils, Kommandant van Heerden passed uneventful days in Weezen, fishing the river, reading the novels of Dornford Yates and wondering why, since he had called on the Heathcote-Kilkoons, they had not got in touch with him at the hotel. On the fourth day he pocketed his pride and approached Mr Mulpurgo who, being an authority on everything else, seemed the most likely person to explain the mysteries of English etiquette.

He found Mr Mulpurgo hiccuping softly to himself in an old rose arbour in the garden. The Kommandant seated himself on the bench beside the English lecturer.

'I was wondering if you could help me,' he began. Mr Mulpurgo hiccuped loudly.

'What is it?' he asked nervously. 'I'm busy.'

'If you had been invited to stay with some people in the country,' the Kommandant said, 'and you arrived at the hotel and they didn't come and visit you, what would you think?'

Mr Mulpurgo tried to figure out what the Kommandant was getting at.

'If I had been invited to stay with some people in the country,' he said, 'I don't see what I'd be doing at a hotel unless of course they owned the hotel.'

'No,' said the Kommandant, 'they don't.'

'Then what would I be doing at a hotel?'

'They said the house was full.'

'Well is it?' Mr Mulpurgo inquired.

'No,' said the Kommandant, 'they're not there.' He paused. 'Well they weren't there when I went the other day.'

Mr Mulpurgo said it sounded very odd.

'Are you sure you got the dates right?' he asked.

'Oh yes. I checked them,' the Kommandant said.

'You could always phone them.'

'They're not on the phone.'

Mr Mulpurgo picked up his book again. 'You seem to be in a bit of a quandary,' he said. 'If I were you I think I'd pay them another call and if they're not there go home.'

The Kommandant nodded uncertainly. 'I suppose so,' he said. Mr Mulpurgo hiccuped again. 'Still got flatulence?' the

Kommandant asked sympathetically. 'You should try holding your breath. That sometimes works.'

Mr Mulpurgo said he had already tried a number of times without result.

'I once cured a man of hiccups,' the Kommandant continued reminiscently, 'by giving him a fright. He was a car thief.'

'Really,' said Mr Mulpurgo, 'what did you do?'

'Told him he was going to be flogged.'

Mr Mulpurgo shuddered. 'How simply awful,' he said.

'He was too,' said the Kommandant. 'Got fifteen strokes ... Stopped his hiccups though.' He smiled at the thought. Beside him the English lecturer considered the terrible implications of that smile and it seemed to him, not for the first time, that he was in the presence of some elemental force for whom or which there were no questions of right or wrong, no moral feelings, no ethical considerations but simply naked power. There was something monstrous in the Kommandant's simplicity. There had been nothing even remotely metaphorical about the Kommandant's 'Dog eats dog.' It was no more than a fact of his existence. In the face of the reality of this world of brute force, Mr Mulpurgo's literary aspirations assumed a nonentity.

'I suppose you approve of flogging,' he asked knowing the answer.

'It's the only thing that really works,' said the Kommandant. 'Prison's no good. It's too comfortable. But when a man has been flogged, he doesn't forget it. It's the same with hanging.'

'Always assuming there's an after-life,' Mr Mulpurgo said. 'Otherwise I should have thought hanging was as good a way of forgetting as you could think of.'

'After-life or no after-life, a man who's been hanged doesn't commit any more crimes, I can tell you,' said the Kommandant.

'And is that all that matters to you?' Mr Mulpurgo asked. 'That he doesn't commit any more crimes?'

Kommandant van Heerden nodded.

'That's my job,' he said, 'that's what I'm paid to do.'

Mr Mulpurgo tried again.

'Doesn't life mean anything to you? The sacredness of life, its beauty and joy and innocence?'

'When I eat a lamb chop I don't think about sheep,' said the Kommandant. Mr Mulpurgo hiccuped at the imagery.

'What a terrible picture of life you have,' he said. 'There seems no hope at all.'

The Kommandant smiled. 'There's always hope, my friend,' he said patting Mr Mulpurgo's shoulder and levering himself up from the seat at the same time. 'Always hope.'

The Kommandant stumped off and presently Mr Mulpurgo rose from the arbour and walked into Weezen.

'Extraordinary number of drunks there are about these days,' Major Bloxham remarked next morning at breakfast. 'Met a fellow in bar last night. Lectures in English at the University. Can't have been more than thirty. Blind drunk and kept shouting about a purpose in liquidity of all things. Had to take him back to the hotel. Some sort of Spa.'

'Don't know what young people are coming to,' said the Colonel. 'If it isn't drink, it's drugs. Whole country's going to the dogs.' He got up and went out to the kennels to see how Harbinger was getting on.

'Spa?' asked Mrs Heathcote-Kilkoon when the Colonel had left. 'Did you say Spa, Boy?'

'Sort of run-down sort of place. Takes guests,' said the Major.

'Then that must be where the Kommandant is staying,' Mrs Heathcote-Kilkoon said. She finished her breakfast and ordered the Rolls and presently, leaving the Colonel and Major Bloxham discussing the seating at the Club dinner that evening, she drove over to Weezen. Club dinners were such boring affairs, so boring and unreal. People in Zululand lacked the chic which had made life so tolerable in Nairobi. Too *raffiné*, she thought, falling back on that small stock of French words with which she was *au fait* and which had been *de rigueur* among her friends in Kenya. That was what was such a change about the Kommandant. No one could possibly accuse him of being *raffiné*.

'There's something so earthy about him,' she murmured as

126

she parked outside the Weezen Spa and went inside.

There was something fairly earthy about the Kommandant's room when she finally found it and knocked on the door. The Kommandant opened it in his underwear, he had been changing to go fishing, and shut it again hurriedly. By the time he opened it again properly apparelled Mrs Heathcote-Kilkoon, who had spent the interval studying the enamel plaque on the door, had drawn her own conclusions as to the origins of the smell.

'Do come in,' said the Kommandant, demonstrating once again that lack of refinement Mrs Heathcote-Kilkoon found so attractive. She entered and looked dubiously around.

'Don't let me interrupt you,' she said glancing significantly at the taps and tubes.

'No, not at all. I was just about . . .'

'Quite,' said Mrs Heathcote-Kilkoon hurriedly. 'There's no need to go into the details. We all have our little ailments I daresay.'

'Ailments?' said the Kommandant.

Mrs Heathcote-Kilkoon wrinkled her nose and opened the door.

'Though to judge from the smell in here, yours are rather more serious than most.' She stepped into the corridor and the Kommandant followed her.

'It's the sulphur,' he hastened to explain.

'Nonsense,' said Mrs Heathcote-Kilkoon, 'it's lack of exercise. Well, we'll soon put that right. What you need is a good gallop before breakfast. What's your seat like?'

Kommandant van Heerden rather huffily said that as far as he knew there was nothing wrong with it.

'Well, that's something,' said Mrs Heathcote-Kilkoon.

They went out through the revolving doors and stood on the terrace where the air was fresher. Something of the acerbity went out of Mrs Heathcote-Kilkoon's manner.

'I'm so sorry you've been stranded here like this,' she said. 'It's all our fault. We looked for you at the hotel in town but I had no idea that this place existed.'

She leaned voguishly against the balustrade and contemplated the building with its stippled portico and faded legend. The Kommandant explained that he had tried to phone but that he couldn't find the number.

'Of course you couldn't, my dear,' said Mrs Heathcote-Kilkoon taking his arm and leading him down into the garden. 'We don't have one. Henry's so secretive, you know. He plays the stock market and he can't bear the thought of anyone listening in and making a killing in kaffirs because he's heard Henry telling his broker to buy Free State Gedulds.'

'That's understandable,' said the Kommandant completely at sea.

They wandered down the path to the river and Mrs Heathcote-Kilkoon chattered away about life in Kenya and how she missed the gay times of Thomson's Falls.

'We had such a lovely place, Littlewoods Lodge, it was called after ... well never mind. Let's just say it was named after Henry's first big *coup* and of course there were acres and acres of azaleas. I think that's why Henry chose Kenya in the first place. He's absolutely mad about flowers, you know and azaleas don't do awfully well in South London.'

The Kommandant said the Colonel must have been keen on flowers to come all the way to Africa just to grow them.

'And besides there was the question of taxes,' Mrs Heathcote-Kilkoon continued, 'I mean once Henry had won the pools ... I mean when Henry came into money, it simply wasn't possible for him to live in England with that dreadful Labour government taking every penny in taxes.'

Presently, when they had walked beside the river, Mrs Heathcote-Kilkoon said she must be getting back.

'Now don't forget tonight,' she said as the Kommandant helped her into the Rolls, 'dinner's at eight. Cocktails at seven. I'll look forward to seeing you. *Au 'voir*,' and with a wave of her mauve glove she was gone.

'You've done what?' Colonel Heathcote-Kilkoon spluttered when his wife returned to say that the Kommandant was coming to dinner. 'Don't you realize it's Berry Night? We can't have some damned stranger sitting in on the Club dinner.'

'I've invited him and he's coming,' insisted Mrs Heathcote-Kilkoon. 'He's been sitting in that ghastly spa for the past week giving himself enemas out of sheer boredom simply because Boy's such an idiot he had to go and drink in the wrong bar.'

'Oh, I say,' expostulated Major Bloxham, 'that's hardly fair.'

'No, it isn't,' said Mrs Heathcote-Kilkoon, 'it isn't fair. So he's coming to dinner tonight, Club or no Club, and I expect you both to behave yourselves.'

She went up to her room and spent the afternoon dreaming of strong silent men and the musky smell of the Kommandant. Outside in the garden she could hear the click of the Colonel's secateurs as he worked off his irritation on the ornamental shrubbery. By the time Mrs Heathcote-Kilkoon came down for tea the bush that had formerly resembled a chicken had assumed the new proportions of a parrot. So, it seemed, had the Colonel.

'Yes, my dear.' 'No, my dear,' the Colonel interjected as Mrs Heathcote-Kilkoon explained that the Kommandant would fit in perfectly well with the other members of the Club.

'After all, it's not as though he's illiterate,' she said. 'He's read the Berry books and he told me himself he was a fan of the Master.'

She left the two men and went to the kitchen to supervise the Zulu cook who among other things was desperately trying to figure out how to cook *Filet de boeuf en chemise strasbourgeoise*.

Left to themselves the two men smiled knowingly.

'Nothing like having a buffoon at a dinner,' said the Colonel. 'Should be quite fun.'

'The court jester,' said the Major. 'Get him pissed and have a lark. Might even debag the bugger.'

'That's an idea,' said the Colonel. 'Teach the swine some manners, eh?'

In his room at the Spa Kommandant van Heerden studied his book *Etiquette for Every Man* and tried to remember which fork to use for fish. At six he had another makeshift bath and sprayed himself all over with deodorant to neutralize the smell of sulphur. Then he put on the Harris Tweed suit he had had made for him at Scurfield and Todd, the English tailors in Piemburg, and which the coloured maid had pressed meticulously for him and at seven drove up to White Ladies. The gravel forecourt was crowded with cars. The Kommandant parked and went up the steps to the front door which was opened by the Zulu butler. Mrs Heathcote-Kilkoon came down the hall to receive him.

'Oh, my God,' she said by way of welcome, appalled at the Kommandant's suit – everyone else was wearing dinner jackets – and then with a greater show of *savoir-faire*, 'Well never mind. It can't be helped,' ushered the Kommandant into a room filled with smoke and talk and people.

'I can't see Henry just at the moment,' she said judiciously, steering the Kommandant to a table where Major Bloxham was dispensing drinks. 'But Boy'll make you a cocktail.'

'What's your poison, old man,' Major Bloxham asked.

The Kommandant said he'd appreciate a beer.

The Major looked askance. 'Can't have that, my dear fellow,' he said. 'Cocktails you know. The good old Twenties and all that. Have an Oom Paul Special,' and before the Kommandant could ask what an Oom Paul Special was, the Major was busy with a shaker.

'Very tasty,' said the Kommandant sipping the drink which consisted of apple brandy, Dubonnet and, to make it Special, had an extra slug of vodka.

'Glad you like it,' said the Major. 'Knock it back and you can have a Sledge Hammer,' but before the Kommandant could experience the effects of a mixture of brandy, rum, and apple brandy on top of the Oom Paul Mrs Heathcote-Kilkoon whisked him as discreetly as the crowd would allow away to meet Henry. The Colonel regarded Kommandant van Heerden's suit with interest.

'Glad you could make it, Kommandant,' he said with an affability his wife found disturbing. 'Tell me, do Boers always wear Harris Tweed to dinner parties?'

'Now, Henry,' Mrs Heathcote-Kilkoon interjected before the Kommandant could reply, 'The Kommandant was hardly prepared for formality in the country. My husband,' she continued to the Kommandant, 'is such a stickler for . . .' The rest of the sentence was drowned by the boom of an enormous gong and as the reverberations died away the Zulu butler announced that dinner was served. It was half past seven. Mrs Heathcote-Kilkoon hurled herself across the room and after a brief and bitter exchange of views in which she called the butler a black oaf twice, the hostess turned with a ceramic smile to the gathering. 'Just a misunderstanding about times,' she said, and with some further remark about the difficulty of getting decent servants mingled serenely with the crowd. The Kommandant, finding himself deserted, finished his Oom Paul and went over to the bar and asked for a Sledge Hammer. Then he found himself a quiet corner beside a goldfish which matched his suit and surveyed the other guests. Apart from the Colonel, whose bilious eye marked him out as a man of distinction, the other men were hardly what the Kommandant had expected. They seemed to exude an air of confident uncertainty and their conversation lacked that urbane banter he had found in the pages of *Berry & Co*. In a little group near him a small fat man was explaining how he could get a fifty per cent discount off on fridges while someone else was arguing that the only way to buy meat was wholesale. The Kommandant moved slowly round the room catching a sentence here and there about roses and the July Handicap and somebody's divorce. At the make-shift bar, Major Bloxham gave him a Third Degree.

'Appropriate, old boy, what?' he said, but before the Kommandant could drink it, the gong had reverberated again and not wishing to waste the cocktail the Kommandant poured it into the goldfish bowl before going in to dinner.

'You're to sit between La Marquise and me,' Mrs Heathcote-Kilkoon said as they stood awkwardly around the long table in the dining-room. 'That way you'll be safe,' and the Kommandant presently found himself next to what he took to be a distinctly queer man in a dinner jacket who kept calling everyone darling. He shifted his chair a little closer to Mrs Heathcote-Kilkoon, uncomfortably aware that the man was eyeing him speculatively. The Kommandant fiddled with the silver and wondered why he found the Colonel's eye on him. In a moment of silence the man on his right asked him what he did.

131

'Do?' said the Kommandant suspiciously. The word had too many meanings for an easy answer.

La Marquise discerned his embarrassment. 'For a living, darling, do for a living. Not me for God's sake. That I do assure you.' Round the table everyone laughed and the Kommandant added to it by saying that he was a policeman. He was about to say that he'd seen some fucking poofters in his time but ... when Mrs Heathcote-Kilkoon whispered, 'She's a woman,' in his ear. The Kommandant went from pink to pale at the thought of the gaffe he had been about to commit and took a gulp of the Australian Burgundy which it appeared the Colonel thought was almost the equal of a Chambertin '59.

By the time the coffee had been served and the port was circulating the Kommandant had quite recovered his self-confidence. He had scored twice, quite accidentally, off La Marquise, once by asking her if her husband was present, and the second time by leaning across her to reach for the salt, and jostling what there was of her well disguised bosom. On his left, flushed with wine and the Kommandant's pervasive manliness, Mrs Heathcote-Kilkoon pressed her leg discreetly against his, smiling brightly and fingering her pearls. When the Colonel rose to propose the toast to the Master, Mrs Heathcote-Kilkoon nudged him and indicated a photograph over the mantelpiece. 'That's Major Mercer,' she whispered, 'Dornford Yates.' The Kommandant nodded and studied the face that peered back disgustedly from the picture. Two fierce eyes, one slightly larger than the other; and a bristly moustache; the romantic author looked like a disgruntled sergeant major. 'I suppose that's where the word authority comes from, author,' thought the Kommandant, passing the port the wrong way. In deference to La Marquise the ladies had not withdrawn and presently the Zulu waiter brought round cigars.

'Not your Henry Clays, just Rhodesian Macanudos,' said the Colonel modestly. The Kommandant took one and lit it.

'Ever tried rolling your own?' he asked the Colonel and was surprised at the suffused look on his face.

'Certainly not,' said Colonel Heathcote-Kilkoon, already irritated by the erratic course of the port. 'Whoever heard of anyone rolling his own cigars?'

'I have,' replied the Kommandant blandly. 'My ouma had a farm in the Magaliesburg and she grew tobacco. You have to roll it on the inside of your thigh.'

'How frightfully oumanistic,' La Marquise said shrilly. When the laughter died down, the Kommandant went on.

'My ouma took snuff. We used to grind that down for her.'

The circle of flushed faces examined the man in the Harris Tweed suit whose grandmother took snuff.

'What a colourful family you have,' said the fat man who knew how to get discounts on fridges and was startled to find the Kommandant leaning across the table towards him with a look of unmistakable fury.

'If I weren't in someone else's house,' snarled the Kommandant, 'you would regret that remark.' The fat man turned pale and Mrs Heathcote-Kilkoon placed her hand restrainingly on the Kommandant's arm.

'Have I said something wrong?' the fat man asked.

'I think Mr Evans meant that your family is very interesting,' Mrs Heathcote-Kilkoon explained in a whisper to the Kommandant.

'It didn't sound like that to me,' said the Kommandant. At the end of the table Colonel Heathcote-Kilkoon, who felt that he needed to assert his authority somewhere, ordered the waiters to bring liqueurs. It was not a wise move. Major Bloxham, evidently still piqued by the failure of his Oom Paul Special and Sledge Hammer to render the Kommandant suitable for debagging, offered him some Chartreuse. As his port glass filled with the stuff, the Kommandant looked at it interestedly.

'I've never seen a green wine before,' he said finally.

'Made from green grapes, old boy,' said the Major and was delighted at the laugh he got. 'Got to drink it all in one go.' Mrs Heathcote-Kilkoon was not amused.

'How low can you get, Boy?' she asked unpleasantly as the Kommandant swallowed the glassful.

'How high can you get?' said the Major jocularly.

La Marquise added her comment. 'High? My dears,' she shrieked, 'you should sit here to find out. Absolute Gorgonzola I do assure you,' a remark which led to a misunderstanding with the waiter who brought her the cheese board. Through it all Kommandant van Heerden sat smiling happily at the warmth spreading through him. He decided to apologize to the fat man and was about to when the Major offered him another glass of Chartreuse. The Kommandant accepted graciously in spite of a sharp kick from Mrs Heathcote-Kilkoon.

'I think we should all join the Kommandant,' she said suddenly, 'we can't let him drink by himself. Boy, fill all the port glasses.'

The Major looked at her questioningly. 'All?' he asked.

'You heard me,' said Mrs Heathcote-Kilkoon, looking vindictively from the Major to her husband. 'All. I think we should all drink a toast to the South African Police in honour of our guest.'

'I'm damned if I'm going to drink a whole port glass of Chartreuse for anyone,' said the Colonel.

'Have I ever told you how Henry spent the war?' Mrs Heathcote-Kilkoon asked the table at large. Colonel Heathcote-Kilkoon turned pale and raised his glass.

'To the South African Police,' he said hurriedly.

'To the South African Police,' said Mrs Heathcote-Kilkoon with more enthusiasm, and watched carefully while the Colonel and Major Bloxham drank their glasses dry.

Happily unaware of the tension around him, the Kommandant sat and smiled. So this was how the English spent their evenings, he thought, and felt thoroughly at home.

In the silence that followed the toast and the realization of what a large glass of Chartreuse could do to the liver, Kommandant van Heerden rose to his feet.

'I should like to say how honoured I feel to be here tonight in this distinguished gathering,' he said, pausing and looking at the faces that gazed glaucously back at him. 'What I am going to say may come as something of a surprise to you.' At the end of the table Colonel Heathcote-Kilkoon shut his eyes and shuddered. If the Kommandant's speech was going to be anything like his taste in clothes and wines, he couldn't imagine what to expect. In the event he was pleasantly surprised.

'I am, as you know, an Afrikaner,' continued the

134

Kommandant. 'Or as you British say a Boer, but I want you to know that I admire you British very much and I would like to propose a toast to the British Empire.'

It took some time for the Colonel to realize what the Kommandant had just said. He opened his eyes in amazement and was appalled to see that the Kommandant had taken a bottle of Benedictine and was filling everyone's glass.

'Now, Henry,' Mrs Heathcote-Kilkoon said when the Colonel looked imploringly at her, 'for the honour of the British Empire.'

'Dear God,' said the Colonel.

The Kommandant finished replenishing the port glasses and raised his own.

'To the British Empire,' he said and drank it down, before staring with sudden belligerence at the Colonel who had taken a sip and was wondering what to do with the rest.

'Now, Henry,' said Mrs Heathcote-Kilkoon. The Colonel finished his glass and slumped miserably in his chair.

The Kommandant sat down happily. The sense of disappointment that had so marred the early part of the evening had quite disappeared. So had La Marquise. With a brave attempt at one last 'darling' she slid, elegant to the last, beneath the table. As the full effects of Kommandant van Heerden's devotion to the British Empire began to make themselves felt, the Zulu waiter, evidently anxious to get to bed, hastened the process by producing both the cheese board and the cigars.

Colonel Heathcote-Kilkoon tried to correct him.

'Stilton and cigars don't go toge . . .' he said before stumbling from the room. Behind him the party broke up. The fat man fell asleep. Major Bloxham was ill. And Mrs Heathcote-Kilkoon pressed a great deal more than her leg against the Kommandant. 'Take me . . .' she said before collapsing across his lap. The Kommandant looked fondly down at her blue rinsed curls and with unusual gallantry eased her head off his flies and stood up.

'Time for bed,' he said and lifting Mrs Heathcote-Kilkoon gently from her seat carried her to her room closely followed by the Zulu butler who suspected his motives.

As he laid her on her bed Mrs Heathcote-Kilkoon smiled in

her sleep. 'Not now, darling,' she murmured, evidently dreaming. 'Not now. Tomorrow.'

The Kommandant tiptoed from the room and went to thank his host for a lovely evening. There was no sign of the Colonel in the dining-room where the Dornford Yates Club lay inertly on or under the table. Only Major Bloxham showed any signs of activity and these were such as to prevent any conversation.

'Totsiens,' said the Kommandant and was rewarded for his Afrikaans farewell by a fresh eructation from the Major. As the Kommandant glanced round the room he noticed a movement under the table. Someone was evidently trying to revive La Marquise though why this should require the removal of her trousers the Kommandant couldn't imagine. Lifting the table cloth he peered underneath. A face peered back at him. The Kommandant suddenly felt unwell. 'I've had too much,' he thought recalling what he had heard about DTS and dropping the cloth hurriedly he rushed from the room. In the darkness of the garden the click of the cicadas was joined erratically by the sound of the Colonel's secateurs but Kommandant van Heerden had no ear for them. His mind was on the two eyes that had peered back at him from beneath the table cloth – two beady eyes and a horrid face and the face was the face of Els. But Konstabel Els was dead. 'I'll be seeing pink elephants next,' he thought in horror as he got into his car and drove dangerously back to the Spa where presently he was trying to purge his system by drinking the filthy water in his room.

CHAPTER TEN

Kommandant van Heerden was not alone in suffering from the illusion that he was having hallucinations. In Piemburg Luitenant Verkramp's efforts to extirpate subversive elements in the body politic were resulting in the appearance of a new and bizarre outbreak of sabotage, this time in the streets of the city. Once again the violence had its origins in the devious nature of the Security chief's line of communication with his agents.

628461's 'drop' for Thursday was in the Bird Sanctuary. To be precise it was in a garbage can outside the Ostrich Enclosure, a convenient spot from everybody's point of view because it was a perfectly logical place to drop things into, and just the sort of place for a Security cop disguised as a hobo to get things out of. Every Thursday morning 628461 sauntered through the Bird Sanctuary, bought an ice cream from the vendor and wrapped his message in sticky silver paper and deposited it in the garbage can while ostensibly observing the habits of the ostriches. Every Thursday afternoon Security Konstabel van Rooyen, dressed authentically in rags and clutching an empty sherry bottle, arrived at the Bird Sanctuary and peered hopefully into the garbage can only to find it empty. The fact that the message had been deposited and then removed by an intermediary never occurred to anyone. 628461 didn't know that Konstabel van Rooyen hadn't collected his message and Konstabel van Rooyen had no idea that agent 628461 even existed. All he knew was that Luitenant Verkramp had told him to collect sticky pieces of ice-cream paper from the bin and there weren't any.

On the Thursday following the Kommandant's departure, 628461 coded an important message informing Verkramp that he had persuaded the other saboteurs to act in concert for once, with a view to facilitating their arrest while on a job for which they could all be hanged. He had suggested the destruction of the Hluwe Dam which supplied water for all of Piemburg and half Zululand, and, since no one could blow a dam by himself, he had urged that they all take part. Much to his surprise all eleven seconded his proposal and went home to code messages to Verkramp warning him to have his men at the dam on Friday night. It was with a sense of considerable relief that he was finally going to get some sleep that 628461 walked to the Bird Sanctuary on Thursday morning to deposit his message. It was with genuine alarm that he observed 378550 following him and with positive consternation became aware as he was buying his ice cream that 885974 was watching him from the bushes on the other side. 628461 ate his ice cream outside the hoopoe cage to avoid drawing attention to the garbage can by the Ostrich enclosure. He ate a second ice cream half an hour later staring wearily at the peacocks. Finally after an hour he bought a third Eskimo Pie and walked casually over to the Ostriches. Behind him 378550 and 885974 watched his movements with intense curiosity. So did the ostriches. 628461 finished his Eskimo Pie and dropped the silver paper in the garbage can and was just about to leave when he became aware that all his surreptitious efforts had been in vain. With an avidity that came from their having been kept waiting for an hour the ostriches rushed to the fence and poked their heads into the garbage can and one lucky bird swallowed the ice-cream wrapper. 628461 forgot himself.

'Damnation and fuck,' he said. 'They've got it. The bloody things'll eat anything.'

'Got what?' asked 378550 who thought that he was being addressed and was glad of the chance to drop his role as shadow.

628461 pulled himself together and looked at 378550 suspiciously.

'You said "They've got it",' 378550 repeated.

628461 tried to extricate himself from the situation. 'I said, "I've got it",' he explained. ' "I've got it. They'll eat anything." '

378550 was still puzzled. 'I still don't see it,' he said.

'Well,' said 628461 desperately trying to explain what the omnivorousness of ostriches had to do with his devotion to the cause of world Communism, 'I was just thinking that we could get them to eat gelly and let them loose and they'd blow up all over the place.'

378550 looked at him with admiration. 'That's brilliant,' he said. 'Absolutely brilliant.'

'Of course,' 628461 told him, 'we'd have to put the explosive in something watertight first. Get them to swallow it. Fix a fuse and bingo, you've got the perfect sabotage weapon.'

885974 who didn't want to be left out of things in the bushes came over and joined them.

'French letters,' he suggested when the scheme was put to him. 'Put the gelignite in French letters and tie the ends, that'd keep it watertight.'

An hour later in Florian's café they were discussing the plan with the rest of the saboteurs. 745396 objected on the grounds that ostriches might eat anything but he doubted if even they would be foolish enough to swallow a contraceptive filled with gelignite.

'We'll try it out this afternoon,' said 628461 who felt that 745396 was somehow impugning his loyalty to Marxist Leninism and the motion was put to the vote. Only 745396 still objected and he was voted down.

While the rest of the group spent the lunch hour coding messages to Verkramp to warn him that the Hluwe Dam project was cancelled and that he might expect an onslaught of detonating ostriches. 885974 who had thought of French letters in the first place, was deputed to purchase twelve dozen of the best.

'Get Crêpe de Chine,' said 378550, who had had an unfortunate experience with another brand, 'they're guaranteed.'

885974 went into a large chemists' on Market Street and asked the young man behind the photographic counter for twelve dozen Crêpe de Chine.

'Crêpe de Chine?' asked the assistant, who was obviously new to the job. 'We don't sell Crêpe de Chine. You need a haberdashers' for that. This is a chemist shop.'

885974 who was already embarrassed by the quantity he had to ask for turned very red.

'I know that,' he muttered. 'You know what I mean. In packets of three.'

The assistant shook his head. 'They sell it in yards,' he said, 'but I'll ask if we have it,' and before 885974 could stop him had shouted across the shop to a girl who was serving some customers at the counter there.

'This gentleman wants twelve dozen Crêpe de Chine, Sally. We don't sell stuff like that do we?' he asked, and 885974 found himself the object of considerable interest to twelve middle-aged women who knew precisely what he wanted even if the assistant didn't and were amazed at the virility suggested by the number he required.

'Oh for God's sake, never mind,' he muttered and hurried from the shop. In the end he managed to get what he wanted by buying six toothbrushes and two tubes of hair cream at other chemist shops and asking for Durex Fetherlites.

'They seemed more suitable,' he explained when he met the other agents outside the Ostrich enclosure in the afternoon. With a unity of purpose noticeably absent from their previous gatherings the agents applied themselves to the business of getting an ostrich to consume high-explosive concealed in a rubber sheath.

'Better try one with sand first,' 628461 suggested, and was presently scooping each into a Durex Fetherlite, an occupation which caused some disgust to a lady who was feeding the ducks on a nearby pond. He waited until she had moved off before offering the contraceptive to the ostrich. The bird took the sheath and spat it out. 628461 got a stick and managed to retrieve the thing from the enclosure. A second attempt was equally unsuccessful and when a third try to introduce half a pound of latex-covered earth into the bird's digestive system failed, 628461 suggested coating the thing with ice cream.

'They seemed to like it this morning,' he said. He was getting sick of scrabbling through the fence for obviously well-filled condoms. Finally, after 378550 had bought two ice-creams and a chocolate bar and the sheath had been smeared with ice cream by itself and chocolate by itself and then with a mixture of the two, the proceedings were interrupted by the arrival of a Sanctuary warden fetched by the lady who had been feeding the ducks. 628461 who had just rescued the French letter from the ostriches' enclosure for the eighth time stuffed it hurriedly into his pocket.

'Are these the men you saw trying to feed the ostriches with foreign matter?' the warden asked.

'Yes, they are,' said the lady emphatically.

The warden turned to 628461.

'Were you trying to induce the bird to digest a quantity of something or other contained in the thing this lady says you were?' he asked.

'Certainly not,' said 628461 indignantly.

'You were too,' said the lady, 'I saw you.'

'I'll ask you to move along,' said the warden.

As the little group moved off 745396 pointed out how right he had been.

'I told you ostriches weren't so dumb,' he said and put 628461's back up still further. He'd just discovered that the sheath in his back pocket had burst.

'I thought you were supposed to get Crêpe de Chines,' he grumbled to 885974 and tried to empty his pocket of earth, chocolate, ice cream and ostrich droppings.

'What am I going to do with twelve dozen Frenchies?' 885974 asked.

It took 378550 to come up with a solution. 'Popcorn and honey', he said suddenly.

'What about it?' 628461 asked.

'Coat them with popcorn and honey and I guarantee they'll swallow the things.'

At the first shop they came to 378550 bought a packet of popcorn and a pot of honey and taking a contraceptive from 885794 went back to the Bird Sanctuary to try his recipe out.

'Worked like a treat,' he reported ten minutes later. 'Swallowed the thing in one gulp.'

'What do we do when we've filled them all up and set the fuse?' 745396 asked doubtfully.

'Lay a trail of popcorn into the centre of town, of course,' 628461 told him. The group dispersed to collect their stocks of gelignite and that night at nine gathered at the Bird Sanctuary. The sense of mutual suspicion which had so informed their earlier meetings had been quite replaced by a genuine cameraderie. Verkramp's agents were beginning to enjoy themselves.

'If this works,' 628461 said, 'there's no reason why we shouldn't try the zoo.'

'I'm damned if I'm feeding contraceptives to the lions,' 745396 said.

'No need to feed them anything,' said 885974 who didn't feel like buying any more French letters. 'They'd be explosive enough on their own.'

If Verkramp's agents were cheerful, the same couldn't be said of their chief. The conviction that something had gone seriously wrong with his plans to end Communist subversion had gathered strength with the discovery by the armourer that large stocks of high-explosive and fuses were missing from the police armoury.

He reported his findings or lack of them to Luitenant Verkramp. Coming on top of a report by the police bomb-disposal squad that the detonators used in all the explosions were of a type used in the past solely by the South African Police, the armourer's news added weight to Verkramp's slow intuition that he might in some curious way have bitten off more than he could chew. It was an insight he shared with five ostriches in the Bird Sanctuary. What had seemed at the outset a marvellous opportunity to fulfil his ambitions had developed into something from which there was no turning back. Certainly the ostriches viewed it in that light as the secret agents discovered to their alarm when they released the loaded birds from their enclosure. Gregarious to the last and evidently under the impression that there was more to come in the way of popcorn-coated contraceptives, the five ostriches strode after the agents as the latter headed for town. By the time the mixed herd and flock had reached the end of Market Street the agents were in a state of near panic.

'We'd better break up,' 628461 said anxiously.

'Break up? Break up? We'll fucking disintegrate if those birds don't get the hell out of here,' said 745396 who had never approved of the project from the start and who seemed to have attracted the friendship of an ostrich that weighed at least 300 lbs unloaded and which had a fifteen-minute fuse. The next moment the agents had taken to their heels down side roads in an effort to shake off the likely consequences of their experiment. Undaunted, the ostriches strode relentlessly and effortlessly behind them. At the corner of Market and Stanger Streets 745396 leapt on to the platform of a moving bus and was appalled to see through the back window the silhouette of his ostrich loping comfortably some yards behind. At the traffic lights at Chapel Street it was still there. 745396 hurled himself off the bus and dashed into the Majestic Cinema which was showing *Where Eagles Dare*.

'Show's over,' said the Commissionaire in the foyer.

'That's what you think,' said 745396 with his eye on the ostrich which was peering inquisitively through the glass doors. 'I just want to use the toilet.'

'Down the stairs to the left,' the Commissionaire told him and went out to the pavement to try to move the ostrich on. 745396 went down to the toilet and locked himself in a cubicle and waited for the explosion. He was still there five minutes later when the Commissionaire came down and knocked on the door.

'Is that ostrich anything to do with you?' he asked as 745396 tore paper off the roll to prove that he was using the place for its proper purpose.

'No,' said 745396 without conviction.

'Well, you can't leave it outside like that,' the Commissionaire told him, 'it'll interfere with the traffic.'

'You can say that again,' said 745396.

'Say what again?' asked the Commissionaire.

'Nothing,' shouted 745396 frantically. He had reached the end of his tether. So it appeared had the ostrich.

'One last question, do you usually—' said the Commissionaire and got no further. An extraordinary sensation of silence hit him to be followed by a wall of flame and a gigantic bang. As the front of the Majestic Cinema crumbled into the street and the lights went out agent 745396 slowly slumped on to the cracked seat of the toilet and leant against the wall. He was still there when the rescue workers found him next day, covered in plaster and quite dead.

Throughout the night rumours that Piemburg had been invaded by hordes of self-detonating ostriches spread like wildfire. So did the ostriches. A particularly tragic incident occurred at the offices of the Zululand Wild Life Preservation Society where an ostrich which had been brought in by a bird-lover exploded while being examined by the society's vet.

'I think it's got some sort of gastric disorder,' the man explained. The vet listened to the bird's crop with his stethoscope before making his diagnosis.

'Heartburn,' he said with a finality that was entirely confirmed by the detonation that followed. As the night sky erupted with bricks, mortar, and the assorted remains of both bird-lover and vet, the premises of the Wild Life Preservation Society, historically important and themselves subject to a preservation order by the Piemburg Council, disappeared for ever. Only a plume of smoke and a few large feathers, emblematic as some dissipated Prince of Wales, floated lethargically against the moon.

In his office Acting Kommandant Verkramp listened to the muffled explosions with a growing sense of despair. Whatever else was in ruins, and by the sound of it a large section of the city's shopping centre must be, his own career would shortly join it. In a frantic attempt to allay his alarming suspicions he had just searched the few messages from his secret agents only to find there confirmation that his plan if not their efforts had misfired. Agent 378550 had said that the sabotage group consisted of eleven men. Agent 885974 had said the same. So had 628461. There was a terrible congruency about the reports. In each case eleven men reported by his agent. Verkramp added one to eleven and got twelve. He had twelve agents in the field. The conclusion was inescapable and so it seemed were the consequences. Desperately searching for some way out of the mess he had got himself into, Luitenant Verkramp rose from the desk and crossed to the window. He was just in time to see a large ostrich loping purposefully down the street. With a muttered curse Verkramp opened the window and peered after the bird. 'This is the end,' he snarled and was astonished to see that at least one of his orders was obeyed. With a violent flash and a blast wave that blew out the window above him the ostrich disintegrated and Verkramp found himself sitting on the floor of his office with the inescapable conviction that his sanity was impaired.

'Impossible. It can't have been an ostrich,' he muttered, staggering back to the window. Outside the street was littered with broken glass and in a bare blackened patch in the middle of the road two feet were all that remained of the thing that had exploded. Verkramp could see that it had been an ostrich because the feet had only two toes.

In the next twenty minutes Luitenant Verkramp acted with maniacal speed. He burnt every file that could connect him with his agents, destroyed their messages and finally, ordering the police armourer to change the lock on the armoury door, left the police station in the Kommandant's black Ford. An hour later, having visited every bar in town, he had run two of his agents to earth drinking to the success of their latest experiment in sabotage in the Criterion Hotel in Verwoerd Street.

'Fuzz,' said 628461 as Verkramp entered the bar. 'Better break up.' 885974 finished his drink and went out. 628461 watched him go and was surprised to see Verkramp follow him out.

'He's making an arrest,' he thought and ordered another beer. A moment later he looked up to find Verkramp glowering down at him.

'Outside,' said Verkramp brusquely. 628461 left his bar stool and went outside and was surprised to find his fellow-saboteur sitting unguarded in the police car.

'I see you've got one of them,' 628461 said to Verkramp, and climbed in beside 885974.

'Them? Them?' Verkramp spluttered hysterically. 'He's not them. He's us.'

'Us?' said 628461, mystified.

'I'm 885974. Who are you?'

'Oh, my God,' said 628461.

Verkramp climbed into the driving seat and stared back malevolently.

'Where are the others?' he hissed.

'The others?'

'The other agents, you idiot,' Verkramp shouted. For the next two hours they searched the bars and cafés while Verkramp fulminated on the evils of sabotaging public utilities and detonating ostriches in a built-up area.

'I send you out to infiltrate the Communist movement and what do you do?' he shouted. 'Blow up half the bloody town, that's what you do. And you know where that's going to get you, don't you? On the end of the hangman's rope in Pretoria Central.'

'You might have warned us,' said 628461 reproachfully. 'You could have told us there were other agents in the field.'

Verkramp turned purple.

'Warned you?' he screamed. 'I expected you to use your common sense, not go around looking for one another.'

'Well, how the hell were we to know we were all police agents?' 885974 asked.

'I should have thought even idiots like you could tell the difference between a good Afrikaner and a Communist Jew.'

885974 thought about this.

'If it's that easy,' he said finally, clinging precariously to some sort of logic, 'I don't see how we're to blame. I mean the Communist Jews must be able to see we're good Afrikaners just by looking at us. I mean what's the point of sending out good Afrikaners to look for Communist Jews if Communist Jews can . . .'

'Oh, shut up,' shouted Verkramp, who was beginning to wish that he hadn't brought up the subject in the first place.

By midnight seven other agents had been found in various parts of the city and the police car was getting rather crowded.

'What do you want us to do now?' 378550 asked as they drove round the park for the fifth time looking for the three remaining agents. Verkramp stopped the car.

'I ought to arrest you,' he snarled, 'I ought to let you stand trial for terrorism but—'

'You won't,' said 885974 who had been giving the matter some thought.

'Why won't I?' Verkramp shouted.

'Because we'll all give evidence that you ordered us to blow up the transformer and the gasometer and the—'

'I did nothing of the sort. I told you to find the Communist saboteurs,' Verkramp yelled.

'Who gave us the keys of the police armoury?' 885974 asked. 'Who supplied the explosives?'

'And what about the messages we sent you?' 628461 asked.

Verkramp stared through the windshield and contemplated a short and nasty future, at the end of which stood the hangman in Pretoria Central Prison.

'All right,' he said. 'What do you want me to do?'

'Get us past the road blocks. Get us down to Durban and

146

give us each 500 rand,' 885974 said, 'and then forget you ever saw us.'

'What about the other three agents?' Verkramp asked.

'That's your problem,' 885974 said. 'You can find them tomorrow.'

They drove back to the police station and Verkramp collected the money and two hours later nine agents climbed out at Durban airport. Luitenant Verkramp watched them disappear into the terminal and then drove back to Piemburg. At the road block on the Durban road the sergeant waved him through for the second time and made a note of the fact that the Acting Kommandant looked drawn and ill. By four in the morning Verkramp was in bed in his flat staring into the darkness and wondering how he was going to find the other three agents. At seven he got up again and drove down to Florian's café. 885974 had advised him to look for them there. At eleven the Kommandant's car passed through the Durban Road check-point yet again and this time the Acting Kommandant had with him two men. By the time he returned eleven agents had left Piemburg for good. 745396 was in the city morgue waiting to be identified.

At Weezen Spa Kommandant van Heerden slept more soundly than his hallucination had led him to expect. He woke next morning with something of a hangover but felt better after a large breakfast in the Pump Room. In the far corner the two elderly ladies with short hair continued their endlessly whispered conversation.

Later in the morning the Kommandant walked into Weezen in the hope of bumping into Mrs Heathcote-Kilkoon who had murmured something about 'Tomorrow' as he put her to bed. He had just reached the main road and was trudging along it when a horn sounded loudly behind him and caused him to jump off the road. He looked round furiously and found Major Bloxham at the wheel of the vintage Rolls.

'Hop in,' shouted the Major. 'Just the man I'm looking for.'

The Kommandant climbed into the front seat and was glad to notice that the Major wasn't looking very well.

147

'To tell the truth,' said the Major when the Kommandant asked if he had recovered from the evening's entertainment, 'I'm not on top form this morning. Have to hand it to you, you Boers know how to hold your liquor. I wonder you made it back to the Spa last night.'

Kommandant van Heerden smiled at the compliment. 'It takes more than a couple of glasses to put me under the table,' he murmured modestly.

'By the way,' said the Kommandant as they drove into Weezen, 'talking of tables, is the woman in the dinner jacket all right?'

'What? La Marquise, you mean?' asked the Major. 'Funny you should mention her. As a matter of fact she's not herself or himself, difficult to tell which, you know, this morning. Said she was feeling a bit off colour.'

In his seat Kommandant van Heerden went very white. If the words 'off colour' meant anything at all in the context, and the Kommandant felt sure they did, he could well believe La Marquise was speaking the truth. There was now little doubt in his mind that he had not imagined seeing Els under the table. Removing the trousers of a drunk Lesbian was just the sort of unchivalrous act that had all the hallmarks of Konstabel Els. But Konstabel Els was dead. The Kommandant wrestled with the problem of Els resurrected until they arrived outside the Weezen Bar.

'Hair of the dog,' said the Major and went into the bar. The Kommandant followed him in.

'Gin and peppermint for me,' said Major Bloxham. 'What's yours, old boy?'

The Kommandant said he'd have the same but his mind was still elsewhere.

'Did she say what had happened?' he asked.

Major Bloxham looked at him curiously.

'You seem to have quite a thing about her,' he said finally. 'Intriguing, what?' The Kommandant looked at him sharply, and the Major continued, 'Let me see, I remember she said something rather queer at breakfast. Oh I know. She said, "I feel absolutely buggered." That's right. Seemed rather a coarse sort of thing for a woman to say.'

Beside him the Kommandant couldn't agree. If he had seen Els under the table he was pretty sure the lady was speaking no more than the simple truth. Serves the silly bitch right for dressing up in men's clothes, he thought.

'By the way Daphne sent a message,' said the Major, 'wants to know if you'll come out with the hunt tomorrow.'

The Kommandant dragged his thoughts away from the problem of Els and the transvestite Lesbian and tried to think about the hunt.

'I'd love to,' he said, 'but I'd have to borrow a gun.'

'Of course it's only a drag hunt,' continued the Major before it dawned on him that the Kommandant shot foxes. A similar dreadful misunderstanding existed in the Kommandant's mind.

'Drag hunt?' he said, looking at the Major with some disgust.

'Gun?' said Major Bloxham with equal revulsion. He looked hastily round the bar to make sure no one was listening before leaning over to the Kommandant.

'Look, old boy,' he said conspiratorially, 'a word to the wise and all that but if you'll take my advice I wouldn't go round broadcasting, well, you know what I mean.'

'Do you mean to tell me that Colonel Heathcote-Kilkoon ...' stuttered the Kommandant, trying to imagine what the Colonel looked like in drag.

'Exactly, old boy,' said the Major. 'He's terribly touchy about that sort of thing.'

'I'm not in the least surprised,' said the Kommandant.

'Just keep it under your hat,' said the Major. 'What about another drink? Your turn, I think.'

The Kommandant ordered two more gin and peppermints and by the time they had arrived had begun to think he understood Major Bloxham's role in the Heathcote-Kilkoon family. The Major's next remark confirmed it.

'Bottoms up,' he said and lifted his glass.

The Kommandant put his down on the bar and looked at him sternly.

'It's illegal,' he said, 'I suppose you realize that.'

'What is, old boy?' asked the Major.

149

It was the Kommandant's turn to look round the bar hastily.

'Drag hunts,' he said finally.

'Really? How extraordinary. I had no idea,' said the Major. 'I mean it's not as though anyone gets hurt or anything.'

The Kommandant shifted uneasily on his stool.

'I suppose that depends which end you're on,' he muttered.

'A bit exhausting for the poor bugger out front. I mean, running all that way but it's only twice a week,' said the Major.

Kommandant van Heerden shuddered.

'You just tell the Colonel what I've said,' he told the Major. 'Tell him it's strictly illegal.'

'Will do, old boy,' said the Major, 'though it beats me why it should be. Still you'd know about these things, being in the police and all that.'

They sat and finished their drinks in silence, each occupied with his own thoughts.

'Are you absolutely sure it's illegal, old boy,' Major Bloxham asked finally, 'I mean it's not as though it's cruel or anything. There's no actual kill.'

'I should fucking well hope not,' said the Kommandant, highly incensed.

'We just pop a kaffir out after breakfast with a bag of aniseed round his middle and an hour later we all go after him.'

'Aniseed?' the Kommandant asked. 'What's the aniseed for?'

'Gives him a bit of a scent you know,' the Major explained.

Kommandant van Heerden shuddered. Scented kaffirs being chased across country by men in their fifties dressed as women was more than he could stomach.

'What does Mrs Heathcote-Kilkoon think about it?' he asked anxiously. He couldn't see an elegant lady like her approving of drag hunting at all.

'What? Daphne? She loves it. I think she's keener than anyone else,' said the Major. 'Got a wonderful seat, you know.'

'So I've noticed,' said the Kommandant who thought the

comment about Mrs Heathcote-Kilkoon's anatomy quite un-called for. 'And what does she wear?'

Major Bloxham laughed. 'She's one of the old school. Hard as nails. Wears a topper for one thing . . .'

'A topper? Do you mean she wears a top hat?' asked the Kommandant.

'Nothing less, old boy, and she doesn't spare the whip I can tell you. God help the man who refuses a fence. That woman will give him what for.'

'Charming,' said the Kommandant trying to imagine what it must be like to get what for from Mrs Heathcote-Kilkoon wearing nothing less than a top hat.

'We can give you a good mount,' said the Major.

The Kommandant anchored himself to his stool firmly.

'I daresay you can,' he said sternly, 'but I wouldn't advise you to try.'

Major Bloxham stood up.

'Got cold feet, eh?' he said nastily.

'It's not my feet I'm worried about,' said the Kommandant.

'Well, I'd better be getting back to White Ladies,' said the Major and moved towards the door. Kommandant van Heerden finished his drink and followed him out. He found the Major getting into the Rolls.

'By the way, just as a matter of interest,' the Kommandant said, 'what do you wear on these . . . er . . . occasions?'

Major Bloxham smiled obscenely.

'Pink, old boy, pink. What else do you think a gentleman wears?' and he let in the clutch and the Rolls moved off leaving the Kommandant filled once more with that sense of dis-illusionment which seemed to come whenever he put the ideal figures of his imagination to the test of reality. He stood for a moment and then wandered up into the square and stood look-ing up at the face of the Great Queen. For the first time he understood the look of veiled disgust he saw there. 'No wonder,' he thought, 'It can't have been much fun being Queen of a nation of pansies.' Thinking how symbolic it was that a pigeon had defecated on her bronze forehead he turned and walked slowly back to the Spa for lunch.

*   *   *

'Illegal?' shouted Colonel Heathcote-Kilkoon when the Major reported what the Kommandant had said. 'Hunting's illegal? Never heard such tommyrot in my life. Man's a liar. Afraid of horses I shouldn't wonder. What else did he say?'

'Admitted he shoots foxes,' said the Major.

Colonel Heathcote-Kilkoon exploded.

'Damn me, I always said the fellow was a scoundrel,' he shouted. 'And to think I've ruined my liver drinking toasts with a swine like that.'

'Don't shout, Henry dear,' Mrs Heathcote-Kilkoon said, coming in from the next room, 'I don't think my head can stand it and besides, Willy's dead.'

'Willy's dead?' asked the Colonel. 'Fit enough yesterday.'

'Go and look for yourselves,' said Mrs Heathcote-Kilkoon sadly. The two men went through to the next room.

'Good God,' said the Colonel as they looked at the goldfish bowl. 'Wonder how that happened?'

'Probably drank himself to death,' said Major Bloxham lightly. Colonel Heathcote-Kilkoon looked at him coldly.

'I don't think that's very funny,' he said and stalked out of the house. Major Bloxham wandered disconsolately onto the the stoep where he found La Marquise standing staring at the view.

'And only man is vile, eh?' he said amiably. La Marquise looked at him angrily.

'Darling, you have a wonderful knack of saying the right thing at the wrong time,' she snapped, and waddled off painfully across the lawn leaving the Major wondering what had got into her.

CHAPTER ELEVEN

The sense of disillusionment which had been Kommandant van Heerden's first reaction to Major Bloxham's disclosures gave way, as he walked back to the Spa, to several new suspicions. Looking back over his recent experiences, the invitation to stay at White Ladies and his subsequent relegation to Weezen Spa, the blatant neglect he had suffered for several days after his arrival, and the overall feeling that in some indefinable way he was not welcome, the Kommandant began to feel that he had some cause for grievance. Nor was that all. The disparity which existed between the behaviour of the Heathcote-Kilkoons and that of the heroes of Dornford Yates' novels was glaring. Berry & Co didn't end up blind drunk under the table unless some French crook had drugged their champagne. Berry & Co didn't invite alcoholic Lesbians to dinner. Berry & Co didn't go riding round the country dressed ... Well, now he came to think of it, there was that story in *Jonah & Co* where Berry dressed up as a woman. But above all Berry & Co didn't consort with Konstabel Els, late or not. That was for sure.

Lying on his bed in Colonic Irrigation No 6 the Kommandant nursed his suspicions until what had begun as disillusionment turned into anger.

Nobody's going to treat me like this he thought, recalling the various insults he had had to put up with, particularly from the fat man, at the dinner. Colourful family indeed, he thought, I'll colourful you. He got up and stared at the image of himself in the mottled mirror.

'I am Kommandant van Heerden,' he said to himself and puffed out his chest in an assertion of authority and was surprised at the large surge of pride that followed this avowal of his own identity. For a moment the gap between what he was and what he would like to have been closed and he viewed the world with all the defiance of a self-made man. He was just considering the implications of this new self-satisfaction when there was a knock at the door.

'Come in,' shouted the Kommandant and was surprised to see Mrs Heathcote-Kilkoon standing in the doorway.

'Well?' said the Kommandant peremptorily and unable in so short a time to make the change from brusque authority to common courtesy the new situation clearly demanded. Mrs Heathcote-Kilkoon looked at him submissively.

'Oh darling,' she murmured. 'Oh my darling.' She stood meekly before him and looked down at her immaculate mauve gloves. 'I feel so ashamed. So terribly ashamed. To think that we've treated you so badly.'

'Yes. Well,' said the Kommandant uncertainly but still sounding as though he were interrogating a suspect.

Mrs Heathcote-Kilkoon subsided onto the bed where she sat staring at her shoes.

'It's all my fault,' she said finally, 'I should never have asked you to come.' She glanced round the horrid room to which her offer of hospitality had condemned the Kommandant and sighed. 'I should have known better than to imagine Henry would behave decently. He's got this thing about foreigners, you see.'

The Kommandant could see it. It explained for one thing the presence of La Marquise. A French Lesbian would appeal unnaturally to a transvestite Colonel.

'And then there's that wretched club of his,' Mrs Heathcote-Kilkoon continued. 'It's not so much a club as a secret society. Oh I know you think it's all terribly innocent and harmless but you don't have to live with it. You don't understand how vicious it all is. The disguise, the pretence, the shame of it all.'

'You mean it's not real?' the Kommandant asked trying to understand the full import of Mrs Heathcote-Kilkoon's outburst.

Mrs Heathcote-Kilkoon looked up at him in amazement.

'Don't tell me they fooled you too,' she said. 'Of course it's not real. Don't you see? We're none of us what we pretend to be. Henry's not a Colonel. Boy's not a Major. He's not even a boy, come to that and I'm not a lady. We're all playing parts, all terrible phonies.' She sat on the edge of the bed and her eyes filled with tears.

'What are you then?' the Kommandant demanded.

'Oh God,' moaned Mrs Heathcote-Kilkoon, 'need you ask?'

She sat there crying while the Kommandant fetched a glass of water from one of the many washbasins.

'Here, take some of this,' he said proffering the glass. 'It will do you good.'

Mrs Heathcote-Kilkoon took a sip and stared at the Kommandant frantically.

'No wonder you're constipated,' she said finally putting the glass down on the bedside table. 'What must you think of us, letting you stay in this awful place?'

The Kommandant, for whom the day seemed to have become one long confessional, thought it better not to say what he thought though he had to agree that Weezen Spa wasn't very nice.

'Tell me,' he said, 'if the Colonel isn't a Colonel, what is he?'

'I can't tell you,' said Mrs Heathcote-Kilkoon, 'I've promised never to tell anyone what he did in the war. He'd kill me if he thought I'd told you.' She looked up at him imploringly. 'Please just forget what I've said. I've done enough damage already.'

'I see,' said the Kommandant drawing his own conclusions from the Colonel's threat to kill her if she let his secret out. Whatever Henry had done during the war it was evidently hush-hush.

Mrs Heathcote-Kilkoon, judging that her tears and the admission she had just made sufficiently atoned for the discomfort of the Kommandant's accommodation, dried her eyes and stood up.

'You're so understanding,' she murmured.

'I wouldn't say that,' said the Kommandant truthfully.

Mrs Heathcote-Kilkoon went over to the mirror and began to repair the calculated ravages to her make-up.

'And now,' she said with a gaiety that surprised the Kommandant, 'I'm going to drive you over to the Sani Pass for tea. It'll do us both good to get out and you could do with a change of water.'

That afternoon was one the Kommandant would never forget. As the great car slid noiselessly over the foothills of the mountains leaving a great plume of dust to eddy over the fields and kaffir huts they passed, the Kommandant resumed something of the good nature he had so recently lost. He was sitting in a car that had once belonged to a Governor-General and in which the Prince of Wales had twice ridden during his triumphal tour of South Africa in 1925 and beside him there sat if not, evidently, a proper lady at least a woman who possessed all the apparent attributes of one. Certainly the way she handled the car excited the Kommandant's admiration and he was particularly impressed by the perfect timing she displayed in allowing the car to steal up behind a black woman with a basket on her head before squeezing the bulb of the horn and causing the woman to leap into the ditch.

'I was in the Army during the war and I learnt to drive then,' she said when the Kommandant complimented her on her skill. 'Used to drive a thirty hundredweight truck.' She laughed at the memory. 'You know everyone says the war was absolutely awful but actually I enjoyed it enormously. Never had so much fun in my life.'

Not for the first time, Kommandant van Heerden considered the strange habit of the English of finding enjoyment in the oddest places.

'What about the ... er ... Colonel? Did he have fun too?' asked the Kommandant for whom the Colonel's wartime occupation had become a matter of intense curiosity.

'What? On the Underground? I should think not,' said Mrs Heathcote-Kilkoon before realizing what she had just done. She pulled the car into the side of the road and stopped before turning to the Kommandant.

'That was a dirty trick,' she said, 'getting me to talk like that and then asking what Henry did during the war. I suppose that's a professional trick of the police. Well, it's out now,' she continued in spite of the Kommandant's protestations, 'Henry was a guard on the Underground. The Inner Circle as a matter of fact. But for God's sake promise me never to mention it.'

'Of course I won't mention it,' said the Kommandant whose respect for the Colonel had gone up enormously now that he knew he'd belonged to the inner circle of the underground.

'What about the Major? Was he in the underground too?' Mrs Heathcote-Kilkoon laughed.

'Dear me no,' she said. 'He was some sort of barman at the Savoy. Where do you think he learnt to make those lethal concoctions of his?'

The Kommandant nodded appreciatively. He'd never thought of Major Bloxham as being a legal type but he supposed it was possible.

They drove on and had tea at the Sani Pass Hotel before returning to Weezen. It was only as they were approaching the town that the Kommandant brought up the question that had been bothering him all day.

'Do you know anyone called Els?' he asked. Mrs Heathcote-Kilkoon shook her head.

'No one,' she said.

'Are you quite sure?'

'Of course I'm sure,' she said. 'I'd hardly be likely to forget anyone with a name like Else.'

'I don't suppose you would,' said the Kommandant thinking that anyone who knew Els under any name was hardly likely to forget the brute. 'He's a thin man with little eyes and he has a flat sort of head, at the back as if someone has hit him with a blunt instrument several times.'

Mrs Heathcote-Kilkoon smiled. 'That's Harbinger to the life,' she said. 'Funny you should mention him. You're the second person to ask about him today. La Marquise said something odd about him at lunch when his name came up. She said, "I could a tale unfold." A funny sort of thing to say about Harbinger. I mean he's not exactly cultured is he?'

'No, he's not,' said the Kommandant emphatically and with a shrewd understanding of La Marquise's remark.

'Henry got him from the Weezen jail, you know. They hire out prisoners for a few cents a day and we've kept him ever since. He's our odd-job man.'

'Yes, well, I daresay he is,' said the Kommandant, 'but I'd keep an eye on him all the same. He's not the sort of fellow I'd want hanging about the place.'

'Funny you should say that,' said Mrs Heathcote-Kilkoon yet again. 'He told me once that he had been a hangman before he took to a life of crime.'

'Before?' said the Kommandant in astonishment but Mrs Heathcote-Kilkoon was too busy manoeuvring the car through the gates of Weezen Spa to hear him.

'You *will* come out with the hunt tomorrow?' she said as the Kommandant climbed out. 'I know it's an awful lot to ask after what you have had to put up with already but I would like you to come.'

The Kommandant looked at her and wondered what to say.

He had enjoyed the afternoon drive and he didn't want to offend her.

'What would you like me to wear?' he asked cautiously.

'That's a point,' Mrs Heathcote-Kilkoon said. 'Look why don't you come over now and we'll see if you can get into Henry's togs.'

'Togs?' said the Kommandant wondering what obscure feminine garment a tog was.

'Riding things,' said Mrs Heathcote-Kilkoon.

'What sort of things does Henry ride in?'

'Ordinary breeches, riding breeches.'

'Ordinary ones?'

'Of course, what on earth do you think he wears? I know he's pretty odd but he doesn't ride around in the raw or anything.'

'Are you sure?' asked the Kommandant.

Mrs Heathcote-Kilkoon looked at him hard.

'Of course I'm sure,' she said. 'What on earth makes you think otherwise.'

'Nothing,' said the Kommandant, meaning to have a chat with Major Bloxham at the earliest opportunity. He climbed into the car again and Mrs Heathcote-Kilkoon drove back to White Ladies.

'There you are,' she said half an hour later as they stood in the Colonel's dressing-room. 'They fit you perfectly.'

The Kommandant looked at himself in the mirror and had to admit that the breeches looked rather splendid on him.

'You even dress the same side,' continued Mrs Heathcote-Kilkoon with a professional eye.

The Kommandant looked around the room curiously.

'Which side do you dress?' he asked and was amazed at the laughter his remark produced.

'Naughty man,' said Mrs Heathcote-Kilkoon finally, and much to the Kommandant's surprise kissed him lightly on the cheek.

In Piemburg the question of naughty men was one that was beginning to bother Luitenant Verkramp. The dispatch of his eleven remaining secret agents had not, after all, seen the end

158

of his problems. Arriving at the police station the morning after their departure he found Sergeant Breitenbach in a state of unusual agitation.

'A fine mess you've got us into now,' he said when Verkramp asked him what was wrong.

'You mean those ostriches?' Verkramp inquired.

'No, I don't,' said the Sergeant, 'I mean the konstabels you've been giving shock treatment to. They're queer.'

'I thought those ostriches were pretty queer,' said Verkramp who still hadn't got over the sight of one blowing up almost under his nose.

'Well you haven't seen the konstabels,' Sergeant Breitenbach told him and went to the door. 'Konstabel Botha,' he shouted.

Konstabel Botha came into the office.

'There you are,' said Sergeant Breitenbach grimly. 'That's what your bloody aversion therapy's been and done. And he used to play rugby for Zululand.'

At his desk Luitenant Verkramp knew now that he was going mad. He'd felt bad enough faced with exploding ostriches but they were as nothing to the insanity he felt now confronted with the famous footballer. Konstabel Botha, hooker for Zululand, six foot four and sixteen stone, minced into the room wearing a yellow wig and with his mouth smudged hideously with lipstick.

'You lovely man,' he simpered to Verkramp, sauntering like some modish elephant about the office.

'Keep your hands off me, you bastard,' snarled the Sergeant but Luitenant Verkramp wasn't listening. The inner voices were there again and this time there was no stopping them. With his face livid and his eyes staring Verkramp collapsed screaming in his chair. He was still screaming and babbling about being God, when the ambulance arrived from Fort Rapier and he was carried downstairs struggling furiously.

Sergeant Breitenbach sat beside him in the ambulance and was there when they arrived at the hospital. Dr von Blimenstein, radiant in a white coat, was waiting.

'It's all right now. You're quite safe with me,' she said and with one swift movement had pinned Verkramp's arm between his shoulderblades and was frogmarching him into the ward.

'Poor bastard,' thought Sergeant Breitenbach gazing with alarm at her broad shoulders and heavy buttocks, 'you've got it coming to you.'

He went back to the police station and tried to think what to do. With a wave of sabotage on his hands, thirty-six irate citizens in prison and two hundred and ten queer konstabels out of a total force of five hundred, he knew he couldn't cope. Half an hour later urgent messages were going out to all police stations in the area asking them to contact Kommandant van Heerden. In the meantime, as a method of isolating the disaffected konstabels, he gave orders that they should be put through their paces on the parade ground and sent Sergeant de Kok down there to give them drill. It was not a particularly happy choice, as Sergeant Breitenbach found when he went down to see how things were going. The two hundred konstabels minced and pirouetted across the parade ground alarmingly.

'If you can't stop them marching like that, you'd better get them out of sight,' he told the Sergeant. 'It's that sort of thing gives the South African Police a bad name.'

'You've done what?' Colonel Heathcote-Kilkoon shouted when his wife told him she had invited the Kommandant to the hunt. 'A man who shoots foxes? In my breeches? By God, I'll see about that.'

'Now, Henry,' said Mrs Heathcote-Kilkoon, but the Colonel had already left the room and was hurrying to the stables where Harbinger was grooming a chestnut mare.

'How's Chaka?' he asked. As if in answer a horse in one of the stalls gave his door a resounding kick.

The Colonel peered cautiously into the darkened interior and studied an enormous black horse that stirred restlessly inside.

'Saddle him up,' said the Colonel vindictively and left Harbinger wondering how the hell he was ever going to get a saddle on the beast.

'You can't possibly ask the Kommandant to ride Chaka,' Mrs Heathcote-Kilkoon told the Colonel when he said what he had done.

'I'm not asking a man who shoots foxes to ride any of my damned horses,' said the Colonel, 'but if he chooses to he can take his chance on Chaka and good luck to him.'

A dreadful banging and the sound of curses from the direction of the stables suggested that Harbinger was not having an easy job saddling Chaka.

'Be it on your own head if the Kommandant gets killed,' said Mrs Heathcote-Kilkoon but the Colonel was unimpressed.

'Any man who shoots foxes deserves to die,' was all he said.

When Kommandant van Heerden arrived it was to find Major Bloxham resplendent in a scarlet coat standing on the steps.

'I thought you said you always wore pink,' said the Kommandant with a touch of annoyance.

'So I do, old boy, so I do. Can't you see?' He turned and went into the house followed by the Kommandant who wondered if he was colour-blind. In the main room people were standing about drinking and the Kommandant was relieved to note that they were all dressed appropriately for their sex. Mrs Heathcote-Kilkoon in a long black skirt was looking quite lovely if a little pale while the Colonel's complexion matched that of his coat.

'I suppose you'll be wanting another green chartreuse,' he said, 'or perhaps yellow would suit you better this morning.'

The Kommandant said the green would suit him fine and Mrs Heathcote-Kilkoon presently drew him into a corner.

'Henry's got it into his head you go around shooting foxes,' she said, 'and he's absolutely furious. I think you ought to know he's given you the most awful horse.'

'I've never even seen a fox,' said the Kommandant with simple honesty. 'I wonder where he got that idea from.'

'Well, it doesn't much matter. He's got it and you've got Chaka. You can ride, can't you? I mean really ride.'

Kommandant van Heerden drew himself up proudly.

'Oh yes,' he said. 'I think I can ride.'

'Well I do hope you're right. Chaka's a dreadful brute. Don't for goodness sake, let him get away from you.'

The Kommandant said he certainly wouldn't and a few

161

minutes later everyone trooped out to the yard where the hounds were waiting. So was Chaka. Massive and black, he stood some way apart from the other horses and at his head there stood the figure of a man with small eyes and a non-existent forehead.

It was difficult for Kommandant van Heerden, who in the excitement of going hunting had forgotten all about ex-Konstabel Els, to make up his mind which animal most dismayed him. Certainly the prospect of even mounting a horse as monstrous as Chaka was hardly pleasing but at least it offered a way of avoiding Els if very little, he was about to say, else. With a speed and vigour that quite took the Colonel by surprise, the Kommandant reached up and hauled himself into the saddle and from these commanding heights surveyed the throng. Below him hounds and horses milled about while the other riders mounted and then with Els on a nag vigorously blowing a horn the hunt moved off. Behind them the Kommandant urged Chaka forward tentatively. I am going foxhunting like a real Englishman, he thought as he dug his heels in a second time. It was the last coherent thought he had for some time. With a demonic lurch the great black horse shot out of the yard and into the garden. As the Kommandant desperately clung to his seat it was apparent that wherever he was going it wasn't hunting. The hounds had strung out in quite a different direction. As a rockery disappeared beneath him, as an ornamental bush looked up and disintegrated, and as the Colonel's roses shed both their labels and their petals in his wake the Kommandant was only aware that he was travelling at a great height and at a speed which seemed incredible. Ahead of him loomed the azalea bushes of which Colonel Heathcote-Kilkoon was so proud and beyond them the open veldt. Kommandant van Heerden shut his eyes. There was no time for prayer. The next moment he was airborne.

The Kommandant's startling gallop caused mixed reactions among the huntsmen. Immaculately sidesaddled and with her top hat perched on her neat blue curls Mrs Heathcote-Kilkoon watched the Kommandant disappear over the azaleas with a combination of disgust at her husband and admiration for the Kommandant. Whatever else he might be, the Kommandant was clearly not a man to baulk at fences.

'See what you've done now,' she shouted at the Colonel who was staring at the destruction left in the wake of his retreating guest. To add to his annoyance Mrs Heathcote-Kilkoon turned her bay and galloped off in pursuit of the Kommandant churning the lawn up still more as she went.

'Got rid of the blighter,' said Major Bloxham cheerfully.

'Damned Boer,' said the Colonel. 'Shoots foxes and smashes my best roses.'

Behind them Harbinger blew his horn again happily. He'd always wanted to see what would happen if he stuffed a quid of tobacco up the great black horse's arse and now he knew.

So did Kommandant van Heerden, though he wasn't aware of the specific cause of Chaka's urgency. Still in the saddle after the first enormous jump he tried to recall what Mrs Heathcote-Kilkoon had said about not letting the horse get away from him. It seemed an uncalled-for piece of advice. If the Kommandant could have thought of any way of letting the horse get away from him without breaking his neck in the process he would have been glad to do so. As it was his only hope of survival seemed to lie in staying with the beast until it ran out of wind. With all the fortitude of a man for whom there were no alternatives, the Kommandant hunched in the saddle and watched a stone wall hurtle towards him. The wall had evidently been built with giraffes in mind. Certainly no horse could clear it. As he landed on the other side Kommandant van Heerden had the distinct impression that the animal he was riding was no horse at all but some mythical creature he'd seen portrayed so eloquently on petrol pumps. Ahead there lay open veldt and in the far distance the shadowy outlines of a wood. One thing he was determined on and that was that no horse, mythical or not, was going to career through a wood full of trees with him on its back. It was better to break one's neck on the open ground than to emerge legless on the far side of a dense wood. With a determination to end his journey one way or another the Kommandant grasped the reins firmly and heaved.

To Mrs Heathcote-Kilkoon, galloping desperately after him, the Kommandant appeared in a new light. He was no longer the coarsely attractive man of reality she had formerly seen him as but the hero of her dreams. There was something reminiscent of a painting she had once seen of Napoleon crossing the Alps on a prancing horse about the figure that soared over the wall no one had been known to attempt before. With a caution entirely justified by her longing for her new idol, Mrs Heathcote-Kilkoon chose a gate and emerged on the other side to find to her astonishment that both the Kommandant and Chaka had vanished. She galloped towards the wood and was horrified to see both horse and rider motionless on the ground. She rode up and dismounted.

When Kommandant van Heerden came to, it was to find his head cradled in the dark lap of Mrs Heathcote-Kilkoon who was bending over him with a look of maternal admiration on her face.

'Don't try to move,' she said. The Kommandant wiggled his toes to see if his back was broken. His toes wiggled reassuringly. He lifted a knee and the knee moved. His arms were all right too. There seemed to be nothing broken. The Kommandant opened his eyes again and smiled. Above him beneath a ring of tinted curls Mrs Heathcote-Kilkoon smiled back and it seemed to Kommandant van Heerden that there was in that smile a new acknowledgement of some deep bond of feeling between them, a meeting of two hearts and minds alone on the open veldt. Mrs Heathcote-Kilkoon read his thoughts.

'Ant-bear hole,' she said with suppressed emotion.

'Ant-bear hole?' asked the Kommandant.

'Ant-bear hole,' Mrs Heathcote-Kilkoon repeated gently.

The Kommandant tried to think what ant-bear holes had to do with his feelings for her and apart from the rather bizarre notion that they should get into one together couldn't think of anything. He contented himself with murmuring 'Ant-bear hole, with as much emotion as possible and closed his eyes again. Beneath his head her plump thighs formed a delightful pillow. The Kommandant sighed and nestled his head against her stomach. A feeling of supreme happiness welled up inside him marred only by the thought that he would have to mount that ghastly horse again. It was a prospect that he had no intention of hastening. Mrs Heathcote-Kilkoon dashed his hopes.

'We can't stay here,' she said. 'It's far too hot.'

The Kommandant who had begun to suspect that some large insect had begun to crawl up the inside of his breeches had to agree. Slowly he lifted his head from her lap and climbed to his feet.

'Let's go into the woods,' Mrs Heathcote-Kilkoon said. 'You need to rest and I want to make sure you haven't broken anything.'

Now that the Kommandant was up he could see what she had meant by ant-bear hole. The great black horse lay on its side, its neck broken and one foreleg deep in a hole. With a sigh of relief that he would never have to ride the beast again and that his horsemanship had been vindicated after all by the aardvark, the Kommandant allowed himself to be helped quite unnecessarily into the shade of the wood. There in an open dell shaded by the trees Mrs Heathcote-Kilkoon insisted that he lie down while she examined him for broken bones.

'You may have concussion,' she said as her experienced hands unbuttoned his jacket. In the next few moments Kommandant van Heerden began to think that she must be right. What the great English lady was doing to him must be some result of brain damage. As she stood above him and unbuckled her skirt he knew he was seeing things. I'd better just lie still until it passes over, he thought and shut his eyes.

Two miles away the hounds had picked up the scent of Fox and, with the hunt in full pursuit and Harbinger occasionally blowing his horn, were off across country.

'Wonder what happened to that damned Boer,' Major Bloxham shouted.

'I daresay he's all right,' the Colonel shouted back, 'Daphne's probably looking after him.'

Presently the hounds veered to the left and headed for a wood and ten minutes later, still mutely absorbed in their pursuit, had left the open ground and were deep in the undergrowth. The scent was stronger here and the hounds quickened their pace. Half a mile ahead Kommandant van Heerden followed suit.

He wasn't quite so mute but his absorption matched that of the pack. Above him clad only in her boots and spurs and with her top hat clinging elastically to the top of her tinted head, Mrs Heathcote-Kilkoon shouted encouragement to her new mount, occasionally lashing him on with her crop. They were so deeply engrossed in one another that they were oblivious to the crackling undergrowth that signalled the approach of the hunt. 'Jill, Jenny, Daphne, my sweet,' moaned the Kommandant unable even now to shake off the notion that he was figuring in one of Dornford Yates' novels. Mrs Heathcote-Kilkoon's imagination, sharpened by years of frustration, was more equestrian.

'Ride a cock horse to Banbury Cross to see a fine lady upon a white horse,' she shouted and was astonished to find that her invitation had been accepted.

Out of the woods raced the pack and the Kommandant who had been on the point of reaching his second climax became suddenly aware that the tongue that was licking his face was of a length and texture quite unusual in a lady of Mrs Heathcote-Kilkoon's breeding. He opened his eyes and found himself looking into the face of a large foxhound which slobbered and panted disgustingly. The Kommandant looked wildly around. The dell was filled with dogs. A tide of tails waved above him and out above them all Mrs Heathcote-Kilkoon sat impaled upon him beating around her with her riding crop.

'Down Jason. Down Snarler. Down Craven. Down van Heerden,' she yelled, her topper bobbing as vigorously as her breasts.

Kommandant van Heerden stared crazedly up at the underside of Snarler and tried to get the dog's paw out of his mouth. He had never realized before how horrible a hot dog smelt. Obedient as ever to his mistress Snarler sat – and got up promptly when the Kommandant, dreading death by suffocation, bit him. Relieved for a moment of this threat of asphyxia the Kommandant raised his head only to have it submerged a moment later by the press. The brief glimpse he had had of the outside world presented so awful a prospect that he preferred the stinking obscurity to be found under the foxhounds. Colonel Heathcote-Kilkoon and the other members of the hunt had emerged from the woods and were surveying the scene in amazement.

'Good God, Daphne, what on earth do you think you're doing?' the Kommandant heard the Colonel shout angrily.

Mrs Heathcote-Kilkoon rose to the occasion magnificently.

'What the hell do you think I'm doing?' she screamed with a display of righteous indignation the Kommandant found extraordinarily impressive but which seemed calculated to raise a question in her husband's mind the Kommandant would have preferred to remain unanswered.

'I've no idea,' shouted the Colonel who couldn't for a moment imagine what his wife was doing in the middle of a dell without her clothes. Mrs Heathcote-Kilkoon answered him. 'I'm having a shit,' she shouted with a coarseness that Kommandant van Heerden found personally humiliating but entirely apposite.

The Colonel coughed with embarrassment. 'Good God, I'm terribly sorry,' he muttered but Mrs Heathcote-Kilkoon was determined to pursue the advantage she had gained.

'And if you were gentlemen you'd turn your backs and get the hell out of here,' she screamed. Her words were immediately effective. The huntsmen turned their horses and galloped back the way they had come.

As the tide of foxhounds slowly ebbed the Kommandant found himself, naked and covered with muddy paw-marks, staring up at the lady of his and Heathcote-Kilkoon's choice. With a reluctance that did him credit she detached herself from him and stood up. Breathless with fear and a new admiration for her the Kommandant scrambled to his feet and began to look for his breeches. He knew now what British sang-froid meant.

'And I've got a stiff upper lip,' he said feeling the effects of Snarler's hindpaw.

'About the only thing stiff you have got,' said Mrs Heathcote-Kilkoon frankly.

In the bushes on the edge of the dell Harbinger giggled softly. He'd never pretended to be a gentleman and he'd always wanted to see the Colonel's wife in the nude.

CHAPTER TWELVE

As they dressed in the dell Kommandant van Heerden and Mrs Heathcote-Kilkoon were filled with post-coital depression.

'It's been so nice to meet a real man for a change,' she murmured. 'You've no idea how tiresome Henry can be.'

'I think I have,' said the Kommandant who wasn't likely to forget his recent nightmare ride. And besides the thought of meeting the Colonel again so shortly after having, as the Kommandant delicately put it, had carnal knowledge of his wife was not particularly appealing. 'I think I'll just walk back to the Spa from here,' but Mrs Heathcote-Kilkoon wouldn't hear of it.

'I'll send Boy over with the Land-Rover to pick you up,' she said. 'You're not in a fit state to walk anywhere. Certainly not after your fall and in this heat too.' Before Kommandant could stop her, she had walked out of the wood and had mounted her horse and was riding away.

Kommandant van Heerden sat on a log and considered the romantic experience he had just undergone. 'Undergone's the word for it,' he muttered aloud and was horrified to hear the bushes part behind him and a voice say, 'Lovely bit of stuff, eh?'

The Kommandant knew that voice. He spun round and found Els grinning at him.

'What the hell are you doing here?' he asked. 'I thought you were dead.'

'Me? Dead?' said Els. 'Never.' The Kommandant began to think Els was right. There was something eternal about him like original sin. 'Been having it off with the Colonel's old woman eh?' Els continued with a familiarity the Kommandant found quite nauseating.

'What I do with my spare time is no concern of yours,' he said emphatically.

'Might be of some concern to the Colonel,' Els said cheerfully, 'I mean he might like to know—'

'Never mind what Colonel Heathcote-Kilkoon might like to know,' interrupted the Kommandant hurriedly. 'What I'd like to know is why you didn't die in Piemburg Prison with the Governor and the Chaplain.'

'That was a mistake,' said Els. 'I got muddled up with the prisoners.'

'Understandably,' said the Kommandant.

Els changed the topic.

'I'm thinking of coming back into the police,' he said. 'I'm tired of being Harbinger.'

'You're thinking of what?' said the Kommandant. He tried to raise a laugh but it didn't sound very convincing.

'I'd like to be a konstabel again.'

'You must be joking,' said the Kommandant.

'I'm not,' said Els. 'I've got my pension to think about and there's that reward money I'm owed for capturing Miss Hazelstone.'

The Kommandant considered the reward money and tried to think of an answer.

'You died intestate,' he said finally.

'I didn't, you know,' said Els. 'I died in Piemburg.'

The Kommandant sighed. He had forgotten how difficult it was to get Els to understand the simplest facts of law.

'Intestate means you died without making a will,' he explained only to find Els looking at him with interest.

'Have you made a will?' Els asked fingering his horn threateningly. He looked as though he was going to blow it.

'I don't see what that's got to do with it,' he said.

'The Colonel's got a legal right to kill you for stuffing his wife,' said Els. 'And that's what he'd do if I blew this horn and called him back.'

Kommandant van Heerden had to admit that for once Els was right. South African law reserved no penalties for husbands who shot their wives' lovers. In his career as a police officer the Kommandant had had occasion to reassure a number of men who were feeling some alarm on this account. To add to his own alarm Els raised his horn to his lips.

'All right,' said the Kommandant, 'what do you want?'

'I've told you,' said Els, 'I want my old job back.'

The Kommandant was beginning to prevaricate when the sound of a Land-Rover approaching determined the issue.

'All right, I'll see what I can do,' he said, 'though how I'm going to explain how a coloured convict is really a white konstabel, God only knows.'

'No point in spoiling the shit for a ha'p'orth of tar,' said Els making use of an expression he had picked up from Major Bloxham.

'Hear you've been having a bit of trouble, old boy,' said the Major when the Land-Rover stopped beside the body of Chaka. 'Always said that black bastard was a menace.' The Kommandant climbed in beside him and murmured his agreement but the black bastard he had in mind was not the dead horse. In the back of the truck Konstabel Els smiled happily. He was looking forward to shooting kaffirs quite legally again.

As they approached the house the Kommandant saw Colonel and Mrs Heathcote-Kilkoon standing at the top of the steps waiting for them. Once again their reactions came as a complete surprise to him. The woman with whom but an hour before he had enjoyed what could without exaggeration be called a touching intimacy now stood erect and coldly detached at the front door while her husband was exhibiting signs of evident embarrassment quite out of keeping with his role.

'Dreadfully sorry,' he muttered opening the door of the Land-Rover for the Kommandant, 'shouldn't have given you that horse in the first place.'

The Kommandant tried to think of a suitable reply to this apology.

'Ant-bear hole,' he said falling back on an expression which seemed to cover a multitude of situations.

'Quite,' said the Colonel. 'Damned nasty things. Should have been stopped.' He led the way up the steps and Mrs Heathcote-Kilkoon stepped forward to greet the Kommandant.

'So nice of you to come,' she said.

'Good of you to have me,' murmured the Kommandant blushing.

'You must try to make it more often,' said Mrs Heathcote-Kilkoon.

They went into the house where the Kommandant was

greeted by La Marquise with a remark about The Flying Dutchman which he didn't particularly like.

'Don't take any notice,' Mrs Heathcote-Kilkoon said, 'I think you were wonderful. They're just jealous.'

For the next few minutes Kommandant van Heerden found himself the centre of attention. The fact that he was the first man to have cleared the high wall, albeit involuntarily, drew murmurs of admiration from everyone. Even the Colonel said he had to take off his hat to him, which considering the loss of Chaka and the state of his garden, not to mention that of his wife, the Kommandant thought was pretty generous of him. He had just explained how he had learnt to ride on his ouma's farm in Magaliesburg and had ridden for the police in Pretoria when the blow fell.

'I must say you take things pretty cool, Kommandant,' the fat man who knew how to get discounts on refrigerators said, 'coming out here and hunting when there's all this trouble in Piemburg.'

'Trouble? What trouble?' he asked.

'What? Do you mean to say you haven't heard?' asked the fat man. 'There's been an outbreak of sabotage. Bomb attacks all over the place. Radio mast down. Electricity cut off. Absolute chaos.'

With a curse Kommandant van Heerden dumped the glass of Cointreau he'd been drinking into the nearest receptacle.

'I'm afraid we haven't a phone,' Mrs Heathcote-Kilkoon told him as he looked wildly round the hall. 'Henry won't have one for security reasons. He's always calling his stock-broker . . .'

The Kommandant was in too much of a hurry to wait and hear about Henry's stock-broker. He dashed down the steps to his car and found, as he might have expected, Els at the wheel. With the feeling that Els' presumption was somehow appropriate to the terrible news he had just received, the Kommandant climbed into the back seat. Disaster was in the air. It was certainly in the herbaceous border, where Els reversed before turning the car down the drive with a spurt of gravel that suggested he was shaking the dust of White Ladies from his feet.

From the terrace Mrs Heathcote-Kilkoon watched them

leave with a feeling of sadness. 'To part is to die a little,' she murmured and went to join the Colonel who was staring morosely into a tank of tropical fish where the Kommandant's drink was already producing some unusual effects.

'So that's how poor Willy went,' said the Colonel.

As they drove into Weezen the Kommandant cursed himself for his own stupidity.

'I might have known Verkramp would foul things up,' he thought and ordered Els to stop at the local police station. The information he was given there did nothing to restore his confidence.

'They do what?' he asked in astonishment when the Sergeant in charge told him that Piemburg had been invaded by hordes of self-detonating ostriches.

'Fly in at night in their hundreds,' said the Sergeant.

'That's a damned lie for a start,' shouted the Kommandant. 'Ostriches don't fly. They can't.'

He went back to the car and told Els to drive on. Whatever ostriches could or couldn't do, one thing was sure. Something had happened in Piemburg to cut the city off from the outside world. The telephone lines had been dead for days.

As the car hurtled along the dirt road towards the head of the Rooi Nek Pass, Kommandant van Heerden had the feeling that he was leaving an idyllic world of peace and sanity and heading back into an inferno of violence at the centre of which sat the diabolical figure of Luitenant Verkramp. He was so immersed in his own thoughts that it only occurred to him once or twice to tell Els not to drive so damned dangerously.

At Sjambok the impression of imminent catastrophe was increased by the news that the road bridges had been blown outside Piemburg. At Voetsak he learnt that the Sewage Disposal plant had been destroyed. After that the Kommandant decided not to stop any more but to drive straight through to Piemburg.

An hour later as they drove down the hill from Imperial View they came to the first tangible evidence of sabotage.

A road block had been set up at the temporary bridge erected to replace the one destroyed by Verkramp's secret agents.

The Kommandant got out to inspect the damage while a konstabel searched the car.

'Got to make a personal check too,' said the konstabel before the Kommandant could explain who he was and ran his hands over the Kommandant's breeches with a thoroughness that was surprising.

'Only obeying orders, sir,' said the konstabel when the Kommandant snarled that he wasn't likely to keep high explosives there. Kommandant van Heerden scrambled into the car. 'And change your shaving lotion,' he shouted. 'You stink to high heaven.'

They drove on into the city and the Kommandant was appalled to notice two konstabels walking down the pavement hand in hand.

'Stop the car,' the Kommandant told Els and got out.

'What the hell do you think you're doing?' he shouted at the two konstabels.

'We're on patrol, sir,' said the men in unison.

'What? Holding hands?' screamed the Kommandant. 'Do you want the general public to think you're fucking queers?'

The two konstabels let go of one another and the Kommandant got back into the car.

'What the hell's been going on round here?' he muttered.

In the front seat Konstabel Els smiled to himself. There had been some changes in Piemburg since he'd last been there. He was beginning to think he was going to enjoy being in the South African Police again.

By the time they arrived at the Police Station the Kommandant was in a vile temper.

'Send me the Acting Kommandant,' he shouted at the konstabel at the Duty desk and went upstairs wondering if his imagination was playing him up or there had been a suggestive leer on the man's face. The first impression that there had been a breakdown in discipline was confirmed by the state of the Kommandant's office. The windows had no glass in them and ashes from the grate had blown all over the room. The Kommandant was just staring at the mess when there was a knock and Sergeant Breitenbach entered.

'What in the name of hell has been happening round here?'

the Kommandant yelled at the Sergeant who was not, he was relieved to note, exhibiting any signs of queerness.

'Well, sir—' he began but the Kommandant interrupted him.

'What do I find when I come back?' he screamed in a voice that made the Duty Konstabel wince on the floor below and several passers-by stop in the street. 'Poofters. Bombs. Exploding ostriches. Do they mean anything to you?' Sergeant Breitenbach nodded. 'I thought they fucking might. I go away on holiday and the next thing I hear is that there's an outbreak of sabotage. Road bridges being blown up. No telephones. Konstabels walking about hand in hand and now this. My own office in a shambles.'

'That was the ostriches, sir,' mumbled the Sergeant.

Kommandant van Heerden slumped into a chair and held his head. 'Dear God. It's enough to drive a man out of his mind.'

'It has, sir,' said the Sergeant miserably.

'Has what?'

'Driven a man out of his mind, sir. Luitenant Verkramp, sir.'

The name Verkramp shook the Kommandant out of his reverie.

'Verkramp!' he yelled. 'Wait till I lay my hands on the swine. I'll crucify the bastard. Where is he?'

'In Fort Rapier, sir. He's off his rocker.'

Kommandant van Heerden absorbed the information slowly.

'You mean . . .'

'He's got religious mania, sir. Thinks he's God.'

The Kommandant stared at him disbelievingly. The notion that any man could think he was God when his creation was as chaotic as Verkramp's had so obviously been seemed inconceivable.

'Thinks he's God?' he mumbled. 'Verkramp?'

Sergeant Breitenbach had given the matter some thought.

'I think that's how the trouble started,' he explained. 'He wanted to show what he could do.'

'He's done that all right,' said the Kommandant limply, looking round his office.

174

'He's got this thing about sin, sir, and he wanted to stop policemen going to bed with black women.'

'I know all that.'

'Well he started off by giving them shock treatment and showing them photographs of naked black women and . . .'

Kommandant van Heerden stopped him.

'Don't go on,' he said, 'I don't think I can stand it.'

He got up and went over to his desk. He opened a drawer and took out a bottle of brandy he kept for emergencies and poured himself a glass. When he'd finished it he looked up.

'Now then begin at the beginning and tell me what Verkramp did.' Sergeant Breitenbach told him. At the end the Kommandant shook his head sadly.

'It didn't work then? This treatment?' he asked.

'I wouldn't say that, sir. It just didn't work the way it was meant to. I mean you'd find it difficult to get any of the konstabels who's been treated into bed with a black woman. We've tried it and they get into a frightful state.'

'You've tried to get a konstabel into bed with a black woman?' asked the Kommandant, who could see himself giving evidence at the inevitable court of inquiry and having to admit that policemen under his command had been ordered to have sexual intercourse with black women as part of their duties.

Sergeant Breitenbach nodded. 'Couldn't do it though,' he said, 'I guarantee that not one of those two hundred and ten men will ever go to bed with a black again.'

'Two hundred and ten?' asked the Kommandant stunned by the scale of Verkramp's activities.

'That's the number, sir. Half the force are gay,' the Sergeant told him. 'And not one of them prepared to sleep with a black woman.'

'I suppose that makes a change,' said the Kommandant looking for some relief in this recital of disasters.

'Trouble is they won't go near a white woman either. The treatment seems to have worked both ways. You should see the letters of complaint we've had from some of the men's wives.'

The Kommandant said he'd prefer not to.

'What about the exploding ostriches?' he asked. 'That have

anything to do with Verkramp's religious mania?'

'Not to my knowledge,' said the Sergeant. 'That was the work of the Communist saboteurs.'

The Kommandant sighed. 'Them again,' he said wearily. 'I don't suppose you've got a lead on them, have you?'

'Well, we have made some progress, sir. We've got the description of the men who were feeding the ostriches French letters . . .' He stopped. Kommandant van Heerden was staring at him wildly.

'Feeding them French letters?' he asked. 'What the hell were they doing that for?'

'The explosive was packed in contraceptives, sir. Fetherlites.'

'Fetherlights?' said the Kommandant trying to imagine what sort of ornithological offal he was on about.

'That's the brand name, sir. We've also an excellent description of a man who bought twelve dozen. Twelve women have come forward who say they remember him.'

'Twelve dozen for twelve women?' said the Kommandant. 'I should bloody well think they can remember him. I should have thought he was unforgettable.'

'They were in the shop when he tried to buy the things,' the Sergeant explained. 'Five barbers have also given us a description which tallies with that of the women.'

The Kommandant tried desperately to visualize the sort of man whose tastes were so indiscriminate. 'He can't have got far, that's for sure,' he said finally. 'Not after that lot.'

'No sir,' said Sergeant Breitenbach. 'He didn't. A man answering his description and with fingerprints that correspond with some of those on the French letters was found dead in the toilet at the Majestic Cinema.'

'I'm not in the least surprised,' said the Kommandant.

'Unfortunately we can't identify him.'

'Too emaciated I suppose,' the Kommandant suggested.

'He was killed by the bomb which went off there,' the Sergeant explained.

'Well have you made any arrests at all?'

The Sergeant nodded. 'Luitenant Verkramp ordered the

arrest of thirty-six suspects as soon as the first bombings occurred.'

'Well that's something anyway,' said the Kommandant more cheerfully. 'Got any confessions out of them?'

Sergeant Breitenbach looked dubious.

'Well, the Mayor says . . .' he began.

'What's the Mayor got to do with it?' asked the Kommandant with a sense of awful premonition.

'He's one of the suspects, sir,' Sergeant Breitenbach admitted awkwardly. 'Luitenant Verkramp said . . .'

But Kommandant van Heerden was on his feet and white with rage.

'Don't tell me what the fucking shit says,' he screamed. 'I go away for ten days and half the town blows up, half the police force turns into raving homosexuals, half the stock of French letters is bought up by some sex maniac, Verkramp arrests the fucking Mayor. What the fuck do I care what Verkramp says. It's what he's done that's worrying me.'

The Kommandant stopped short. 'Is there anything else I ought to know?' he demanded. Sergeant Breitenbach shifted his feet nervously. 'There are thirty-five other suspects in the prison, sir. There's the Dean of Piemburg, Alderman Cecil, the manager of Barclays Bank . . .'

'Oh my God, and I suppose they've all been interrogated,' squawked the Kommandant.

'Yes sir,' said Sergeant Breitenbach who knew precisely what the Kommandant meant by interrogated. 'They've been standing up for the last eight days. The Mayor's admitted he doesn't like the government but he still maintains he didn't blow up the telephone exchange. The only confession we've got that's any use is from the manager of Barclays Bank'

'The manager of Barclays Bank?' asked the Kommandant. 'What's he done?'

'Peed in the Hluwe Dam, sir. It carries the death penalty.'

'Peeing in the Hluwe Dam carries the death penalty? I didn't know that.'

'It's in the Sabotage Act 1962. Polluting water supplies, sir,' the Sergeant said.

'Yes well,' said the Kommandant doubtfully, 'I daresay it is but all I can say is that if Verkramp thinks he can hang the manager of Barclays Bank for peeing in a dam he must be mad. I'm going up to Fort Rapier to see that bastard.'

In Fort Rapier Mental Hospital Luitenant Verkramp was still suffering from acute anxiety brought on by the wholly unexpected result of his experiment in aversion therapy and counter-terrorism. His temporary conviction that he was the Almighty had given way to a phobia about birds. Dr von Blimenstein drew her own conclusions.

'A simple case of sexual guilt together with a castration complex,' she told the nurse when Verkramp refused his dinner on the grounds that it was stuffed chicken and French lettuce.

'Take it away,' he screamed, 'I can't take any more.'

He was equally adamant about feather pillows and in fact anything vaguely reminiscent of what Dr von Blimenstein would insist on calling our feathered friends.

'No friends of mine,' said Verkramp, eyeing a pouter pigeon on the tree outside his window with alarm.

'We've got to try to get to the bottom of this thing,' said Dr von Blimenstein. Verkramp looked at her wildly.

'Don't mention that thing,' he shouted. Dr von Blimenstein took note of this fresh symptom. 'Anal complex,' she thought to herself and sent the Luitenant into panic by asking him if he had ever had any homosexual experiences.

'Yes,' said Verkramp desperately when the doctor insisted on knowing.

'Would you like to tell me about it?'

'No,' said Verkramp who still couldn't get the picture of hooker Botha in a yellow wig out of his mind. 'No. I wouldn't.'

Dr von Blimenstein persisted.

'We're never going to get anywhere unless you come to terms with your own unconscious,' she told him. 'You've got to be absolutely frank with me.'

'Yes,' said Verkramp who hadn't come to Fort Rapier to be frank with anyone.

If, during the day, Dr von Blimenstein gained the impression that sex was at the root of Verkramp's breakdown, his behaviour at night suggested another explanation. As she sat by his bedside and made notes of his ramblings, the doctor noticed a new pattern emerging. Verkramp spent much of his nights screaming about bombs and secret agents and was clearly obsessed with the number twelve. Remembering how frequently she had counted twelve explosions as the saboteurs struck she was hardly surprised that the head of Security in Piemburg should be obsessed by the number. On the other hand she gained the definite impression from Verkramp's sleep-talking that he had had twelve secret agents working for him. She decided to ask him about this new symptom in the morning.

'What does the number twelve mean to you?' she asked when she came to see him next day. Verkramp went pale and began to shake.

'I have to know,' she told him. 'It's in your own interest.'

'Shan't tell you,' said Verkramp who knew, if he knew anything, that it wasn't in his interest to tell her about the number twelve.

'Don't forget that I'm acting in a professional capacity,' said the doctor, 'and that anything you tell me remains a secret between us.'

Luitenant Verkramp was not reassured.

'Doesn't mean anything to me,' he said. 'I don't know anything about number twelve.'

'I see,' said the doctor making a note of his alarm. 'Then perhaps you'd like to tell me about the trip to Durban.'

There was no doubt now that she was close to the heart of Verkramp's neurosis. His reaction indicated that quite clearly. By the time the gibbering Luitenant had been got back into bed and given sedation, Dr von Blimenstein was satisfied that she could effect a cure. She was beginning to think that there were other advantages to be gained from her insight into his problems and the idea of marriage, never far from the doctor's mind, began to re-emerge.

'Tell me,' she said as she tucked Verkramp into bed again, 'is it true that a wife cannot be forced to give evidence against her husband?'

Verkramp said it was and, with a smile that suggested he would do well to meditate on the fact, Dr von Blimenstein left the room. When she returned an hour later, it was to find the patient ready with an explanation for his obsession with the number twelve.

'There were twelve saboteurs and they were—'

'Bullshit,' snapped the doctor, 'utter bullshit. There were twelve secret agents and they were working for you and you took them to Durban by car. Isn't that the truth?'

'Yes. No, No, it's not,' Verkramp wailed.

'Now listen to me. Balthazar Verkramp, if you go on lying I'll have you given an injection of truth drug and we'll get an accurate confession out of you before you know what's happened.'

Verkramp stared panic-stricken from the bed.

'You wouldn't,' he shrieked. 'You're not allowed to.'

Dr von Blimenstein looked round the room suggestively. It was more like a cell than a private room. 'In here,' she said, 'I can do anything I like. You're my patient and I'm your doctor and if you give any trouble I can have you in a straitjacket and there is absolutely nothing you can do about it. Now then, are you prepared to tell me about your problems and remember your secrets are safe with me. As your medical adviser no one can force me to tell them what has passed between us unless of course I was put into the witness box. Then of course I would be under oath.' The doctor paused before continuing, 'You did say that a wife couldn't be forced to give evidence against her husband, didn't you?'

To Verkramp the alternatives he was now facing were, if anything more shocking than exploding ostriches and camp konstabels. He lay in bed and wondered what to do. If he refused to admit that he was responsible for all the bombings and violence in the city, the doctor would use the truth drug to get it out of him and he would have forfeited her good-will into the bargain. If he admitted it openly, he would escape the legal consequences of his zeal only to be led to the altar. There seemed to be little choice. He swallowed nervously, stared round the room for the last uncommitted time and asked for a glass of water.

'Will you marry me?' he said finally.

Dr von Blimenstein smiled sweetly.

'Of course, I will, darling. Of course I will,' and a moment later Verkramp was in her arms and the doctor's mouth was pressed closely over his lips. Verkramp shut his eyes and considered a lifetime of Dr von Blimenstein. It was, he supposed, preferable to being hanged.

When Kommandant van Heerden arrived at Fort Rapier to see the Luitenant it was not surprising that he found his way strewn with extraordinary obstacles. In the first place he found the clerk in the Inquiry Desk at Admissions decidedly unhelpful. The fact that the clerk was a catatonic schizophrenic chosen by Dr von Blimenstein for his general immobility to help out at a time of acute staff shortage led to a sharp rise in the Kommandant's blood pressure.

'I demand to see Luitenant Verkramp,' he shouted at the motionless catatonic and was about to resort to violence when a tall man with an exceedingly pale face interrupted.

'I think he's in Ward C,' the man told him. The Kommandant thanked him and went to Ward C only to find it was filled with manic-depressive women. He returned to Admissions and after another one-sided altercation with the catatonic clerk was told by the tall thin man who happened to be passing through again that Verkramp was definitely in Ward H. The Kommandant went to Ward H and while unable to diagnose what the patients there were suffering from was grateful to note that Verkramp wasn't. He went back to Admissions in a foul temper and met the thin tall man in the corridor.

'Not there?' the man inquired. 'Then he's certainly in Ward E.'

'Make up your mind,' shouted the Kommandant angrily. 'First you say he's in Ward C, then in Ward H and now Ward E.'

'Interesting point you've just raised,' said the man.

'What point?' asked the Kommandant.

'About making up your mind,' said the man. 'It presupposes in the first place that there is a distinction between the mind and the brain. Now if you had said "Make up your brain" the implications would have been quite different.'

'Listen,' said the Kommandant, 'I've come here to see Luitenant Verkramp not swop logic with you.' He went off down the corridor again in search of Ward E only to learn that it was in the Bantu section which made it unlikely Verkramp was in it whatever he was suffering from. The Kommandant went back to Admissions swearing to murder the tall man if he could find him. Instead he found himself confronted by Dr von Blimenstein who pointed out acidly that he was in a hospital and not in a police station and would he kindly behave accordingly. Somewhat subdued by this evidence of authority the Kommandant followed her into her office.

'Now then, what is it you want?' she asked seating herself behind her desk and eyeing him coldly.

'I want to visit Luitenant Verkramp,' said the Commandant.

'Are you parent, relative or guardian?' asked the doctor.

'I'm a police officer investigating a crime,' said the Kommandant.

'Then you have a warrant? I should like to see it.'

The Kommandant said he hadn't a warrant. 'I am Kommandant of Police in Piemburg and Verkramp is under my command. I don't need a warrant to visit him wherever he is.'

Dr von Blimenstein smiled patronizingly.

'You obviously don't understand hospital rules,' she said. 'We have to be very careful who visits our patients. We can't have them being disturbed by casual acquaintances or by being asked questions about their work. After all, Balthazar's problems largely stem from overwork and I'm afraid I hold you responsible.'

The Kommandant was so astonished by hearing Verkramp called Balthazar that he couldn't think of a suitable reply.

'Now, if you could let me have some idea of the sort of questions you wish to put to him, I might be able to assist you,' continued the doctor, conscious of the advantage she had already gained.

The Kommandant could think of a great many questions he would like to put to the Luitenant but he thought it wiser not to mention them now. He explained that he simply wanted to find out if Verkramp could shed any light on the recent series of bombings.

'I see,' Dr von Blimenstein said. 'Now if I understand you rightly, you are quite satisfied with the way the Luitenant handled the situation in your absence?'

Kommandant van Heerden decided that a policy of appeasement was the only one likely to persuade the doctor to allow him to interview Verkramp.

'Yes,' he said, 'Luitenant Verkramp did everything he could to put a stop to the trouble.'

'Good,' said Dr von Blimenstein encouragingly, 'I'm glad to hear you say that. You see it's important that the patient shouldn't be made to feel in any way guilty. Balthazar's problems are largely the result of a long-standing sense of guilt and inadequacy. We don't want to intensify those feelings now, do we?'

'No,' said the Kommandant who could well believe that Verkramp's problem had to do with guilt.

'I take it then, that you are absolutely satisfied with his work and feel that he has handled the situation with skill and an exceptional degree of conscientiousness. Is that correct?'

'Definitely,' said the Kommandant, 'he couldn't have done better if he had tried.'

'In that case I think it is quite all right for you to see him,' Dr von Blimenstein said and switched off the portable tape recorder on her desk. She got up and went down the passage followed by the Kommandant who was beginning to feel that he had in some subtle way been outmanoeuvred. After climbing several flights of stairs they came to yet another corridor. 'If you'll just wait here,' said the doctor, 'I'll go and tell him that you want to see him,' and leaving the Kommandant in a small waiting-room she went off to Verkramp's private room.

'We've got a visitor,' she announced gaily as Verkramp cringed in his bed.

'Who is it?' he asked weakly.

'Just an old friend,' she said. 'He just wants to ask you a few questions. Kommandant van Heerden.'

Verkramp assumed a new and dreadful pallor.

'Now there's no need to worry,' Dr von Blimenstein said, sitting down on the edge of the bed and taking his hand. 'You don't have to answer any questions unless you want to.'

'Well, I don't,' said Verkramp emphatically.

'Then you shan't,' she said, extracting a bottle from her pocket and a lump of sugar.

'What's that?' Verkramp asked nervously.

'Something to help you not to answer any questions, my darling,' said the doctor and popped the lump of sugar into his mouth. Verkramp chewed it up and lay back.

Ten minutes later the Kommandant who was trying to keep his temper at the long wait by reading a magazine about motor cars was horrified by the sound of screams coming from the corridor. It sounded as though one of the patients was enduring the torments of hell.

Dr von Blimenstein came into the room. 'He's ready to see you now,' she said, 'but I want to warn you that he's to be handled gently. This is one of his good days and we don't want to upset him do we?'

'No,' said the Kommandant trying to make himself heard above the demented shrieks. The doctor unlocked a door and the Kommandant peered very nervously inside. What he saw sent him hurriedly back into the corridor.

'No need to be alarmed,' said the doctor and pushed him into the room. 'Just put your questions to him gently and don't excite him.' She locked the door behind him and the Kommandant found himself alone in a small room with a screaming scurrying creature that had when the Kommandant could catch a glimpse of its face some of the features of Luitenant Verkramp. The thin nose, the fierce eyes and the angular shape were those of the Kommandant's second-in-command but there the resemblance ended. Verkramp didn't scream like that, in fact the Kommandant couldn't think what did. Verkramp didn't slobber like that, Verkramp didn't scurry sideways like that, and above all Verkramp didn't cling to the window bars like that.

As the Kommandant pressed himself terrified into a corner by the door he knew that he had made a wasted trip. Whatever else the day had taught him, one thing was quite sure: Luitenant Verkramp's insanity was unquestionable.

'Ugh, ugh, snow man balloon fill up baboon,' shrieked Verkramp and hurled himself from the window bars and disappeared under the bed still shrieking only to reappear precipitously scrabbling for the Kommandant's legs. The Kommandant kicked him off and Verkramp shot across the room and up the window bars. 'Let me out of here,' yelled the Kommandant and found himself beating on the door with a dementia that almost equalled that of Verkramp. An eye regarded him bleakly through the spy hole in the door.

'You're quite sure you've asked him all the questions you want to?' Dr von Blimenstein asked.

'Yes, yes,' shouted the Kommandant desperately.

'And there's no question of Balthazar being held responsible for what has happened?'

'Responsible?' screamed the Kommandant. 'Of course he's not responsible.' It seemed a totally unnecessary question to ask.

Dr von Blimenstein unlocked the door and the Kommandant staggered into the corridor. Behind him Verkramp was still gibbering from the window, his eyes alight with an intensity the Kommandant had no doubt was a sign of incurable insanity.

'One of his good days,' said the doctor, locking the door and leading the way back to her office.

'What did you say was the matter with him?' the Kommandant asked wondering what Verkramp's bad days were like.

'Mild depression brought on by overwork.'

'Good heavens,' said the Kommandant, 'I wouldn't have thought that was mild.'

'Ah but then you've had no experience of mental illness,' said the doctor. 'You judge these things from a lay position.'

'I wouldn't say that,' said the Kommandant. 'Do you think he'll ever recover?'

'Positive,' said the doctor. 'He'll be as right as rain in a few days time.'

Kommandant van Heerden deferred to her professional opinion and with a politeness that sprang from the conviction that she had a hopeless case on her hands thanked her for her help.

'If there's anything I can do at any time,' she told him, 'don't hesitate to call on me.'

With a silent prayer that he would never have to, the Kommandant left the hospital. In his room Luitenant Verkramp continued his trip. It was the first time he'd taken LSD.

CHAPTER THIRTEEN

If Kommandant van Heerden's visit to Fort Rapier Mental Hospital had given him a new and terrible insight into the irrational depths of the human psyche, his next appointment did nothing to remove the impression that everyone in Piemburg had changed for the worse in his absence. Certainly the thirty-six men who stumbled from their cells to receive the Kommandant's profound apologies and expressions of regret were no longer the upstanding and prominent public figures of a fortnight before. The Mayor, whom the Kommandant had decided to see first, couldn't reciprocate the process. His eyes were swollen and black as a result, the Security Sergeant told the Kommandant, of the suspect's having banged himself against the door knob of his cell. Since the cells weren't equipped with door knobs it didn't seem a likely explanation. The rest of the Mayor wasn't in much better shape. He had been kept standing for eight days with a bag over his head and hadn't been allowed to perform his private functions let alone his public ones in the manner to which his office entitled him. As a result he was distinctly soiled and suffering from the delusion that he was presiding at a Mayoral banquet.

'This has been a most unfortunate incident,' the Kommandant began, holding a handkerchief to his nose.

'I'm privileged to be here today in this august assembly,' mumbled the Mayor.

'I would like to proffer my . . .' said the Kommandant.

'Most sincere congratulations on . . .' the Mayor interrupted.

'For this unwarranted action,' said the Kommandant.

'It is not all of us who have the honour . . .'

'In keeping you under lock and key.'

'Serve the public to the best . . .'

'Won't happen again.'

'Look forward to . . .'

'Oh bugger me,' said the Kommandant who had lost track of the conversation. In the end, after being helped by three warders to sign a statement he couldn't even see, let alone read, to say that he had no complaints to make about the way he had been treated and thanking the police for their protection, the Mayor was carried out to a waiting ambulance and allowed to go home.

Several of the other detainees were less amenable to reason and one or two harboured the illusion that the Kommandant was merely a new and more sinister interrogator.

'I know what you want me to say,' the manager of Barclays Bank declared when he saw the Kommandant. 'All right I'll admit it. I am a member of the Anglican Church and a Communist.'

The Kommandant looked at the manager in some confusion. The manager's face was badly bruised and his ankles terribly swollen from standing so long.

'Are you really?' said the Kommandant doubtfully.

'No,' said the manager encouraged by this dubious note. 'I'm not. I hardly ever go to Church. Only when my wife insists and she's a Baptist.'

'I see,' said the Kommandant, 'but you are a Communist.'

'Oh my God,' wailed the manager, 'would I be a bank manager if I was a Communist?'

The Kommandant pushed the form indemnifying the police across the desk. 'I don't give a stuff what you are so long as you sign this form,' he said irritably. 'If you refuse I'm going to charge you with sabotage.'

'Sabotage,' croaked the manager in terror, 'but I haven't committed sabotage.'

'By your own admission you've peed in the Hluwe Dam and that constitutes sabotage in terms of the General Laws Amendment Act of 1962.'

'Peeing in a dam?'

'Polluting the public water supply. Carries the death penalty.' The manager signed the form and was helped out.

By the time the Kommandant had dealt to his own satisfaction with the detainees, it was already late at night and he was still faced with the intractable problem of the wave of bombings. True there had been no explosions since the ostriches had destroyed themselves and so many public buildings but public confidence would only be restored when the saboteurs were caught. The Kommandant left the prison and told Els to drive him back to the police station.

As he mounted the steps and passed the Duty desk where a konstabel was soliciting a man who had come in to complain that his car had been stolen, the Kommandant realized the enormity of the task before him. With a demoralized force of policemen he had to defend the city against saboteurs so well organized that they used police high-explosive for their bombings and who, apart from one dead man in the toilet of the Majestic Cinema, were wholly unidentifiable. It was a task that would have defeated a lesser man and Kommandant van Heerden had no illusions. He was a lesser man.

He ordered a mixed grill from a Greek café and sent for Sergeant Breitenbach.

'These secret agents that Verkramp was always talking about,' he said, 'do you know anything about them?'

'I think you'll find he lost touch with them,' said the Sergeant.

'Not the only thing he's lost touch with, I can tell you,' said the Kommandant with feeling. Verkramp's terrible antics were still fresh in his memory. 'Does anyone else know who they are?'

'No, sir.'

'There must be records,' said the Kommandant.

'Burnt, sir.'

'Burnt? Who burnt them?'

'Verkramp did when he went mad, sir.'

'What, the whole bloody lot?'

Sergeant Breitenbach nodded. 'He had a file called Operation Red Rout. I never saw what was in it but I know he burnt it the night the ostriches went off. They affected him badly, sir, those ostriches. He was a changed man after one exploded in the street out there.'

'Yes, well, that doesn't help us very much,' said the Kommandant, as he finished his mixed grill and wiped his mouth. 'You know,' he continued leaning back in his chair, 'there's been something puzzling me for a long time and that is, why did the Communists bug my house? Verkramp seemed to think they wanted to get something on me. Didn't seem likely. I don't do anything.'

'No sir,' said the Sergeant. He looked round the room rather nervously. 'Do you think Luitenant Verkramp will ever recover, sir?' he asked.

Kommandant van Heerden had no doubts on that score.

'Not a celluloid rat's chance in hell,' he said cheerfully. Sergeant Breitenbach looked relieved.

'In that case, I think you ought to know that those microphones weren't placed there by Communists, sir.' He paused to allow the implications of the remark to sink in.

'You mean . . .' said the Kommandant turning an alarming colour.

'Verkramp, sir,' said the Sergeant hurriedly.

'You mean that bastard bugged my house?' yelled the Kommandant. Sergeant Breitenbach nodded dumbly, and waited for the Kommandant's outburst to exhaust itself.

'He said he had orders from BOSS to do it, sir,' he said when the Kommandant calmed down a little.

'BOSS?' said the Kommandant. 'Orders from BOSS.' A new note of alarm in his voice.

'That's what he said, sir. I don't think he did though,' Sergeant Breitenbach told him.

'I see,' said the Kommandant trying to think why the Bureau of State Security should be so interested in his private life. The idea was not reassuring. People who interested BOSS frequently fell out of tenth-storey windows in Security Headquarters in Johannesburg.

'I think it was all part of his insanity, sir,' the Sergeant continued, 'part of his purity campaign.'

The Kommandant looked at him weakly.

'Dear God,' he said. 'Are you trying to tell me that all Verkramp's talk about Communist agents was simply an excuse to find out if I was having an affair?'

'Yes, sir,' said Sergeant Breitenbach desperately determined not to say whom the Kommandant was thought to be having an affair with.

'Well all I can say is that Verkramp's lucky to be in an insane asylum. If he weren't I'd have the bastard reduced to the ranks.'

'Yes sir,' said the Sergeant. 'No explosions tonight.' He was anxious to change the topic of conversation away from the Kommandant's private life. Kommandant van Heerden looked out through his glassless windows and sighed.

'None last night. None the night before. None since Verkramp went into the loony bin. Odd that, isn't it?' he said

'Very odd sir.'

'All the attacks coincided with Verkramp's being in charge,' continued the Kommandant. 'All the high-explosive came from the police armoury. Very odd indeed.'

'Are you thinking what I'm thinking?' asked the Sergeant.

Kommandant van Heerden looked at him intently.

'I'm not thinking about what I'm thinking and I'd advise you to do the same,' he said. 'It doesn't bear thinking about.' He relapsed into silence and considered the appalling prospect revealed by Sergeant Breitenbach's information. If there had been no Communist agents involved in the bugging of his house ... He stopped himself following that train of thought. And what was BOSS's interest in the business? Again it seemed a dangerous line to follow.

'Well, all I know is that we've got to produce those saboteurs in court and have them convicted or my job isn't going to be safe. There's going to be a public outcry about this and someone's got to stand on the scaffold.' He got up wearily. 'I'm going to bed,' he said, 'I've had enough for one day.'

'Just one more thing, sir, that I think you ought to consider,' said the Sergeant. 'I've been doing some calculations about the bombings.' He put a piece of paper in front of the Kommandant. 'If you look here you'll see that there were twelve explosions on each of the nights in question. Right?' Kommandant van Heerden nodded. 'The day before you left on holiday, Luitenant Verkramp ordered twelve new keys cut for the police armoury.' He paused and the Kommandant sat down again and held his head.

'Go on,' he said finally. 'Let's get it over.'

'Well, sir,' continued the Sergeant, 'I've been checking the men who picked up the messages from the secret agents and it begins to look as if there were twelve agents too.'

'Are you trying to tell me that Verkramp organized these attacks himself?' the Kommandant asked and knew that it was an unnecessary question. It was obvious what Sergeant Breitenbach thought.

'It begins to look like it, sir,' he said.

'But what the hell for? It doesn't make fucking sense,' shouted the Kommandant frantically.

'I think he was mad all the time, sir,' said the Sergeant.

'Mad?' shouted the Kommandant. 'Mad? He wasn't just mad. He was fucking insane.'

By the time Kommandant van Heerden got to bed that night he was almost insane himself. The extraordinary events of the day had taken their toll. As he passed a fitful night tossing and turning in his bed, images of exploding ostriches and homosexual policemen mingled disturbingly with Mrs Heathcote-Kilkoon clad in nothing but a top hat and boots riding an enormous black horse over a landscape pitted with bomb craters while Els smiled demonically in the background.

In Fort Rapier Mental Hospital the author of most of the Kommandant's misfortunes spent a pretty unpleasant night himself. True it wasn't as bad as the trip he'd been on during the day but it was bad enough to convince Dr von Blimenstein that she might have misjudged the strength of the dose she had given him.

Only Konstabel Els slept well. Ensconsed in Verkramp's flat which he was ostensibly guarding, he had found the Luitenant's stock of girlie magazines and having leafed through them had gone to sleep dreaming about Konstabel Botha whose yellow wig Els though most fetching. Once or twice he twitched in his sleep like a dog dreaming of a hunt. In the morning he got up and drove round to the Kommandant's house where muttered curses from the kitchen suggested that the Kommandant was not finding the editorial in the *Zululand Chronicle* much to his taste.

'I knew it, I knew it,' he shouted brandishing the offending article which accused the police of incompetence, the torture of innocent people and a general inability to maintain law and order. 'They'll be demanding a Court of Inquiry next. What the hell is this country coming to? How the hell do they expect me to maintain law and order when half my men are fucking fairies?'

Mrs Roussouw was shocked. 'Language,' she said tartly. 'Walls have ears.'

'And that's another thing,' snapped the Kommandant, 'do you realize I've been living in what amounts to an auditorium for the past month? This place has more bugs . . .'

But Mrs Roussouw had heard enough. 'I won't have you say that,' she said. Outside the window Konstabel Els grinned to himself and listened to the ensuing argument with a deepening sense of pleasure. By the time Kommandant van Heerden left the house Mrs Roussouw had been persuaded to stay on as housekeeper but only after the Kommandant had been forced to apologize for his criticism of her work.

At the police station another group of irate women were waiting for the Kommandant when he arrived.

'Deputation of policemen's wives, sir,' said Sergeant Breitenbach when the Kommandant had negotiated the stairs where the women were gathered.

'What the hell do they want?' the Kommandant demanded.

'It's to do with their husbands being queer,' the Sergeant explained. 'They've come to demand redress.'

'Redress?' squawked the Kommandant. 'Redress? How the hell can I redress them?'

'I don't think you quite understand,' said the Sergeant, 'they want you to do something about their husbands.'

'Oh, all right. Show them in,' said the Kommandant wearily. Sergeant Breitenbach left the room and presently the Kommandant found himself confronted by twelve large and clearly frustrated women.

'We've come here to register an official complaint,' said the largest lady who was evidently the spokesman for the group.

'Quite,' said the Kommandant, 'I quite understand.'

'I don't think you do,' said the woman. The Kommandant looked at her and thought that he did.

192

'I gather that this matter concerns your husbands,' he said.

'Exactly,' said the large woman. 'Our husbands have been subject to experiments which have deprived them of their manhood.'

The Kommandant wrote the complaint down on a piece of paper.

'I see,' he said, 'and what do you expect me to do about it?'

The large woman looked at him distastefully.

'We want this matter straightened out without delay,' she said. The Kommandant sat back and stared at her.

'Straightened out?'

'Yes,' said the large lady emphatically.

The Kommandant tried to think what to do. He decided to try flattery.

'I think the remedy is in your own hands,' he said with a suggestive smile. It was clearly the wrong thing to have said.

'How disgusting,' shouted the woman, 'how utterly revolting.'

Kommandant van Heerden turned bright red.

'No please,' he said, 'please ladies ...' but there was no holding the women.

'It'll be carrots and candles next,' shouted one woman.

'Ladies, you misunderstand me,' said the Kommandant desperately trying to calm them down. 'All I meant was that if you'll only get together...'

In the pandemonium that ensued Kommandant van Heerden could be heard saying that he was sure that if they took a firm stand and all pulled together ...

'For God's sake take a grip on yourselves,' he yelled as the women stood round his desk shouting. Sergeant Breitenbach entered the room and with the help of two heterosexual konstabels restored order.

In the end a distinctly dishevelled Kommandant told the ladies that he would do what he could.

'You may rest assured that I shall bend over backwards to see that your husbands return to their conjugal duties,' he said and the women filed out of the office. On the stairs Konstabel Els asked several of them if he could be of any assistance and made three appointments for the evening. When they had all left the Kommandant asked Sergeant Breitenbach to have photographs of nude men taken.

'We'll have to do the thing in reverse,' he said.

'Black men or white men, sir?'

'Both,' said the Kommandant, 'we don't want any more cock-ups.'

'Don't you think we ought to get the advice of a proper psychiatrist?' the Sergeant inquired.

Kommandant van Heerden considered the matter.

'Where do you think Verkramp got the idea from in the first place?' he asked.

'He had been reading a book by a professor called Ice Ink.'

'Sounds a funny sort of name for a professor,' said the Kommandant.

'Sounds a funny sort of professor,' said the Sergeant, 'and I still think we ought to get a proper psychiatrist to help.'

'I suppose so,' the Kommandant agreed doubtfully. The only psychiatrist he knew was Dr von Blimenstein and he was wary of asking her for assistance.

By the end of the morning he had revised his opinion. A deputation of Piemburg's businessmen had been to see him with a view to forming a group of vigilantes to assist the police in their so far fruitless efforts to protect life and property from the terrorists and the Kommandant had received several summonses from lawyers alleging that their clients, namely the Mayor and thirty-five other prominent citizens, had been illegally detained and tortured. To cap it all he had received a telephone call from the Commissioner of Police in Zululand demanding the immediate apprehension of the men responsible for the sabotage attacks.

'I hold you personally responsible, van Heerden,' shouted the Commissioner who had been looking for an excuse to demote the Kommandant for years. 'Understand that. Personally responsible for what has occurred. Either we have some action or I'll be asking for your resignation. Understand?'

The Kommandant understood and put down the receiver with the look of a very large rat in a very tight corner.

In the next half hour the consequences of the Commissioner's threat began to make themselves felt.

'I don't care who they are,' shouted the Kommandant at Sergeant Breitenbach, 'I want every group of eleven men arrested on sight.'

'What, even the Mayor and the Aldermen?' asked the Sergeant.

'No,' screamed the Kommandant. 'Not the Mayor and the Aldermen but every other suspicious group.'

As usual Sergeant Breitenbach equivocated.

'I think that would be asking for trouble, sir,' he pointed out.

'Trouble?' yelled the Kommandant. 'What do you think we've got already? It's my neck that's on the block and if you think I'm going to give that fucking Commissioner the opportunity to lop it off you've got another think coming.'

'It's BOSS I'm thinking about, sir,' said the Sergeant.

'BOSS?'

'Luitenant Verkramp's agents were presumably men from the Bureau of State Security in Pretoria, sir. If we arrested them I don't think BOSS would appreciate it.'

The Kommandant looked frantically at him.

'Well what the hell do you want me to do?' he asked with a growing sense of hysteria. 'The Commissioner tells me to arrest the men who did the bombings. You tell me that I'll have BOSS up in arms if I do. What the fuck can I do?'

Sergeant Breitenbach had no idea. In the end the Kommandant countermanded his orders to arrest all groups of eleven men and dismissing the Sergeant sat at his desk confronted with a problem that seemed insoluble.

Ten minutes later he had arrived at a solution and he was about to send Els down to the cells to collect eleven black prisoners who were going to blow themselves up in a stolen car filled with police gelignite as proof that the South African Police in general and Kommandant van Heerden in particular could act with speed and efficiency against Communist saboteurs when it occurred to him that the scheme had a flaw. The men seen feeding the ostriches had all been white. With a curse the Kommandant returned to the problem.

'Verkramp must be insane,' he muttered for the umpteenth

time and was just considering the nature of the Luitenant's insanity when he came up with a brilliant solution.

Picking up the phone, the Kommandant rang Dr von Blimenstein and made an appointment to see her after lunch.

'You want me to do what?' Dr von Blimenstein asked when the Kommandant made his suggestion to her. She moved to switch the tape recorder on but the Kommandant reached over and unplugged it.

'You don't seem to understand,' said the Kommandant with a grim determination to get the doctor to see reason. 'You can either co-operate with me or I'll have Verkramp out of here and charge him with wilful destruction of public property and sabotage and he'll stand trial.'

'But you can't possibly expect me to . . .' said the doctor moving towards the door. With a sudden swiftness she jerked it open only to find herself face to face with Konstabel Els. She closed the door hurriedly and came back into the room.

'This is outrageous,' she protested. Kommandant van Heerden smiled horridly.

'You can't arrest my Balthazar,' continued the doctor trying to maintain some fortitude in the face of that smile. 'Why only yesterday you told me that he had handled the whole affair very skilfully and with an exceptional degree of conscientiousness.'

'Skilfully?' bawled the Kommandant. 'Skilfully? I'll tell you how skilful that bastard has been. Your fucking Balthazar has been responsible for the biggest outbreak of sabotage this country has ever seen. Why, compared with him the guerrillas on the Zambesi are playing soldiers. He's been personally responsible for the destruction of four road bridges, two railway lines, a transformer, the telephone exchange, four petrol storage tanks, one gasometer, five thousand acres of sugar cane and a radio mast and you have the nerve to tell me he's been skilful.'

Dr von Blimenstein slumped into her chair and stared at him.

'You've got no proof,' she whimpered finally. 'And besides he's not well.'

Kommandant van Heerden leant across the desk and leered into her face. 'Well?' he asked. 'Well? By the time the hangman's through with him he'll look a bloody sight worse, believe me.'

Dr von Blimenstein did believe him. She shut her eyes and shook her head to rid herself of the Kommandant's leer and the dreadful vision of her fiancé on the gallows. Satisfied that he had made his point the Kommandant relaxed.

. 'After all it's only doing what the poor fellows tried to do themselves and failed,' he explained. 'It's not as though we're asking them to go against their own natural inclinations.'

Dr von Blimenstein opened her eyes and looked at him imploringly.

'But Balthazar and I are engaged to get married,' she said.

It was Kommandant van Heerden's turn to be shocked. The idea of the bosomy doctor married to the apelike creature he had seen scampering about his cell the day before took his breath away. He began to understand the look of abject terror he had seen in Verkramp's eyes.

'Congratulations,' he muttered. 'In that case there's all the more reason for you to do what I'm suggesting.'

Dr von Blimenstein nodded miserably, 'I suppose so,' she said.

'Now then, let's get down to details,' said the Kommandant. 'You will arrange to have eleven patients with a record of suicide attempts placed in an isolation ward. You will then use your perversion therapy to indoctrinate them with Marxist-Leninist ideas . . .'

'But that's impossible,' said the doctor, 'you can't use aversion therapy to give people ideas. You can only cure them of habits.'

'That's what you think,' the Kommandant told her. 'You want to come and look what ideas your Balthazar has managed to give my konstabels. He hasn't cured them of any habits, I can tell you.'

Dr von Blimenstein tried another tack. 'But I don't know anything about Marxist-Leninism,' she said.

'That's a pity,' said the Kommandant and tried to think of someone who did. The only person he knew was serving a twenty-five year sentence in Piemburg Prison.

'Never mind about that,' he said finally, 'I'll arrange for someone to come here who does.'

'And then what are you going to do?' the doctor asked.

Kommandant van Heerden smiled. 'I think you can safely leave the rest to me,' he said and got up. As he left the office he turned and thanked the doctor for her cooperation.

'Remember it's all for the good of Balthazar,' he said and followed by Konstabel Els went out to his car. In her office Dr von Blimenstein considered the terrible task the Kommandant had given her. 'I suppose it's only another form of euthanasia,' she thought and began to draw up a list of suitably suicidal patients. Dr von Blimenstein had always agreed with the form of mental treatment meted out in the Third Reich.

The same could hardly be said of the man in Piemburg Prison who was the next person the Kommandant visited. Sentenced to twenty-five years for his part in the Rivonia conspiracy, about which he had in fact known nothing, Aaron Geisenheimer had spent six years in solitary confinement consoling himself with the thought that a revolution was about to take place which would bring him if not into his own at least out of someone else's – that thought and the Bible, which, thanks to the religious policy of the prison authorities, was the only book the lapsed Jew was allowed to read. Since Aaron Geisenheimer had spent his youth in an obsessive study of the works of Marx, Engels and Lenin and since too he came of a long line of rabbinical scholars, it was hardly surprising that after six years of more or less enforced acquaintanceship with the Holy Writ he was now a mine of scriptural information. He was also no fool, as the prison chaplain knew to his cost. The Chaplain would emerge from Isolation Cell Two after an hour of Christian counselling with Geisenheimer in some doubt as to the divinity of Christ and with a tendency to think of *Das Kapital* as coming somewhere between Chronicles 1 and the Song of Solomon. To make matters worse, Aaron Geisenheimer supplemented his daily ration of thirty minutes in the exercise yard by attending every possible service in the prison chapel where his critical presence forced the Chaplain to raise the intellectual standards of his sermons to the point where they were totally unintelligible to the rest of the congregation while still open to considerable criticism from the Marxist. In the light of the Chaplain's complaints the Governor of the Prison was delighted to hear that Kommandant van Heerden was considering having Geisenheimer transferred to Fort Rapier.

'Do what you like with the bastard,' Governor Schnapps told the Kommandant, 'I'll be glad to get him off my hands. He's even got some of my warders wearing Maoist badges.'

The Kommandant thanked him and went down to Isolation Cell Two where the prisoner was deep in Amos.

'It says here "Therefore the prudent shall keep silence in that time; for it is an evil time,"' Geisenheimer told him when the Kommandant asked if he had any complaints.

Kommandant van Heerden looked round the cell. 'A bit short of space in here,' he said. 'Not room to swing a cat.'

'Yes, there is that to be said for it,' said Geisenheimer.

'Like to move to more spacious accommodation?' the Kommandant inquired.

'*Timeo Danaos et dona ferentis*,' said Geisenheimer.

'Don't you talk Kitchen Kaffir to me,' the Kommandant yelled. 'I asked you if you would like bigger accommodation.'

'No,' said Geisenheimer.

'Why the hell not?' asked the Kommandant.

'It says here "As if a man did flee from a lion, and a bear met him; or went into the house, and leaned his hand on the wall, and a serpent bit him." It seems a sensible point of view.'

Kommandant van Heerden didn't want to take issue with Amos but he was still puzzled.

'Must get a bit lonely here at times,' he said.

Geisenheimer shrugged.

'I believe it's a characteristic of solitary confinement,' he said philosophically.

The Kommandant went back to Governor Schnapps and told him that there was no doubt in his mind that Geisenheimer was out of his. That afternoon the Marxist was transferred to a ward in Fort Rapier Mental Hospital where he found eleven other beds and the complete works of Marx and Lenin kindly supplied by the confiscated books department of the Piemburg Police Station. As the Kommandant delivered them to Dr von Blimenstein he was reminded of the aversion therapy for the homosexual konstabels.

'One other thing,' he said when the doctor explained that

she had had eleven suitable suicides lined up, 'I'd be glad if you'd drop by the Drill Hall this afternoon. I want some advice about getting some queers back to normal.'

CHAPTER FOURTEEN

As the Kommandant drove down to the Drill Hall where Sergeant Breitenbach had assembled two hundred and ten protesting konstabels, he felt pleased with the way things were turning out. Certainly there were still difficulties ahead but at least a start had been made in getting things back to normal. It would take a day or two to get the suicides ready for their arrest and the Kommandant still hadn't made up his mind exactly how to go about it. Studying the back of Konstabel Els' head once again he found consolation in its shape and colour. What human ingenuity and design could not accomplish in the way of destroying inconvenient evidence, Konstabel Els through chance and unthinking malice could, and the Kommandant had frequently cherished the hope that Els would include himself in the process. It seemed unlikely somehow. Chance, it appeared, favoured the Konstabel. It certainly didn't favour those with whom he came into contact and the Kommandant had little doubt that Els would bungle the arrest of the eleven patients to an extent that would eliminate any subsequent attempts to prove them innocent.

By the time they reached the Drill Hall Kommandant van Heerden was in a more cheerful frame of mind. The same could not be said for the two hundred and ten konstabels who were objecting to the idea of undergoing aversion therapy for the second time.

'You've no idea what we might come out as this time, sweetie,' one of them told Sergeant Breitenbach, 'I mean you simply don't know, do you?'

Sergeant Breitenbach had to admit that in the light of what had happened previously he didn't.

'You couldn't be worse than you are,' he said with feeling.

'I don't know,' simpered the konstabel, 'we might be absolute animals.'

'It's a chance I'm prepared to take,' said the Sergeant.

'And what about us, dear? What about us? I mean it's not much fun not knowing what you're going to be from one moment to the next, is it? It's upsetting, that's what it is.'

'What about all the gear we've bought, too?' said another konstabel. 'Cost a small fortune. Bras and panties and all. They won't take it back you know.'

Sergeant Breitenbach shuddered and was just wondering how he was ever going to get them into the hall when the Kommandant arrived and relieved him of the responsibility.

'I'll appeal to their patriotism,' he said looking with evident distaste at Konstabel Botha's wig. He collected a loudhailer and addressed the queers.

'Men,' he shouted. His voice, resonant with doubt, boomed out over the parade ground and into the city. 'Men of the South African Police, I realize that the experience you have lately undergone is not one that you wish to repeat. I can only say that it is in the interest of the country as a whole that I have ordered this new treatment which will turn you back into the fine upstanding body of men you once were. This time a trained psychiatrist will supervise the treatment and there will be no balls-up.' Loud laughter interrupted the Kommandant at this point and a particularly oafish konstabel who appeared to be wearing false eyelashes winked suggestively at him. Kommandant van Heerden, already exhausted by the swift turn of events, lost his cool.

'Listen, you shower of filth,' he screamed voicing his true opinions with an amplification that could be heard two miles away, 'I've seen some arse-bandits in my time but nothing to equal you. A more disgusting lot of gobblers and moffies it's never been my misfortune to meet. By the time I've finished with you I'll have you back to fucking normal.' He singled out the konstabel with the false eyelashes for personal abuse and was just telling him that he'd never look another sphincter in the face without coming over all queer when Dr von Blimenstein arrived and restored order. As the doctor walked slowly but significantly towards them, the konstabels fell silent and eyed her large frame with respect.

'If you don't mind, Kommandant,' she said as the Kommandant's blood pressure fluttered down to something approaching normal, 'I think I'll try a different approach.' Kommandant van Heerden handed her the loudhailer and a moment later her dulcet tones were echoing across the parade ground.

'Boys,' said the doctor using a more appropriate epithet, 'I want you all to think of me,' she paused seductively, 'as a friend, not as someone to be afraid of.' A tremor of nervous excitation ran down the ranks. The prospect of being a friend of someone so redolent of frustrated sex, whatever its gender, obviously appealed to the konstabels. As Doctor von Blimenstein continued her talk the Kommandant turned away satisfied that everything was under control now that the doctor's magnetic hermaphroditism was exerting its influence over the queers. He found Sergeant Breitenbach in the drill hall checking the transformer.

'What a horrible woman,' said the Sergeant. Dr von Blimenstein was telling the konstabels about the pleasures they could expect from heterosexual intercourse.

'The future Mrs Verkramp,' said the Kommandant lugubriously. 'He's proposed to her.' He left the Sergeant mulling over this fresh proof of Verkramp's insanity to deal with another problem. A deputation of ministers from the Dutch Reformed Church had arrived to add their objections to those of the konstabels.

The Kommandant shepherded them into an office at the back of the hall and waited until Dr von Blimenstein had got her patients seated before discussing the problem with the black-coated ministers.

'You have no right to tamper with man's nature,' the Rev Schlachbals said when the doctor arrived. 'God has made us what we are and you are interfering with his work.'

'God didn't make all these men poofters,' said the doctor, her language confirming the minister's opinion that she was the instrument of the devil. 'Man did and man must put the mistake right.'

Kommandant van Heerden nodded in agreement. He thought she had put the case very well. The Rev Schlachbals clearly didn't.

'If man can turn decent young Christians into homosexuals by scientific means,' he insisted, 'the next step will be to turn blacks into whites and then where will we be? The whole of Western Civilization and Christianity in South Africa is at stake.'

Kommandant van Heerden nodded again. It was obvious that the minister had a point. Dr von Blimenstein didn't think so.

'You clearly misunderstand the nature of behavioural psychology,' she explained. 'All we are doing is rectifying mistakes that have been made. We are not altering essential characteristics.'

'You're not trying to tell me that these young men are essentially, er . . . homosexual,' said the dominie. 'You're impugning the moral foundations of our entire community.'

Dr von Blimenstein refused to admit it.

'What absolute nonsense,' she said. 'All I'm saying is that aversion therapy can exert a degree of moral pressure which nothing else can match.'

Kommandant van Heerden, who had been giving some thought to the matter of turning blacks into whites by electric shocks, butted in to point out that if that were the case thousands of blacks would already be white.

'We're always giving them electric shocks,' he said. 'It's part of our normal interrogation procedure.'

The Rev Schlachbals wasn't impressed. 'That's quite different, punishment is good for the soul,' he said. 'What the doctor is doing is tampering with God's work.'

'Are you trying to tell me that God ordained that these konstabels should remain fairies?' the Kommandant asked.

'Certainly not,' said the minister, 'all I'm saying is that she has no right to use scientific means to change them. That can only be accomplished by moral effort on our part. What is needed is prayer. I shall go in to the hall and kneel down . . .'

'You do that,' said the Kommandant, 'and I won't be held responsible for what happens.'

'. . . and pray for the forgiveness of sins,' continued the minister.

In the end it was agreed that the two approaches to the problem should be tried at the same time. Dr von Blimenstein would proceed with the aversion therapy while the Rev Schlachbals conducted a religious service in the hope of effecting a spiritual conversion. The joint effort was entirely successful, though it took the Rev Schlachbals some time to accommodate himself to the prospect of leading the congregation in 'Rock of Ages Cleft for Me' to the accompaniment of slides depicting nude males of both races projected twice lifesize above his head. To begin with the congregation's singing was pretty ragged too but Dr von Blimenstein soon picked up the beat and pressed the shock button most emphatically whenever a particularly high note was called for. Strapped to their chairs, the two hundred and ten konstabels gave vent to their feelings with a fervour the minister found most rewarding.

'It's a long time since I've known a congregation to be so enthusiastic,' he told the Rev Diederichs, who took over from him after three hours.

'God works in a mysterious way,' said the Rev Diederichs.

In Fort Rapier Aaron Geisenheimer was having much the same thought though in his case it was not so much God as the process of history whose ways were so mysterious. The arrival of eleven patients whose intelligence was proclaimed by the fact that the political situation in South Africa had prompted them all to attempt suicide without being foolish enough to succeed gave the eminent Marxist food for thought. So did the attitude of the hospital authorities, who put no obstacle in the way of his lecturing them on the intricacies of dialectical materialism but seemed anxious that he should. Mulling over this extraordinary change in his fortune he came to the conclusion that the police were anxious to obtain fresh evidence for a new trial though why they should want to increase a life sentence any further he could not imagine. Whatever their motives he decided to afford them no opportunity and resolutely refrained from discussing Communism with his new companions. Instead, to give vent to his need for conversation which had been compulsive enough before his confinement and hadn't been improved by six years in solitary, he instructed the eleven men in Biblical history to such good effect that within a week he had rid them all of their suicidal tendencies and had turned them into convinced Christians.

'Goddammit,' snarled the Kommandant inconsequentially when Dr von Blimenstein told him that Geisenheimer wasn't cooperating. 'You'd think the bastard would be only too glad to poison their minds with Marxism. We can't have twelve ardent Christians in the dock.'

'Oh, I don't know,' said the doctor, 'after all you did have the Dean of Johannesburg.'

'That was different,' the Kommandant told her, 'he was a Communist.' He tried to think of some way round the problem. 'Can't you hypnotize the swine or something?'

Dr von Blimenstein could not see what good that would do.

'Tell them to wake up Communists,' said the Kommandant. 'You can do anything with hypnotism. I once saw a hypnotist turn a man into a plank and sit on him.'

Dr von Blimenstein said it was different with ideas.

'You can't make people do things that they wouldn't want to do in their ordinary life. You can't make them act against their own moral sense.'

'I don't suppose that bloke wanted to be a plank,' said the Kommandant, 'not in ordinary life anyway, and as for moral sense I should have thought your suicides have a great deal in common with Communists. All the Communists I've met have wanted to give the vote to the blacks and if that isn't suicidal, tell me what is.'

He left her with the warning that something had to be done quickly. 'Pretoria will be sending down a team of investigators shortly and then we'll all be in the shit,' he said.

Later the same day he had the same trouble with the Rev Schlachbals this time over the introduction of nude women into the treatment for the queers.

'That doctor wants to bring girls up here from the strip clubs in Durban and parade them up and down in front of the boys,' the Rev Schlachbals complained. 'She says she wants to test their reactions. I won't stand for it.'

'It seems a good idea to me,' said the Kommandant.

The Rev Schlachbals looked at him disapprovingly.

'That is as maybe,' he said, 'but it's too much for me. I've stood for men but naked ladies are another matter.'

'Have it your own way,' said the Kommandant. The Rev Schlachbals blushed.

'I don't mean what you mean,' he said and walked out.

The Kommandant gave Dr von Blimenstein permission to go ahead with the test and later in the day several blowsy girls from Durban went through their routine in front of the konstabels while Sergeant Breitenbach went along the rows with a swagger stick making sure that everyone responded properly.

'All present and erect, sir,' he said when he had finished.

Kommandant van Heerden thanked the doctor for her assistance and accompanied her to her car.

'It's been no trouble,' said the doctor, 'I found the whole experience most valuable. It's not every woman can say she's had such a stimulating effect on two hundred and ten men at the same time.'

'Two hundred and eleven, doctor,' said the Kommandant with unusual gallantry and left the doctor with the impression that she had made a conquest. He had just caught sight of Els who was apparently about to rape one of the chorus girls.

'Amazing woman,' said Sergeant Breitenbach, 'I don't envy Verkramp's chances with her.'

'That's one marriage that wasn't made in heaven,' said the Kommandant.

At White Ladies Mrs Heathcote-Kilkoon had come to much the same conclusion about her own marriage to the Colonel. Ever since her brief taste of happiness in the dell, her thoughts had turned again and again to the Kommandant. So had the Colonel's.

'Damned man comes here, ruins my best roses, flogs an expensive horse to death, pollutes a tank of tropical fish, poisons poor Willy and finally goes off with a damned good whipper-in,' he said irritably.

'I had rather a soft spot for Harbinger,' said La Marquise tenderly.

For the most part though, the Kommandant's visit was forgotten and the brief glimpse of fearful reality his presence had given to the members of the Dornford Yates Club lent a new and frenetic gaiety to their efforts to evoke the past. They drove over to Swaziland to gamble at the casino at Piggs Peak in memory of Berry's great coup at San Sebastian in *Jonah & Co.* where he had won four thousand nine hundred and ninety-five pounds. Colonel Heathcote-Kilkoon lost forty before giving up and driving home through a thunderstorm trying to maintain an insouciance he didn't feel. They went racing but again without luck. The Colonel made a point of backing only black horses in memory of Chaka.

'Blue-based baboon,' he said in a voice that carried his unique blend of Inner Circle County across the heads of the crowd. 'That damned jockey was pulling.'

'We should organize our own races, Berry,' said the fat man. 'There was a car race in *Jonah & Co.*'

'By Jove, I do believe he's right,' said La Marquise who was doubling as Piers, Duke of Padua.

'The cars were called Ping and Pong,' Major Bloxham said. 'And the race was from Angoulême to Pau. It was two hundred and twenty miles.'

Next day the dusty roads of Zululand saw the great race from Weezen to Dagga and back and by nightfall the Colonel, as Berry, had made good his losses of the previous days. Admittedly Weezen was hardly Angoulême and Dagga's resemblance to Pau was limited to a view of distant mountains but the Club made good these deficiencies in their own imaginations and by driving with a wholly authentic disregard for other road users. Even Berry & Co. could hardly have complained and among other trophies the Colonel collected two goats and a guinea fowl. In the back seat of the Rolls Mrs Heathcote-Kilkoon did her best to be Daphne but her heart wasn't in it. Much the same could be said for the Duke of Padua, who insisted that the fat man stop at Sjambok while she bought an inflatable ring. That night Mrs Heathcote-Kilkoon told the Colonel she was going down to Piemburg next morning.

'Another perm, eh?' said the Colonel. 'Well don't overdo things. It's Berry Puts Off His Manhood night tomorrow.'

'Yes dear,' said Mrs Heathcote-Kilkoon.

The next day she was up early and on her way to Piemburg. As the great car slid down the Rooi Nek, Mrs Heathcote-Kilkoon felt free and strangely youthful. Chin in air, eyebrows raised, lids lowered, the faintest of smiles hovering about her small red mouth, she leaned back with an indescribable air of easy efficiency which was most attractive. Only the parted lips at all betrayed her eagerness . . .

She was still in a playful mood when she was shown into the Kommandant's office by Sergeant Breitenbach.

'My darling,' she said as soon as the door was shut, and skipped across the room a vision of elegance in mauve silk.

'For God's sake,' spluttered the Kommandant, unwinding her arms from his neck.

'I had to come, I couldn't wait,' said Mrs Heathcote-Kilkoon.

Kommandant van Heerden looked frantically round his office. Something about shitting on one's own doorstep was on the tip of his tongue but he managed not to say it. Instead he asked after the Colonel.

Mrs Heathcote-Kilkoon reclined in a chair. 'He's absolutely furious with you,' she said. Kommandant van Heerden went pale.

'You can't blame him, can you?' she continued. 'I mean, think how you'd feel in his position.'

The Kommandant didn't have to think how he'd feel. He knew.

'What's he going to do?' he asked anxiously, the vision of the cuckold Colonel shooting him looming large in his mind. 'Has he got a gun?'

Mrs Heathcote-Kilkoon leant back and laughed. 'Has he got a gun? My dear, he's got an arsenal,' she said. 'Haven't you seen his armoury?'

The Kommandant sat down hurriedly and got up almost at once. Coming on top of the terrible position Verkramp had put him in, this new threat not only to his position but to his life was the last straw. Mrs Heathcote-Kilkoon sensed his feelings.

'I shouldn't have come,' she said taking the words out of the Kommandant's mouth. 'But I simply had to tell you . . .'

'As if I hadn't got enough fucking trouble on my hands without this,' snarled the Kommandant, his instinct for survival sweeping away what few pretensions he had previously maintained in her company. Mrs Heathcote-Kilkoon adjusted her language to his mood.

'Doesn't Doodoo love his mummy any more?' she cooed.

With rare good taste the Kommandant shuddered.

'Of course he does,' he snapped, taking refuge in the third person from the threat of extinction doodoos brought to mind. He was about to say that he had enough on his fucking plate without jealous husbands when there was a knock on the door and Sergeant Breitenbach entered.

'Urgent telegram for Verkramp, sir,' he said. 'From BOSS. I thought you'd want to see it.' The Kommandant snatched the message from him and stared at it.

'INSTANT EXPLANATION SAB STROKE SUBV PIEMBURG STOP URGENT CARR STROKE INTERRO COMBLIBS STOP DETAIL ACTION STOP SAB STOKE SUBV BOSS TEAM FOLLOWING,' he read and stared at the Sergeant uncomprehendingly. 'What the hell does it mean?' he asked.

Sergeant Breitenbach glanced meaningfully at Mrs Heathcote-Kilkoon.

'Never mind her,' shouted the Kommandant, 'tell me what the thing means.'

Sergeant Breitenbach looked at the telegram.

'Instant explication sabotage subversion Piemburg stop Urgent arrest interrogation Communists and Liberals stop Detail action taken stop Sabotage subversion team from Bureau of State Security following.'

'Oh my God,' moaned the Kommandant for whom the news that a team of investigators from BOSS was on its way came as the final death knell. 'Now what do we do?'

In her chair Mrs Heathcote-Kilkoon sat listening with a sense of being at the heart of the action, where decisions of far-reaching moment were made and real men made up real minds to do real things. It was a strangely exhilarating experience. The gulf between fantasy and fact which years of reading Dornford Yates and playing Daphne to the Colonel's Berry across the dark continent had created in her mind suddenly closed. This was it, whatever it was, and Mrs Heathcote-Kilkoon, so long excluded from It, wanted to be part of It.

'If only I could help you,' she said melodramatically as the door closed behind Sergeant Breitenbach, who had just admitted he couldn't.

'How?' said the Kommandant who wanted to be left alone to think of someone he could arrest before the BOSS team arrived.

'I could be your glamorous spy,' she said.

'We're not short of glamorous spies,' said the Kommandant shortly, 'what we need are suspects.'

'What sort of suspects?'

'Eleven bloody lunatics who know how to use high explosive and hate Afrikanerdom enough to want to put the clock back a thousand years,' said the Kommandant morosely, and was surprised to see Mrs Heathcote-Kilkoon tilt back her lovely head and laugh.

'What's the matter now?' he asked feeling pretty hysterical himself.

'Oh how frightfully funny,' Mrs Heathcote-Kilkoon shrieked. 'How absolutely priceless. Do you realize what you've just said?'

'No,' said the Kommandant as the tinted curls tossed delightfully.

'Don't you see? The Club. Eleven lunatics. Boy, Berry, Jonah ... Oh it's too gorgeous.'

Kommandant van Heerden sat down at his desk, the light of understanding glazing his bloodshot eyes. As Mrs Heathcote-Kilkoon's laughter amazed Sergeant Breitenbach in the next room and awoke in Konstabel Els memories of other days and other places, Kommandant van Heerden knew that his troubles were over.

'Two birds with one stone,' he muttered and pressed the bell for Sergeant Breitenbach.

Twenty minutes later Mrs Heathcote-Kilkoon, somewhat astonished by her rapid dismissal from the Kommandant's office but still chortling over her joke, was at the hairdresser's.

'I think I'll have a black rinse for a change,' she told the assistant with an intuitive sense of occasion.

CHAPTER FIFTEEN

In the Drill Hall, so recently the scene of sexual conversion, Kommandant van Heerden briefed his men.

'The saboteurs are based on a house called White Ladies near Weezen,' he told the assembled officers. 'They are led by an ex-Colonel in the British secret service, one of their top men who served in the inner circle of the underground during the war. His second-in-command is a Major Bloxham and the sabotage group has used as its cover a club organized ostensibly for literary purposes. They are in possession of a considerable quantity of arms and ammunition and I anticipate fierce resistance when we surround the house.'

'How do we know they are the men we are after?' Sergeant Scheepers of the Security Branch asked.

'I realize that this may come as something of a surprise to you, Sergeant,' the Kommandant answered with a smile. 'But we of the uniformed police also have our agents in the field. You Security Branch fellows aren't the only ones to work undercover.' He paused to let this information sink in. 'For the past year Konstabel Els has been working in the Weezen area at considerable risk to himself and disguised as a convict.' Standing to one side of the Kommandant Konstabel Els blushed modestly. 'Thanks to his efforts we were able to infiltrate the Communist organization. Furthermore,' he added before anyone could point out that Konstabel Els was hardly a reliable witness, 'over the past two weeks I have investigated the matter personally and on the spot. I have confirmed Konstabel Els' findings and can vouch for the fact that these people are all avowed enemies of the Republic, maintain unquestioning loyalty to Britain and are utterly ruthless. An attempt was made to kill me while out riding.'

'Is there any other evidence that these men are responsible for the sabotage attacks in Piemburg?' Sergeant Breitenbach asked.

The Kommandant nodded. 'A very good question, Sergeant,' he said. 'In the first place Konstabel Els will go into the witness box and give evidence that he frequently heard the Colonel and his associates discussing the need for a change of government in South Africa. Secondly Els will swear that on the nights the attacks took place the group left the house early and didn't get to bed until dawn. Thirdly and most significantly, a member of the group has turned State's witness and will give evidence that these allegations are all correct. Does that satisfy you, Sergeant?'

'It all seems rather circumstantial, sir,' said Sergeant Breitenbach doubtfully. 'I mean is there any hard evidence?'

'Yes,' said the Kommandant emphatically and rummaging in his pocket produced a small object. 'Have any of you seen one of these?' he asked. It was clear that everyone in the room had seen a police detonator. 'Good,' continued the Kommandant. 'Well, this was found in the stables at White Ladies.'

'By Konstabel Els?' Sergeant Breitenbach inquired.

'By me,' said the Kommandant, and made a mental note to send Els ahead with a police van filled to the roof with gelignite, fuses, detonators and contraceptives to ensure that enough hard evidence to satisfy Sergeant Breitenbach was there when the rest of the force arrived. In the meantime he explained the layout of the house and garden and ordered a full force of Saracen armoured cars, two hundred policemen armed with Sterling machine guns, German guard dogs and Dobermann Pinschers to be deployed.

'Remember we are dealing with professional killers,' he said finally. 'These fellows aren't amateurs.'

By the time Mrs Heathcote-Kilkoon emerged suitably washed, set and permed from the hairdressers she was just in time to see the convoy led by five Saracen armoured cars grinding through the main street. She stood for a moment gazing at the policemen crowding the lorries and admiration for the Kommandant's obvious efficiency swelled in her breast. As the

212

last lorry containing German guard dogs disappeared round the corner she turned and walked back to the police station to tell him once again how much she had missed him, an opinion confirmed by the Sergeant at the Duty desk.

'But where has he gone?' she asked plaintively.

'Sorry, ma'am,' said the Sergeant, 'I'm not allowed to tell you.'

'But isn't there any way I can find out?'

'Well if you follow that convoy, I daresay you'll find him,' said the Sergeant and Mrs Heathcote-Kilkoon went out into the street disappointed and rather hungry. To console herself she went into Lorna's Causerie in Dirk's Arcade and had a pot of tea and some cup cakes.

I'll try again later, she thought. He can't have gone far. But when an hour later she went round to the police station again it was to learn that the Kommandant wouldn't be returning until the following day.

'How extraordinary, you'd think he would have told me,' she said exuding an aura of middle-class charm that had subdued stronger men than the Duty Sergeant.

'This mustn't go any further,' he told her confidingly, 'but they've gone up to Weezen.'

'On manoeuvres?' asked Mrs Heathcote-Kilkoon hopefully.

'To get those saboteurs,' said the Sergeant.

'In Weezen?'

'That's right,' the Sergeant said, 'but don't tell anyone I told you.'

Mrs Heathcote-Kilkoon said she certainly wouldn't and went out into the street astonished by this new turn of events. She was half-way back to the Rolls when the full realization of what she had done dawned on her.

'Oh my God,' she wailed and ran the rest of the way to the Rolls only to find that she'd left the keys somewhere. She searched her bag but the keys weren't there. In a state of utter distraction she ran back to the hairdresser's and came out five minutes later empty-handed. As she stood in the street despairingly a taxi drew up.

Mrs Heathcote-Kilkoon jumped in. 'To Weezen and fast,' she said. The driver turned round and shook his head.

'That's seventy miles,' he said. 'Can't do it.'

'I'll pay you double fare,' Mrs Heathcote-Kilkoon said frantically and opened her bag. 'That'll pay you for the return journey.'

'All right,' said the driver.

'For God's sake hurry,' she told him, 'it's a matter of life and death.'

The taxi moved off and was soon bucketing over the corrugations on the road into the mountains. Far ahead forked lightning on the horizon heralded the approach of a storm.

As the lightning flickered around him and the hailstones rattled on the roof of his van Konstabel Els switched on the windshield wipers and peered into the gloom. Driving with his usual disregard for other traffic on the road, his own life and that of anyone living within half a mile of the van should it explode, Els was looking forward to the evening's entertainment. It would compensate him for the tone of voice Colonel Heathcote-Kilkoon had used to address him in the past. 'I'll Harbinger him,' Els thought with relish. By the time he reached Weezen night had fallen. Els drove on and turned up the drive to White Ladies. With a show of bravado occasioned by his knowledge of the drinking habits of the household he drove the van into the yard at the back of the house and switched off the engine. A black face peered into the van. It was Fox.

'Harbinger,' he said. 'You've come back.'

'Yes,' said Els, 'I've come back.'

Konstabel Els climbed out of the van and went round to the back and opened the doors. Then he turned back and called, 'Fox, you kaffir, come here.' But there was no answer. Responding to the same instinct for self-preservation which marked his namesake he was off across the garden and into the trees and putting as much ground as he could between him and the man in the uniform of the South African Police whom he knew by the name of Harbinger. Fox knew death when he saw it.

Inside the house Colonel Heathcote-Kilkoon and his guests were less discerning.

'Wonder what's happened to Daphne,' the Colonel thought as he dressed for the party. 'Typical of her to be late tonight.'

He peered into the mirror, and was mollified. A frock of pale pink georgette, with long bell-shaped sleeves and a black velvet girdle knotted at one side, fitted him seemingly like a glove. A large Leghorn hat, its black velvet streamers fastened beneath his chin, heavily weighted with a full-blown rose over one eye, threatened to hide his rebellious mop of hair. White silk stockings and a pair of ordinary pumps completed his attire. A miniature apron, bearing the stencilled legend 'An English Rose' upon its muslin, left no doubt about his identity.

'Berry to the life,' he murmured and consulted *Jonah & Co.* Chapter XI to see if there was anything he had left out. Then picking up his bead bag he went downstairs where the others had gathered waiting for revels to begin.

'I'm an Incroyable,' Major Bloxham told La Marquise who had come as Sycamore Tight.

'Absolutely, darling,' she shrieked shrilly.

Colonel Heathcote-Kilkoon's entrance as Berry as An English Rose was greeted with rapturous applause. The Colonel waited for the laughter to die down before addressing his guests.

'As you all know,' he said, 'every year we celebrate our annual meeting with a final re-enactment of one of the great episodes in the life of Berry & Co. Tonight it is Chapter XI of *Jonah & Co*, Berry Puts Off His Manhood. I'm glad to see there has been such a good turn-out this year.'

After a few more words about the necessity of keeping the flag flying in foreign parts which La Marquise took as a compliment, the Colonel told Major Bloxham to switch the record player on and presently was dancing a Tango with him.

'These step-ins of Daphne's are damned tight,' he said as they went into a reverse turn.

'So's La Marquise,' said the Major.

In the darkness outside the window Konstabel Els watched the proceedings with interest. 'I always wondered why he was so keen on roses,' he thought, eyeing the Colonel with new appreciation.

He went back to the van and began to carry the evidence of the Colonel's attempt to overthrow the government of South Africa into the harness room. By the time he had packed several hundred pounds of gelignite on to shelves that had previously held nothing more incriminating than saddle soap he had begun to regret letting Fox escape. Finally when the last carton of Durex Fetherlites had been safely installed, Els lit a cigarette and sat back in the darkness to consider what other measures to take.

'Party seems to be going with a bang,' he heard the fat man tell Major Bloxham from the terrace where the two men were urinating intermittently on to a bed of begonias. Els took the hint and stubbed his cigarette out but the remark had given him a new idea. He crept out of the harness room and presently was carrying buckets of kerosene from the fuel store across the yard and pouring them into the Colonel's wine cellar where they splashed unnoticed over the Australian burgundy. To add to the inflammatory mixture Els then fetched several bundles of gelignite and tossed them into the cellar. Finally, to prevent anyone leaving the house without giving some indication where they had gone, he poured a solution of aniseed on the door-mats before climbing into the van and driving down to the main gate to wait for the police convoy. When there was no sign of it after ten minutes, Els decided to go back and see how the party was getting on.

'Got to kill time,' he muttered as he strolled up through the orchard. Ahead of him White Ladies, brilliantly illuminated for the occasion, exuded an atmosphere of discreet abandon. The Tango had been replaced by the Black Bottom and the Colonel was sitting this one out with La Marquise while Major Bloxham and the fat man were debating what to put into a cocktail called a Monkey Gland. With a fine disregard for the Colonel's herbaceous border Els groped his way round the house and found a window which gave him an excellent view of the proceedings and he was studying An English Rose with an appreciative eye when La Marquise looked up and spotted him.

In the second armoured car Kommandant van Heerden was having second thoughts about giving Els three hundred pounds of gelignite to plant. He was the only person to know the layout and besides I'd have heard it if it had gone off, he thought and consoled himself with the realization that it might not be such a bad thing if Els did bungle the part he had been given to play. No arrests, no trouble with confessions and no Els, and he once again wondered if he had been wise to listen to Mrs Heathcote-Kilkoon. All in all, he decided, he had very little choice in the matter. If she was foolish enough to let her husband know that he had been cuckolded and the Colonel threatened to shoot a member of the South African Police and a senior member at that, he had only himself to blame for what followed. The Kommandant couldn't remember if Mrs Heathcote-Kilkoon had actually said that her husband had threatened to shoot him but in any case the suspicion that he might was enough. More to the point was the appeal the Colonel would make to the Bureau of State Security. If there was one sort of suspect BOSS really liked after Jewish millionaires whose parents had emigrated from Petrograd, it was Englishmen of the old school with links with the Anglican Church. The Colonel's outspoken contempt for Afrikaners would silence any suspicion that he might be entirely innocent while his wartime experience in the underground and his training in explosives made him precisely the sort of man BOSS had been looking for over the years. The Kommandant remembered the Union Jack flying in front of White Ladies. In the eyes of BOSS that alone would damn the Colonel and his Club as traitors.

Finally, to salve what little remained of his conscience, the Kommandant recalled the fate of his grandfather who had been shot after the Battle of Paardeburg by the British.

Tit for tat, he thought and ordered the driver to stop at the police station in Weezen. There he insisted on seeing the Sergeant in charge.

'Colonel Heathcote-Kilkoon a communist?' asked the Sergeant who finally made his appearance in a pair of pyjamas. 'There must be some mistake.'

'Our information is that he's a saboteur trained by British intelligence,' said the Kommandant. 'Have you checked his wartime career in your security reports?'

'What sec . . .' the Sergeant began before realizing his mistake. 'No.'

'I always keep a file copy in case Security HQ lose the one I send them,' said the Kommandant. 'Amazing how many times they have mislaid things I've sent them.' He looked round the police station approvingly. 'Like the way things are done here, Sergeant. About time you had some promotion. The main thing is to keep copies of your security reports.'

He went outside and the Sergeant was amazed at the size of the task force required to arrest Colonel Heathcote-Kilkoon. As if to provide final proof that the Colonel was indeed the Communist saboteur trained by British intelligence, a sudden burst of firing came from the direction of White Ladies. Kommandant van Heerden dived into the Saracen and the Sergeant returned to his office and sat down at his typewriter to draft a report on the Colonel. It was much easier than he had expected, thanks to the forgetfulness of the Kommandant, who had left a specimen of his own report on the desk.

As the convoy moved off again the Sergeant typed out his suspicions. They were dated six months earlier.

'Better late than never,' he thought as he typed.

His view of things was shared by Mrs Heathcote-Kilkoon's taxi driver.

'There's ice on the road,' he told her when she asked him to step on it.

'Nonsense,' said Mrs Heathcote-Kilkoon, 'it's a hot night.'

'There's been a hailstorm, lady and if it isn't ice it's a thin coating of mud and as slippery as hell,' and to prove his point put the car into a slight skid on the next corner.

'You don't want to end up over a cliff,' he went on, righting the car, 'that wouldn't do you no good at all.'

In the back seat Mrs Heathcote-Kilkoon couldn't imagine that anything was going to do her much good. What had started out with less than the emotional force involved in her monthly choice of hairstyle had turned into a paroxysm of uncertainty. Melodramatic mock confessions were one thing. They added spice to the boredom of existence. But armoured cars and convoys of policemen armed with rifles and accompanied by snarling guard dogs were something else again. 'One can have too much of a good thing,' she thought recalling the logistics of her lover's concern. They argued a quite disproportionate devotion, not to mention a terrifying lack of sense of humour.

'I was only joking,' she murmured and was not consoled by the taxi driver's next remark.

'Looks like the army's been through here,' he said as the car slewed through the mud churned up by the convoy. 'Shouldn't be surprised if it wasn't tanks.'

'I should,' said Mrs Heathcote-Kilkoon more correctly and stared apprehensively into the darkness.

In the living-room at White Ladies her husband was doing the same and with even greater apprehension. La Marquise's sudden scream at the sight of the face at the window had provided An English Rose with an opportunity for a display of chivalry calculated to restore the Colonel's confidence in his rightful sex which La Marquise's interest had somewhat undermined.

'I'll deal with the swine,' he shouted and dashed into his study with all the speed his wife's step-ins allowed, to emerge a moment later with a sporting rifle. 'Only one way to deal with intruders,' he said and fired into the garden.

To Konstabel Els flitting across the lawn the accuracy of the shot came as something of a surprise. Aimed at a neatly trimmed bush some twenty yards to his right which to the Colonel's alcholic eye had the look of an intruder, the bullet ricochetted off a rockery and sang unpleasantly past Konstabel Els' head. Els took cover in a sunken garden and unfastened his holster. Outlined against the light in a window he could see the Colonel peering out. Els took careful aim over the Colonel's shoulder and fired and was delighted by the consternation his deliberate near miss caused in the house. As the lights went out and the Colonel shouted orders to keep down, Els crawled away and was presently well hidden in a clump of azaleas, where he could keep an eye on the back door. The Battle of White Ladies had begun.

'God Almighty,' yelled An English Rose as a third bullet, this time from a different part of the garden, ruffled the night air and shattered a vase on the mantelpiece, 'it's a bloody uprising. The natives have risen.' With a vindictiveness that came from the realization that the kaffirs were using more sophisticated weapons than assegais and knobkerries he prepared to defend his corner of Western Civilization against the tide of barbarism he had always expected. Behind him the members of the Dornford Yates Club, sobered by the prospect of an imminent bloodbath, stumbled into the study where Major Bloxham was handing out rifles and ammunition. With a military authority he had never before exercised the Colonel deployed his forces.

'Boy, take the front room. Toby, the kitchen,' he ordered. 'The rest of you spread out in the library and breakfast-room and keep firing.'

'What shall I do?' asked La Marquise.

'Pass the ammunition and keep your powder dry,' shouted the Colonel bitterly. La Marquise crawled into the study and began to undress. If the black hordes were coming, there was no point in maintaining the fiction that she was a man.

'There's no such thing as a fate worse than death,' she muttered in the darkness.

'What's that?' whispered Major Bloxham.

'I said all cats are grey when the candles are out,' said La Marquise.

'You can say that again,' said the Major busily trying to rid himself of his Incroyable costume.

In the azalea bushes Konstabel Els lay and listened to the hail of gunfire issuing from the house. It was going to be a good night. He had no doubt about that now.

In the second armoured car Kommandant van Heerden was less sanguine. The knowledge that he was moving into an area where Konstabel Els was involved in a private war brought back memories of previous holocausts initiated by Els.

'The stupid bastard will probably shoot his own side,' he thought when Sergeant Breitenbach came to ask for orders.

'Open fire at long range,' he told the Sergeant, 'I don't want anyone getting too close.' Presently two hundred policemen had disembarked from the lorries and had crawled into the bushes that marked the boundary of White Ladies and were adding their concentrated fire to that of Els and the Dornford Yates Club.

'Why not send in the armoured cars?' Sergeant Breitenbach asked.

'Certainly not,' said the Kommandant, appalled at the idea that he should be driven into close proximity to Konstabel Els and three hundred pounds of gelignite, not to mention the obviously irate Colonel and whatever weapons he had in his arsenal. 'We'll wear them down first and then move in.'

'Wear them down's about right,' said the Sergeant as the police fire cut a swathe through the ornamental hedges of the Colonel's garden. In the background the hounds of the Dornford Yates pack were giving tongue and lending a new sense of urgency to the snarls of the police dogs in the rear lorries.

Inside the house the realization that they were surrounded and that the black hordes were armed with the very latest in automatic weapons had slowly dawned on most of the defenders. La Marquise was no longer interested. Deserting her post she crawled upstairs to put on some clean underwear in anticipation of her approaching ordeal when she was hit by a burst of machine-gun fire. She was the first casualty of the battle.

In the kitchen the Zulu butler, with greater presence of mind, left the house and made his way to a telephone box on the outskirts of Weezen and dialled the operator.

'Get me the police station,' he told her. The operator wasn't to be told.

'Don't you speak to me like that, kaffir,' she shouted. 'You ask nicely.'

'Yes, missus,' said the butler relapsing into the required tone of servility. 'Ambulance please, missus.'

'Black or white ambulance?' the operator inquired.

The butler considered the question.

'White ambulance, missus,' he said finally.

'It's not for you, is it?' the girl inquired. 'Kaffirs can't ride in white ambulances. They have to be fumigated afterwards.'

'Not for me, missus,' the butler told her. 'For white boss.'

'What address?'

'White Ladies,' said the butler.

'Which white lady's?'

'White Ladies House,' said the butler as a fresh outburst of firing lent urgency to his request.

'I know that, kaffir,' screamed the operator. 'I know white ladies live in houses. I know she doesn't live in a mud hut like you. What I want to know is which white lady's.'

'Mrs Heathcote-Kilkoon,' said the butler.

'Why didn't you say so in the first place?' shouted the operator. The butler put down the receiver and went out into the inhospitable night where his white masters were killing one another with a ferocity he found incomprehensible.

'No point in getting caught in the middle,' he thought and began to walk carefully into Weezen. Occasionally a stray bullet whirred overhead. The butler kept his head down. In the main street he was stopped by a policeman and asked for his pass.

'You're under arrest,' said the konstabel when the butler admitted he hadn't got a pass on him. 'Can't have savages wandering about in the middle of the night without passes.'

'Yes, baas,' said the butler and climbed into the paddy-wagon.

To Konstabel Els the arrival of the police convoy was a mixed blessing. The fact that he was in some sort of no-man's-land between two opposing forces each defending Western Civilization was something of a hazard. As the Colonel's erratic fire swept through the leaves above him and was answered by the burst of machine-gun fire in his rear, Els began to think the time had come to make his presence felt. He crawled through the azaleas until he reached the corner of the house and then made a wild dash into the yard and was about to light a match to ignite the kerosene he had poured into the wine cellar when it occurred to him that he was endangering both the evidence he had planted so carefully in the harness room and his own life. He fetched a hose and took it into the harness room and presently was playing a sprinkler over the gelignite. He was so busy at his work that he was unaware of the figure that flitted heavily across the yard and into the darkness by the kennels. Assured that he had taken every sensible precaution Els shut the door of the harness room and slipped back across the yard.

This ought to flush the buggers out, he thought, striking a match and dropping it into the kerosene before dashing for cover. A moment later a sheet of flame lit the night sky and an explosion erupted in the basement of White Ladies. With considerable satisfaction Konstabel Els peered out of the azaleas and studied his handiwork while behind him the police ceased their fire. There was indeed no need to continue. Apart from the occasional report of an exploding bottle of Australian burgundy buried under tons of rubble the occupants of White Ladies had ended their resistance. Berry Puts Off His Manhood night had ended.

Colonel Heathcote-Kilkoon alone did not stop to watch his house burn. He was too busy stumbling across open ground in search of cover. As he went he cursed his wife for her absence. 'Wouldn't have happened if she'd been here,' he gasped, a tribute less to her power of personality than to the constriction of her pantie girdle which was playing havoc with his innards. Spurred on by shouts that greeted the conflagration of his home and by the need to apprise those of his neighbours who had not been woken by the sound of battle that the natives had risen, An English Rose blundered into a wood and wrestled with his girdle.

'Got to get it off before I burst,' he muttered, only to decide ten minutes later that there was no question of bursting in spite of his vain efforts to get it off. In the end he decided that sleep might deflate him and crawling into the cover of a bush lay still.

From the turret of his armoured car Kommandant van Heerden surveyed what remained of White Ladies with a mixture of satisfaction and regret.

'No doubt about their being the saboteurs now, Sergeant?' he asked Sergeant Breitenbach.

'None at all,' said the Sergeant. 'There's enough gelignite in the stables to blow up half Piemburg.'

Kommandant van Heerden disappeared hurriedly into the armoured car. His muffled voice could be heard urging the driver to get the hell out. Sergeant Breitenbach went round to the back door.

'It's all right,' he told the Kommandant, 'it won't go off. Someone's been playing a hose on it.'

'You sure?' asked the Kommandant. Sergeant Breitenbach said he wouldn't be standing there if he wasn't and the Kommandant finally emerged and stared at the smouldering building. 'Better get the fire brigade here,' he said. 'We don't want any more explosions and I want a body count as soon as possible.'

'How many suspects do you expect?' asked the Sergeant.

'Eleven will do,' said the Kommandant and clambered back into the Saracen to get some sleep.

At the entrance to what had once been her home Mrs Heathcote-Kilkoon's taxi was stopped by a Sergeant and several konstabels armed with machine-guns.

'Sorry, lady,' the Sergeant said, 'but orders is orders and no one is allowed in.'

'But I live here, officer,' said Mrs Heathcote-Kilkoon dredging a seductive smile from the depths of her despair.

'Not any more you don't,' said the Sergeant. 'This is one house you won't be living in again.'

In the back of the taxi Mrs Heathcote-Kilkoon clutched her coat to her and shivered. To add to her troubles the taxi-driver insisted on being paid before he drove her any further.

'How can I pay?' she pleaded. 'All I ever had is in there,' and she pointed to the smudge of smoke that darkened the night sky over the azaleas.

'You said you'd pay me double fare when we got here,' the driver insisted, 'I didn't come all this way for nothing.'

'But I've nothing to give you,' Mrs Heathcote-Kilkoon said wearily.

'We'll see about that,' said the driver and turned the car in the road. Half a mile further on he pulled into the side and climbed into the back seat.

'I suppose it's only fare,' Mrs Heathcote-Kilkoon murmured as his coarse hands fumbled with her panties.

CHAPTER SIXTEEN

It was characteristic of Konstabel Els that his feelings as he watched the end of White Ladies were less ambiguous than those of the Kommandant. If he felt any regret, it was that his efforts at fire-raising had been so completely successful. He had at least hoped that the flames would have driven some survivors of the Dornford Yates Club out into the open where they could be shot down at leisure like men or more correctly as men dressed as women. Els particularly regretted the failure of his late employer to put in an appearance. He had been looking forward to despatching An English Rose with a degree of lingering incivility he felt the Colonel merited.

Long before the ashes were cool, Konstabel Els was busy in the ruins counting the bodies and making quite sure that no one had been overlooked. By the time he had finished he had managed to recover the melted remains of Mrs Heathcote-Kilkoon's jewels and was beginning to think that something else was missing.

Stumbling around in the ashes he counted the bodies again.

'There's only eleven here,' he told Sergeant Breitenbach, who was watching him with some revulsion.

'Who cares?' asked the Sergeant rhetorically.

'I do,' said Els. 'There ought to be thirteen.' He did some mental arithmetic. 'Still wrong,' he said finally. 'There's still one missing.'

'How many servants?' asked the Sergeant.

'I'm not counting kaffirs,' said Els, 'I'm talking about people.'

'Which one is it?'

'Looks like the Colonel,' said Els bitterly. 'Shifty bastard. Typical of him to get away.'

Sergeant Breitenbach said he thought it was very sensible but he went over to the armoured car and knocked on the door.

'What is it now?' the Kommandant asked sleepily.

'Els says the Colonel got away,' said the Sergeant and was amazed at the rapidity with which Kommandant van Heerden responded.

'Get the dogs,' he yelled frantically, 'get the dogs. We've got to find the swine.' As Sergeant Breitenbach gave orders for the Dobermann Pinschers to be released, Konstabel Els went off to the kennels and presently the gravel forecourt was filled with snarling police dogs and slobbering foxhounds, each pack busily disputing the right of the other to be there. In the middle of the seething mass Kommandant van Heerden, appalled at the knowledge that Mrs Heathcote-Kilkoon's irate husband was still at large and doubtless imbued with a new sense of grievance, tried to avoid getting bitten.

'Down Jason, down Snarler,' he yelled vainly trying to repeat the magic formula that had worked so well in the dell. Here it was less successful. Busy about their private business the hounds snapped and snarled at one another in an ever-increasing vortex of confusion and the Kommandant was just beginning to think he was going to be bitten to death when Els rode up on his nag leading Mrs Heathcote-Kilkoon's bay. The Kommandant climbed into the saddle thankfully and looked around.

'I suppose you could say I was MFHDP,' he said proudly. Els blew his horn and the hunt moved off through the gate and across the field.

'What's DP stand for?' Els asked as they followed.

The Kommandant looked at him irritably. 'Police dogs, of course,' he said and spurring the bay galloped after the hounds who had picked up the scent of The English Rose. Compounded of Chanel No 5 and aniseed, it was unmistakable. Even the Dobermann Pinschers loping ominously behind the fox hounds could pick it up. In the light of the early dawn they quickened their pace.

So did Colonel Heathcote-Kilkoon, whose sleep had not deflated him sufficiently to escape from the intractable embrace of his wife's corsets. Stumbling about the thicket in an attempt to rid himself of the beastly things, the Colonel heard the sound of Els' horn and read its message rightly. As the

226

first foxhounds breasted the horizon a mile away the Colonel broke cover and headed for the river. As he ran he scattered the less obdurate accessories of An English Rose. The frock of pale pink georgette, the bell-shaped sleeves, the Leghorn hat and the miniature apron fluttered behind him on the veldt, pathetic remnants of an Imperial dream. At the river bank the Colonel hesitated before diving in. 'Got to lose the scent,' he thought as he surfaced and allowed the current to carry him downstream.

'He's given us the slip,' Els shouted as the hounds milled round the discarded garments.

'I can see that,' said the Kommandant studying the torn fragments of pink with considerable distaste. 'Are you sure it's not Major Bloxham?' he asked. 'He said he always wore pink.'

But Els was already down by the river with the foxhounds and sniffing the air. 'He's gone thataway,' he said finally pointing downstream and blowing his horn set off along the river bank. Kommandant van Heerden followed slowly.

The sun had risen and with it there came to the Kommandant a sudden sense of regret. There was no need to hurry now. Els was on the trail and had scented blood and from long experience the Kommandant knew he would never give up. Besides there was no doubt now that he was safe from BOSS. Verkramp's errors of judgement had been buried in the wreckage of White Ladies and no one would question the Kommandant's efficient handling of the matter now that he had eleven corpses and three hundred pounds of gelignite to prove it. He felt safe at last and with his sense of security there returned the desire to do the gentlemanly thing. Certainly chasing elderly colonels dressed as women across the countryside wasn't a gentlemanly occupation. There was something vaguely sordid about it. With one last glance at the tailless haunches of the Dobermanns gliding menacingly among the willows, the Kommandant turned his bay and rode slowly back to the house. On the way he met Sergeant Breitenbach in an armoured car and with a rejuvenated sense of chivalry pointed in quite the wrong direction. 'They've gone thataway,' he shouted and watched the Sergeant disappear over the hillside. Far down the river Els sounded his horn and the Kommandant thought he heard the cry, 'Gone to earth.' It was followed by the sound of yelping.

In the back of the taxi Mrs Heathcote-Kilkoon had spent her night watching the night sky turn crimson over the taxi-driver's shoulder and had responded with a degree of agitation that lent weight to his conviction that she was actively enjoying what he was doing. As the reflected glow ebbed from the sky Mrs Heathcote-Kilkoon's writhings ebbed with it and the taxi-driver fell asleep. As she detached herself from him and climbed out of the car, it occurred to her to search his pockets for money but she discarded the thought. There was more to be gained in the house. When the armoured cars drove out of the yard in pursuit of her husband, Mrs Heathcote-Kilkoon adjusted her dress and then scrambled through the hedge and walked up to the house. A mound of blackened rubble, it had little to remind her of the past. In any case Mrs Heathcote-Kilkoon was more concerned with the future. She hadn't left the suburbs of South London for the dangers and discomforts of life in Africa for nothing. She climbed the steps which had been the scene of so many welcomes and which still retained something of their old warmth and surveyed the ruins. Then stepping adroitly between her old friends she made her way to her bedroom and began to dig in the ashes.

As the sound of the horn reached him Colonel Heathcote-Kilkoon scrambled out of the river and disappeared into the trees. He stumbled through the undergrowth and five minutes later found himself at the foot of a cliff. He could go no further. Behind him the yelps of the hounds grew more insistent on the far side of the river. The Colonel listened breathlessly for a moment and then turned and searched for somewhere to hide. He found it in an overhang of rock. Crawling inside he found himself in some sort of cave, dark and deep and with a narrow entrance. If only I could block it up, he thought and the next moment, with a presence of mind that had come rather late in life, he was out in the sunlight and struggling with a thorn bush which resolutely defied his efforts to pull it up by the roots. Below him the sound of the pack seemed closer and spurred on by this indication of danger, the Colonel hauled the bush out of the ground, a feat which had it not been for his wife's corsets would certainly have ruptured him. He crawled back into the hole and dragged the thorn bush behind him. That ought to keep them out, he thought grimly, crouching in the darkness oblivious to the paintings of other hunts that glimmered from the walls of the cave.

On the river bank Konstabel Els and the hounds sniffed the air. There was nothing to indicate which way their quarry had gone. Els wondered what he would have done had he been in the Colonel's shoes and came to the conclusion that he would have headed into the thick bush on the far side of the river. Urging his nag forward, Els waded into the water and with the hounds swarming around him crossed over. A few minutes later the leading hounds had picked up the trail and were following a line through the trees. Els pushed on after them and came out into the open to find the pack giving tongue round a thorn bush which appeared to be growing in the most unlikely fashion from inside a cave. Els dismounted and considered the situation while the Dobermann Pinschers snarled and the fox-hounds greeted their old master with a friendliness that was not reciprocated. With reckless disregard for life and limb Els waded into the pack and peered into the thorn bush. A moment later his 'Gone to earth' echoed from the cliff face.

In his burrow Colonel Heathcote-Kilkoon recognized the call and the voice had something familiar about it. Hope surged in his breast. If Harbinger was outside, he was safe. He started to push the thorn bush forward to crawl out but was instantly dissuaded by three Dobermanns who threw themselves into the gap with bared teeth. The Colonel hauled the thorn bush back and tried shouting but his words were drowned by the noise of the pack.

Outside Konstabel Els sat on a rock and lit a cigarette. He was in no hurry. Can't shoot him, he thought recalling the MFH's adamant veto on the shooting of foxes; what I need is a terrier. Els began to cast about for a suitable substitute. Presently he was scrambling among the rocks on one side of the cliff. It was hot work and the sun was up and it took Els half an hour to find what he was looking for. In the end he grabbed a large snake that was sunning itself on a ledge and holding it by the tail made his way back to the earth. The dogs backed away and Els dropped the snake into the thorn bush with a snigger and watched it slither into the darkness. A moment later a convulsive shudder shook the thorn bush to be followed by a scream as the corseted Colonel erupted from his burrow and hurtled across the scree and into the trees. 'Gone away,' yelled Els and watched with a smile as the hounds surged after him. Silly bugger, he thought, he ought to know grass snakes are harmless. Screams and snarls from the bushes marked the end of the hunt and Els pushed his way among the dogs and took out his knife.

To Kommandant van Heerden jogging back to White Ladies the sight that greeted him was full of a poignancy he would never forget. It put him in mind of the heroines in the books of the author whose portrait had once adorned the wall of the dining room. True, Mrs Heathcote-Kilkoon was no slender girl and the magic that clung to her was wholly black, but these discrepancies were as nothing to the vision of tragic grief she presented. The Kommandant left the horse at the gate and crossed the gravel to her side. Only then did Mrs Heathcote-Kilkoon raise her tinted head.

'It's buried . . .' she began, tears ravaging her lovely features. Kommandant van Heerden looked down at the corpse beside her feet and shook his head.

'Not Berry, Daphne. Boy,' he murmured. But Mrs Heathcote-Kilkoon was obviously too far gone in grief to hear.

'My precious treasure . . .' she shrieked and threw herself down to scrabble in the ashes. The Kommandant knelt beside her and shook his head again sadly.

'They've gone for good, my darling,' he whispered and was astonished at the fresh paroxysm of grief that racked her body. Cursing himself for the lack of tact that had made him use an endearment at a time like this, he took her hand in his.

'They've gone to a better world,' he said gazing into her deep grey eyes. Mrs Heathcote-Kilkoon thrust him away imperiously.

'You're lying,' she cried, 'they can't have. They're all I've got,' and disregarding her delicate hands she dug into the rubble. Beside her, overcome by emotion, the Kommandant knelt and watched.

He was still maintaining his steadfast vigil when Els rode up on his nag waving something.

'I've got it. I've got it,' he shouted triumphantly and dismounted. Kommandant van Heerden regarded him bleakly through eyes dimmed by tears and motioned him away. But Els lacked the Kommandant's sense of occasion. He ran up the steps into the ruins eagerly and waved something in the Kommandant's face.

'Look at that. Isn't it a fine one?' he shouted. Kommandant van Heerden shut his eyes in horror.

'For God's sake, Els, there's a time and a place ...' he shouted dementedly but Els was already daubing his cheeks and forehead.

'You're blooded,' he shouted, 'you're blooded.'

The Kommandant rose frantically to his feet.

'You swine,' he screamed, 'You filthy swine.'

'I thought you'd like the brush,' Els said in a puzzled tone of voice. It was obvious that he was cut to the quick by the Kommandant's rejection of his offering. So it appeared was Mrs Heathcote-Kilkoon. As the Kommandant turned to make his apologies for Konstabel Els' appalling lapse of taste, the Colonel's widow struggled to her feet.

'It's mine, you thief,' she screamed and lunged at Els furiously. 'You had no right to take it, I want it back,' a claim whose justice the Kommandant had to admit while deploring the fact that Mrs Heathcote-Kilkoon should want to make it.

'Give it to her,' he shouted at Els, 'it's hers by right,' but before Els could proffer his ghastly souvenir, Mrs Heathcote-Kilkoon, evidently intent on more practical reparation for the loss of her conjugal rights, had hurled herself on the konstabel and was tearing at his trousers.

'Dear God,' bawled the Kommandant as Els fell back into the ashes.

'Help,' screamed Els evidently imbued with the same suspicion as to her intentions.

'It's mine,' shrieked Mrs Heathcote-Kilkoon, clawing at Els' pants. Kommandant van Heerden shut his eyes and tried to shut out too the screams from Els.

'That it should come to this,' he thought and was trying to reconcile this new evidence of feminine fury with that gentle image of Mrs Heathcote-Kilkoon he had nurtured in the past when with a shriek of triumph the Colonel's widow got to her feet. The Kommandant opened his eyes and stared at the strange object in her hand. It was not, he was thankful to note, what he had expected. Mrs Heathcote-Kilkoon's hand held a dark lump of metal in whose misshapen surface there gleamed here and there large brilliant stones. Twisted and melted though they were, the Kommandant could still recognize traces of Mrs Heathcote-Kilkoon's bijouterie. Clutching the great ingot to her breast she looked once more the woman he had known.

'My darlings,' she shrieked, her voice radiant with frenetic gaiety, 'my precious darlings.'

The Kommandant turned sternly to Els who was still lying prone and shaken by his recent experience.

'How many times have I told you not to nick things?' he demanded. Els smiled weakly and got to his feet.

'I was only looking after them,' he said by way of explanation.

The Kommandant turned away and followed Mrs Heathcote-Kilkoon down the steps.

'Have you a car?' he asked solicitously. Mrs Heathcote-Kilkoon shook her head.

'Then I'll send for a taxi,' said the Kommandant.

A fresh pallor blanched Mrs Heathcote-Kilkoon's face.

'You've got to be joking,' she muttered before collapsing in a dead faint in his arms.

'Poor thing,' thought the Kommandant, 'it's all been too much for her.' He picked her up and carried her gently over to a Saracen. As he lowered her to the floor he noticed that she still clutched the nugget in her limp hand.

'The British bulldog,' he thought and closed the door.

* * *

When the police convoy finally left White Ladies Mrs Heathcote-Kilkoon had revived sufficiently to sit up. She was still obviously stunned by the change in her fortunes and the Kommandant tactfully didn't bring the subject up. Instead he busied himself with some paperwork and ran over in his mind things he had still to do.

He had left Sergeant Breitenbach with a small body of men to guard the scene of the crime and had arranged for photographs of the cache of high-explosives and detonators in the harness room to be supplied to the press. He would write up a full report on the affair for the Commissioner of Police and forward a copy to BOSS and he would announce to the press that another revolutionary conspiracy to overthrow the Republic had been nipped in the bud. He might even hold a press conference. In the end he decided not to on the grounds that journalists were a breed of men who didn't make the job of the police in South Africa any easier and he saw no reason why they should rely on him for their information. He had, in any case, more important matters to worry about than public opinion.

There was for instance the problem of the Colonel's widow and, while he had every sympathy for her in her present plight, the Kommandant was alive to the possibility that the distressing action he had been forced to take might well have ended the good feeling she had once felt for him. As the convoy approached Piemburg the Kommandant inquired as to her plans.

'Plans?' asked Mrs Heathcote-Kilkoon roused from her silent reverie. 'I have no plans.'

'You have friends in Umtali,' said the Kommandant hopefully. 'They would surely put you up.'

Mrs Heathcote-Kilkoon nodded. 'I suppose so,' she said.

'Better than a police cell,' said the Kommandant and explained that he ought to hold her as a witness. 'Of course if you give me your word not to leave the country . . .' he added.

That evening the Rolls stopped at the Customs Post at Beit Bridge.

'Anything to declare?' asked the Rhodesian Customs officer.

'Yes,' said Mrs Heathcote-Kilkoon with feeling. 'It's good to be back with one's own kith and kin.'

'Yes, ma'am,' said Customs Officer Van der Merwe and waved her through. As she drove through the night Mrs Heathcote-Kilkoon began to sing to keep herself awake.

'Rule Britannia, Britannia rules the waves, Britons never never will be slaves,' she shrieked happily as the car knocked an African cyclist into the ditch. Mrs Heathcote-Kilkoon was too tired to stop. 'Teach him to drive without lights,' she thought and put her foot on the accelerator. In the glove compartment a fortune in gold and diamonds rolled unevenly about.

In the week that followed the Kommandant was kept too busy to worry about Mrs Heathcote-Kilkoon's disappearance. The team of Security men who came down from Pretoria to report on the affair were sent up to Weezen to investigate.

'Try the storekeeper,' the Kommandant suggested. 'Very helpful fellow.' The Security men tried the storekeeper and were infuriated by his refusal to speak Afrikaans.

'I've seen enough coppers,' he told them, 'to last me a lifetime. I've ordered one off the premises already and I'm ordering you. This is Little England and you can get the hell out.'

By the time they returned to Pretoria they could find nothing to criticize in the Kommandant's handling of the affair. The fact that the victims of police action were found on examination to be wearing women's clothes in the case of the men and a jockstrap in the case of La Marquise added weight to the Kommandant's claim that the safety of the Republic had been threatened. Even in the Cabinet the Kommandant's handling of the affair received a friendly reception.

'Nothing like the threat of terrorism to keep the electorate on our side,' said the Minister of Justice. 'We could do with an incident like this before every election.'

At Fort Rapier Luitenant Verkramp viewed the outcome of the affair in a different light. Now that the immediate cause of his insanity had been removed, Verkramp had regained sufficient rationality to regard his proposal to Dr von Blimenstein as a temporary aberration.

'I must have been mad,' he told the doctor when she reminded him of their engagement.

Dr von Blimenstein looked at him reproachfully.

'After all I've done for you,' she said finally.

'Done for me is about right,' said Verkramp.

'I'd planned such a lovely honeymoon too,' the doctor complained.

'Well I'm not going,' said Verkramp. 'I've had enough trips to last me a lifetime.'

'Is that your last word?' asked the doctor.

'Yes,' said Verkramp.

Dr von Blimenstein left the room and ordered the nurse to put Verkramp under restraint. Ten minutes later Verkramp was in a straitjacket and Dr von Blimenstein was closeted with the Hospital Chaplain.

That afternoon Kommandant van Heerden, visiting Fort Rapier to inquire about Aaron Geisenheimer, found Dr von Blimenstein dressed, rather ostentatiously, he thought, in a picture hat and a shark-skin suit.

'Going somewhere?' he asked. In the rush of events he had forgotten about Verkramp's impending marriage.

'We're honeymooning in Muizenberg,' said the doctor.

Kommandant van Heerden sat down suddenly in a chair.

'And Verkramp's quite well?' he asked.

In the light of the Kommandant's gallantry at their last meeting Dr von Blimenstein overlooked the imputation.

'A touch of last-minute nerves,' she said, 'but I think it'll go off without a hitch.' She hesitated before continuing, 'I know it's a lot to ask but I wonder if you would be best man?'

Kommandant van Heerden tried to think what to say. The thought that he would be in any way instrumental in joining the author of so many of his misfortunes to a woman as totally unloveable as Dr von Blimenstein had its appealing side. The thought of the doctor as Mrs Verkramp had nothing to recommend it.

'I suppose Verkramp has given up all idea of returning to his post?' he inquired hopefully. Dr von Blimenstein was pleased to reassure him.

'You've nothing to worry about,' she said. 'Balthazar will be on duty just as soon as we get the honeymoon over.'

'I see,' said the Kommandant, rising. 'In that case I think I had better see him now.'

'He's in Hypnotherapy,' said the doctor as the Kommandant went out into the corridor. 'Tell him I won't be long.'

The Kommandant went down the passage and asked a nurse the way. At Hypnotherapy the nurse opened the door and smiled.

'Here's your best man,' she said and ushered the Kommandant into the ward where Verkramp was sitting up in bed surrounded by an inferno of chrysanthemums.

'You too?' Verkramp groaned as the Kommandant entered and sat down on a chair by the bed.

'Just popped in to see if there was anything you needed,' said the Kommandant. 'I had no idea you were getting married.'

'I'm not getting married,' said Verkramp, 'I'm being married.'

'I see they've given you a clean straitjacket for the occasion,' said the Kommandant anxious to keep off controversial topics.

'Won't be needing that in a minute,' said the nurse. 'Will we?' She picked up a hypodermic and pulling back the bedclothes rolled Verkramp on to his stomach.

'I don't want ...' shouted Verkramp but the nurse had already plunged the needle into his backside. By the time she withdrew it the Kommandant was feeling distinctly agitated while Verkramp had relapsed into an unusual torpor.

'There we are,' said the nurse propping him up again and unfastening his straitjacket. 'No need for this horrid old thing now, is there?'

'I do,' said Verkramp.

The nurse smiled at the Kommandant and left the room.

'Listen,' said the Kommandant, appalled at what he had just witnessed, 'is it true that you don't want to marry this woman?'

'I do,' said Verkramp. The Kommandant, who had been on the brink of assuring him that there was no need for him to go through with the marriage looked nonplussed.

'But I thought you said you didn't,' he said.

'I do,' said Verkramp.

'There's still a chance to change your mind,' said the Kommandant.

'I do,' said Verkramp.

'Well I'm damned,' muttered the Kommandant. 'You certainly change your mind quickly.'

'I do,' said Verkramp. At that moment the nurse returned with the ring.

'Does he often go into this "I do" routine?' the Kommandant asked as he slipped the ring into his pocket.

'It's a new treatment that Dr von Blimenstein has developed,' the nurse told him. 'It's called CIRS.'

'I should think it must be,' said the Kommandant.

'Chemically Induced Repetitive Syndrome,' the nurse explained.

'I do,' said Verkramp.

'Good God,' said the Kommandant suddenly realizing the full implications of the treatment. If Dr von Blimenstein could get Verkramp unwillingly to the altar by chemically induced hypnosis and get him saying 'I do' all the way there, she could do anything. Kommandant van Heerden visualized the outcome. Hundreds of innocent and respectable citizens could be induced to confess to sabotage, membership of the Communist party, training in guerrilla warfare and any crime you cared to name. Worse still, Dr von Blimenstein was not the sort of woman to hesitate when it came to advancing her husband's career by such dubious methods. The Kommandant was just considering this new threat to his position as Chief of Police when the bride arrived with the hospital Chaplain and a bevy of patients who had been raked in as bridesmaids. A tape recorder struck up the wedding march and the Kommandant slipping the ring into Verkramp's hand left the room. He had no intention of being best man at a wedding that marked the end of his own career. He went out on to the parade ground and wandered miserably among the inmates cursing the irony of fate that had saved him from the consequences of Verkramp's deliberate attempts to oust him only to destroy him now. It would have been better to have let Verkramp take the rap for the activities of his secret agents than to have allowed him to marry Dr von Blimenstein. The Kommandant was just wondering if there was anything he could do even at this late hour when he became aware of a disturbance outside Hypnotherapy. Dr von Blimenstein was being escorted, weeping, from the makeshift chapel.

Kommandant van Heerden hurried across.

'Something go wrong?' he asked eagerly.

'He said "I do",' the nurse explained. Dr von Blimenstein wept uncontrollably.

'But I thought he was supposed to,' said the Kommandant.

'Not when the Chaplain asked if anyone present knew of any reason why these two should not be joined in holy wedlock,' the nurse explained. A broad smile broke across the Kommandant's face.

'Oh well,' he said cheerfully, 'Verkramp seemed to know his own mind after all,' and slapping the disconsolate doctor on the back with 'You can't win them all', he went into the ward to congratulate the ex-bridegroom.

With Konstabel Els, his problem was rather different. The telephone call from the taxidermist at the Piemburg Museum verged on the hysterical.

'He wanted me to stuff it,' the taxidermist told the Duty Sergeant.

'What's wrong with stuffing a fox's brush?' asked the Sergeant who couldn't see what all the fuss was about.

'But I keep telling you it wasn't a fox's brush. It was a phallus,' screamed the taxidermist.

'A false what?' the Sergeant asked.

'Not a false anything. A real phallus.'

'You're not making much sense, you know,' said the Sergeant.

The taxidermist took a deep breath and tried again. In the end the Sergeant put him through to the Kommandant who knew exactly what the man was talking about.

'No need to worry,' he said soothingly, 'I'll take the matter in hand at once.'

The taxidermist looked at the phone with disgust.

'You do that small thing,' he said and put the receiver down thankfully. Kommandant van Heerden sent for Els.

'I thought we'd seen the last of that beastly thing,' he said. Els looked downcast.

'I wanted to keep it as a souvenir,' he explained, 'I was thinking of having it mounted.'

'Mounted?' shouted the Kommandant. 'You must be out of your mind. Why can't you give it a rest?'

Els said he would try.

'You'll do more than that,' the Kommandant told him. 'If I catch you flashing the thing again, I'll book you.'

'What with?' Els asked.

'Indecent Exposure,' snarled the Kommandant. Els went away to get rid of his trophy.

As the weeks passed and Piemburg resumed its slow routine the memory of exploding ostriches and the outbreak of sabotage passed into the safe hands of local legend. Kommandant van Heerden was well content to see it go. Looking back over the events of those days he found himself wondering at the great difference between life and literature. It doesn't do to read too much, he thought, recalling the fate that literary endeavours had held in store for Colonel Heathcote-Kilkoon and the members of the Dornford Yates Club. Instead the Kommandant chose to carry on the traditions of the English gentleman in practice. He added the foxhounds of the Colonel's pack to the police kennels where they struck up friendly relations with the Dobermann Pinschers and he put Konstabel Els in charge of them. Els, it seemed, had a way with dogs. The Kommandant acquired a horse and ordered a crimson hunting coat from the tailors and twice a week he could be seen riding to hounds in Chaste Valley with Els on a nag and a convict running for his life with a bag of aniseed tied round his middle. Sometimes he even invited Dr von Blimenstein, who was quite fond of riding. It seemed the least he could do for the poor woman now that Verkramp had jilted her and in any case he felt it was wise to keep on the right side of her.

All in all he was well content. Whatever had happened, the Values of Western Civilization were still safe in Piemburg and as MFHDP Kommandant van Heerden maintained those traditions which went with the heart of an English gentleman.

Selected Bestsellers

All these books are available at your local bookshop or newsagent, or can be ordered direct from the publisher. Indicate the number of copies required and fill in the form below

Name_____
(block letters please)
Address_____

_____

Send to Pan Books (CS Department), Cavaye Place, London SW10 9PG
Please enclose remittance to the value of the cover price plus:

25p for the first book plus 10p per copy for each additional book ordered to a maximum charge of £1.05 to cover postage and packing Applicable only in the UK

While every effort is made to keep prices low, it is sometimes necessary to increase prices at short notice. Pan Books reserve the right to show on covers and charge new retail prices which may differ from those advertised in the text or elsewhere